The Empty Mirror

LISA EL HAFI

Published 2022

Cover Design: Jennifer Stimson

Editing: Hott + Hadley Writing Consultancy

Author Photo Credit: Adam Valenstein

DEDICATION

To my grandfather, Dr. Michael Austin, and my mother, Nancy Austin Laufbahn. Thank you for your love and the mystery.

CONTENTS

FRANCES

READING, PENNSYLVANIA, 1915

Four girls hopped onto the Carsonia Avenue trolley, the last barely making the step before the car began to roll down the hill. Sonia, a dark, plump girl, was hindered not only by her weight, but also by the constraints of her attire. Only she, of the group of girls, wore a fitted and formal wool dress. The other girls, each with a different shade of blonde hair, ranging from strawberry to flaxen, wore casual dresses and pinafores. They were dressed for an afternoon of active fun. Betsy and Patricia were both pretty girls, fair-complexioned, blue-eyed with cherubic faces. Frances, on the other hand, had luminous blue eyes, a slightly pouty mouth, all set in a beautiful oval-shaped face. She was the tallest of the four and seemed to be on the brink of adolescence, even though she had several months before she would turn eleven.

It was three o'clock on a Friday afternoon. School had let out a little early and they had been planning their outing to Carsonia Park all week. Some of their friends had been last week and apparently there were some new rides. Betsy and Patricia wanted to walk around the lake and look for rabbits and ducks. Frances wanted to stand outside the Casino, which was really a dance hall, and look at the dresses the ladies were wearing. She had a keen interest in fashion for a ten-year-old and loved to draw pictures of tall, elegant ladies in the latest fashions.

All too often Frances' mother criticized her for being a dreamer. "Just come back down to earth," she would scold. "I don't know what you are looking for. After all, you have loving parents and a comfortable home."

This rebuke hurt Frances because she had known since she was eight years old that she had been adopted. Her mother's comment also cut deep because she knew how much her parents loved her. And as the daughter of a successful small-town doctor, she lacked for nothing. Her father indulged her every whim.

Yes, it was true that she had a nice home and parents who adored her. Everyone liked her. She glanced at her friends who were jubilant about the outing to Carsonia Park. And although she had been looking forward to the excursion, she suddenly fell into a melancholy humor. When she thought of the city of Reading, she visualized a gloomy gray landscape. Factories were made of gray concrete and black smoke poured out of the chimneys into a leaden sky. Downtown was a combination of squat brick department stores and streets of identical rowhomes. Even the newer homes, built in the exclusive neighborhood that separated Reading from Mount Penn, were built in the German style with heavy gray stone or brown bricks.

The Austin's lived in the recently developed suburb of Mount Penn. Many families were moving further out in search of cleaner air, trees, and grass. Within a few years there was an elementary school and a large high school. It was much more pleasant than downtown, but it was dull. Her parents' friends were all the same, interested in Temple activities and the mundane activity of small-town life, bridge for the ladies and golf for the men. Her teachers were mediocre, and her classes were tedious. If she hadn't been such an avid reader, Frances sometimes felt that she might go mad with boredom.

The September breeze blew through the trolley's open

windows and tousled their hair, except for Sonia. Her hair was pulled back in tight braids that reached her waist. She turned to Frances, who sat next to her, and whispered. "Frances, I shouldn't have let you talk me into coming with you. By the time we get there I'll only have an hour before I will have to rush home. If I am not dressed for Temple by five, I just don't know what my mother will do. I suppose you are going to miss Sabbath services again. My mother says that the rabbi is not at all happy about your absences."

"Oh, stop with the rabbi. I don't care what he thinks or what your mother thinks. I am fed up with Friday nights at Temple. I am bored with the same kids, Morgensterns, Dinnersteins and all the other Cohens, who aren't even related to my mother's family. Look at Betsy and Patricia. When I'm with them I have such fun. We talk about different things: clothes, their travels, and sometimes they even talk about boys. And by boys, I don't mean Howard Finkel. Patricia thinks Dennis Franklin is cute. I know we're too young to go with boys, but we can think about it."

Sonia arched her brow and spoke in a sarcastic tone. "So, we're not good enough for you, Miss blondie, so and so. I suppose I'm boring too."

"Not you, Sonia," she said, softening her tone. "We have been friends since we were tiny, and your mother is friends with my mother. But I want to be friends with people that are not in the same crowd."

"You mean with Gentiles," said Sonia, visibly annoyed and hurt.

"Yes, with the Gentiles. If you don't want to play with Christian girls, it's just as bad as what some of them do to us. If you tried, you could fit in. Why do you think I invited you today?"

The trolley stopped and the girls quickly jumped off and headed for the lake. Betsy took Patricia's hand and pulled her along, as she looked back at Sonia and Frances.

"Hurry, I want to see the lake before it gets dark. If there are any animals, we won't be able to make them out after the sun goes down. Then we can go over to the rides and the casino. Is that alright, Frances?

"Sure. Let's get going," said Frances giving Sonia an encouraging glance.

Later, the clear blue sky began to darken as the sun descended to the horizon. The wind picked up and the girls hugged themselves to ward off the chill. Sonia looked up at the large clock over the entrance to the park and turns to Frances in a panic.

"I have to go. Are you coming Frances? You'll still have time to change for Temple."

"No Sonia," she snapped. "I won't be in Temple tonight."

The three friends walked towards the Casino where Frances commented on the dresses that the young ladies were wearing, explaining which were fashionable and which were very last year.

As they rode down Carsonia Avenue on the trolley, Frances stared out the window silently evoking the events of the day: the gay crowds, beautiful women, the beauty of the lake and most of all the joy of fitting in with the most popular girls in her school. Yet, as often happened when she reached the summit of contentment, she abruptly fell into a deep melancholy for no clear reason. It was if something, no someone were missing. When she was younger, it was not a feeling, but something more concrete. She shared her happiest moments, as well as all her worries, with an imaginary friend, a sweet little girl about her age. Over the years, the friend's appearances became few and far between. But every once and a while she felt not her presence, but her existence. She never discussed these feelings with her friends, and especially not with her parents. She wondered if other girls had similar experiences, but no one had ever spoken of it. But as these feelings were becoming infrequent, she told herself that she was growing up and that it was a childhood folly that would dissipate as she matured.

ADDIE

PHILADELPHIA, PENNSYLVANIA, 1915

"Addie, come inside," Rose called opening the door of her smart duplex house. "Your Uncle Barry is stopping by in an hour. I want you to get cleaned up. Take off those play clothes and put on your new dress."

A group of girls, breathless and flushed from jumping rope, all glanced up at Mrs. Strauss, Addie's mother. Addie, her face turning even redder from embarrassment, tried to ignore her mother and ran to take her turn at jumping.

"Adelaide Strauss, come here this moment," called her mother with a menacing tone.

Addie knew better than to defy her mother when she used that tone. She turned to her friends. "Sorry girls, I got to go." As she approached the narrow porch, which was diminished even more by a railing that demarcated her side from the neighbor's, she saw that her mother was holding out a new dress, embroidered with lace with sleeves lined with mother of pearl buttons.

This puzzled Addie since her mother was extremely thrifty, especially when it came to luxuries such as new dresses.

"Hurry my girl. Go wash up and then I'll help you put this on. I don't want you to tear the lace or lose any buttons."

"Mama, why all the fuss?" said Addie. "It's only Uncle Barry."

Suddenly she noticed that her mother had a new coiffure. Her long blonde hair was swept up in a complicated fashion. Addie realized that she must had been to a professional hairdresser at considerable expense.

As Rose was helping her daughter into the new dress and brushed her long blonde hair, she became unexpectedly serious. She scrutinized her daughter, turning her this way and that, adjusting the dress.

"Barry is coming over today to talk to you. We have made some plans and he insists on telling you himself. He didn't want me to say a word. And Lord knows why, he wants your approval. Personally, I find it ridiculous to even ask the opinion of a ten-year-old girl. Why I will do as I please. Well, never mind. I see him parking his car. You'll know soon enough."

Barry Lutz stood on the front porch. A middle-aged man of forty, he was tall and lanky, not particularly handsome, but pleasant looking. Rose had met him in the law office where she worked as a legal secretary. He first appeared around a year ago to deliver new typewriters and other office equipment. Because the stenographers needed to learn how to operate the various innovations on the machines, he spent several days with them, and Rose and he began to step out together. Their relationship had become serious and a week ago he proposed. Though she could hardly say that she loved him, she liked him very much. What is more, he offered security and a brighter future.

The doorbell rang. "Addie, please open the door for Uncle Barry. I just need to check my hair."

Addie opened the door and Barry gave her one of his bear hugs. She giggled and tried to reach her arms around his neck to return the hug. "Hi, Uncle Barry. I didn't know that you were coming by today, and Mama says you have something particular to discuss with me. I am all ears."

"Hello, sweetheart," he said, putting on a gallant air. "Where is your Mama?"

"Mama is here," said Rose, as she descended the stairs. "Let's go sit in the living room. Sit down like I taught you, Addie. Cross your legs at the ankles."

"My, my," said Barry. How did I get so lucky to have the attention of two beautiful ladies?"

Rose glanced at him trying to hide her impatience. "Come on, Barry. The poor girl is dying of curiosity. Let's let her in on our secret."

Addie's heartbeat wildly and her mouth was dry. "Please, one of you please tell me what is going on."

"Okay, calm down," he said. "I wanted to tell you the news myself. I have asked your mother to marry me and beyond all my expectations, she has accepted."

Addie jumped out of her chair, clapping her hands. Then hugging her mother, she said, "Mama, I am so happy for you, and of course for Barry. Will you marry soon?"

"Yes, quite soon," said Rose. "But Barry hasn't finished. Please go sit down."

Barry looked at her in his usual gentle manner, but he appeared jittery. Out of the blue Addie started to cry. "Mama, are you going to leave me behind? I have always felt that you didn't really want me. Now that you are going to marry Uncle Barry, you're going to have me adopted or leave me with a neighbor. Then you'll have a new baby with him."

"Stop it!" Rose snapped. "You are absurd. Never wanted you indeed. You have no idea how much I wanted you. Would you please calm down and let Barry finish?"

"Nothing could be further from the truth," he assured her. "When we marry, I plan to adopt you. Would you mind changing your name to Addie Lutz?"

Addie's throat tightened as she tried to control her tears. "I'm sorry. I don't know what made me say those awful things. I would be proud and happy to be your daughter. I have always dreamed of having a father."

She rose and sat next to him on the sofa, kissing him gently on the cheek.

"Good, good," said Rose. "I knew that she would be pleased, Barry. Now tell her the rest."

"The rest?" she said, her eyes widening.

"Well, this is the sticky part," he said. "It took me some smooth talking to convince Rose. By gum if I could understand why she resisted at first. The fact is that we will all be moving to New York City. Your Uncle Barry, I mean your Papa if you don't mind, has gotten a promotion. I will be getting, what we call in the sales business, a new territory. I'll be working for the same company, but I will call on offices in New York and New Jersey."

Addie was stunned. She had never thought of leaving her house and her friends in Philadelphia. But taking in the entire situation, her mother's happiness, and the idea of finally having a father, after a minute of consideration, she considered herself a very lucky girl.

Rose walked up from the IRT and crossed 115th Street. She held Addie's hand with an overabundance of caution. Addie tried to shake her hand loose.

"Come on, Mama. I'm not a five-year-old. I've been playing on the street since I was even younger than that."

"This is New York, not Philadelphia," Rose snapped. "Until we get to know the neighborhood and the neighbors, you will stay where I can keep an eye on you."

"School starts in two weeks. I hope you don't plan to walk me back and forth. I met a girl a few days ago who says that we are in the same grade. We plan to walk together, and she has a group of friends who all live on our block."

"Who is this girl? Do I know her?" Rose said, appearing leery.

"Dina Del Vecchio. Her family lives down the block in one of the newer buildings.

She has been so nice to me. She even invited me over for dinner. She is always bragging what a great cook her mother is. Can I go sometime, Mama?"

"I suppose so," her mother said. "At least she's not from a Jewish family. Italians are usually very friendly, not stuck up like the Jews. And it's true that women are good cooks."

"Why do you always say such mean things about Jews? More than half our neighbors are Jewish and the few girls that I have met are awfully nice. Dina said that the smartest kids in our school are Jewish. Don't you want me to be friends with the smart kids?"

"I have my reasons. I would rather you restrict your social circle to Protestants, even Catholics, if you must. You will see that Jews stick together. They don't want anything to do with us. They consider themselves to be superior people, the chosen people. Well, I choose to have nothing to do with them. And neither should you."

Bewildered and disappointed, Addie knew better than to press the point any further. But she was even more determined to make friends with Jews, Catholics, or anyone she met when she started school.

FRANCES

BRYN MAWR COLLEGE, 1922

Frances couldn't believe her eyes when she had opened the letter from Bryn Mawr. Sure, she was the smartest girl in her class, but it was a class of forty students graduating from Mt. Penn High. Reading was not known as a Mecca of intellectuals. But she had written her essay carefully and had stressed all her extracurricular activities: editor of the school paper, debate club and captain of the hockey team. Of course, she made no mention of her time spent in the Temple Oheb Shalom Youth Group, which was limited to serving on a committee responsible for decorating for Hanukah. She imagined that the Admissions Department did not suspect that she was Jewish. After all, with a name like Frances Austin, people make assumptions. She had not been concerned when they called her for an interview. After all, even if they suspected, she assumed that they would have the tact not to ask.

Yet somehow, they must have known. Her parents were from Philly and her mother's large family were prominent. Apparently, they knew because when she got to her room, her roommate introduced herself.

"Hi, I am Rachael Aronson," said a rail-thin brunette who was unpacking her large suitcase. "I took the bed near the window. I hope you don't mind."

She approached Frances and shook her hand, then greeted Dr. and Mrs. Austin. "I hope you don't mind if I am completely honest. But I was a little confused when the hall proctor told me that I would be rooming with Frances Austin. You see, there aren't many of us here and they always have us room together. So naturally, well, you understand. I prefer to share with a Jewish girl like myself."

Minnie smiled and tried to make the girl feel comfortable. "This kind of thing happens quite often. Yes, Frances Austin does sound goyish. Would you do me a favor, Rachael?"

"Why of course, Mrs. Austin. Anything within reason."

"Could you see that my girl gets to temple from time to time. You are Reform, aren't you? I just assumed that a college girl would be Reform. I'll give you a list of some temples that are nearby."

Frances' mouth was pinched, and she turned her head trying to ignore her mother. She didn't want to argue. Her parents would be leaving soon and then she would do as she pleased. Still, she didn't want her roommate to get the wrong impression. After kissing her mother and father goodbye at their car, she walked back to her room. Oddly, she felt a lump in her throat and had to fight back tears when she kissed her father. But by the time she walked into the dormitory room, she had recovered her composure.

"Rachael, just so we are clear, I have no intention of attending services at temple. As a matter of fact, I don't practice my religion. Do you understand?"

"Sure, I understand," she said with a smirk. "You want to pass as a goy. You won't get away with it on campus. So, I can only assume that you want to keep your secret from the boys at Penn. Don't worry. I won't say a word. It's not likely that I will be invited to any mixers or frat parties. So, you needn't worry."

It was the end of September, and the leaves began to change turning the campus into a riot of reds, yellows, and browns. The Gothic buildings, at first intimidated Frances. Reading had offered nothing to compare with the remarkable historical architecture. Soaring grey stone buildings, long arcades in the Cloisters, and buildings with turrets, gargoyles and stone owls were set among beautiful landscaping designed by Vaux and Olmstead. The Great Hall held a beautiful statue of Athena, the Goddess of Wisdom. Frances spent her time getting accustomed to the rhythm of classes, scheduled meals, and hours of study in the beautiful M. Carey Thomas library. She took her studies seriously, having decided to concentrate on American and English literature with a smattering of French and World History. Her grades were high, and the teachers wrote encouraging, sometimes glowing comments on her papers.

At the end of October, the student body took part in Lantern Night an annual Bryn Mawr tradition, when first-year students gather in The Cloisters and receive lanterns from sophomores. This symbolized the passing of the light of knowledge from one class to another. Frances adored the traditions, and she felt happy to be part of a community of intelligent women. The fall term flew by, and she fell in with a swell crowd of girls, not one of them Jewish. Her closest friend, Alice Bradford, was from Chicago, the daughter of a wealthy manufacturer. She was also extremely literary and was in most of Frances' classes. Alice's circle included Caroline Pierson and Mary Stevenson, both from Stamford, Connecticut. They were debutantes, so they were constantly flitting back and forth from Philly to New York to try on dresses, choose orchestras, and make out invitations. They both wanted to bob their hair before the coming out parties, but their mothers threatened to send them to finishing schools in Switzerland if they dared cut off their beautiful hair. Frances expected to see them with short hair in the spring term after their balls.

Edna Parker, a tall redheaded, freckled girl, was in her French class. She had paired up with her to write up and perform dialogues about dining out in a restaurant in Paris.

Edna didn't quite fit into her crowd, but Frances told the girls that because she had a brother, who was a senior at Penn and was the president of one of the best fraternities, they had better let her join the group.

Of course, Frances only saw Rachael in their dormitory room. In the beginning Frances made an effort to be friendly. She even tagged along a few times with her roommate when she met her group of friends for lunch. But seeing how they isolated themselves from the other girls and made such a fuss about the difficulty of staying kosher, she started skipping lunch altogether. Rachael didn't approve of her desire to be friends with the goyim. But that was just too bad. If she hadn't fallen in with the Jewish crowd in Reading with all her mother's pressure, she wasn't going to give in now. The atmosphere got a bit icy in the room, and Frances was considering asking for a single room. But the term was almost over, and she decided to wait and see if things improved in January.

Her parents spoiled her during the vacation with Hanukah presents and rich foods. They invited the Bashes and her friend Sonia's family for Sabbath dinner. Sonia had started a job as a stenographer at a steel mill in Bethlehem. Frances felt bad for her because she was a bright girl and had dreamed of going to college and perhaps even pursuing the law. But her parents didn't have the means. It occurred to Frances that she had been refused little in her life. Usually, she would only have to ask her mother once, at most twice for a new dress or permission to go to a party. If Mother refused, she would get her way by complaining to Father. And for the first time she understood what it might be like to have to give up on dreams and settle for what life offers.

She spent several evenings with her friends Patricia and Betsy. Both were home from Penn State. Of course, they had both bobbed their hair, but she couldn't imagine that the barbers upstate had much experience with the latest in women's coiffures.

"I love your bob, Betsy," she fibbed.

"Thanks," said Betsy. "Patricia and I went to a barber the same day on a dare. Since he is the only one in town who is willing to cut girls' hair, we didn't have much choice. I'm going downtown tomorrow to have it fixed up."

"I love it," said Patricia. "And so do the boys. I was asked out by three boys the day I had it cut. So, spill Frances. Have you got a fella yet? The Penn boys must be calling you every night."

"Not yet," said Frances. "We have some parties lined up in January, even a debut in New York. But I have been concentrating on my classes. I know it sounds out of character, but I have become quite the bookworm."

"Not really," said Betsy, rolling her eyes. "You were second in the class, and you hardly cracked a book. If you don't watch out you might turn into an egghead or one of those Greenwich Village intellectuals, if you find your way to New York one day."

"Wouldn't I just love to go to New York," sighed Frances. "But first I have to get my Bryn Mawr pedigree. Apparently, it carries a lot of weight if a gal wants to make a splash in advertising or in publishing."

A melodious automobile horn signaled the arrival of Bobby Kendall. He was driving the girls over to Steve Koch's house for a party. Steve's father could always be counted on to have a stock of imported gin, and he was a good sport about letting his son share it with his friends, if they didn't overdo it. Frances rarely drank, not that she particularly approved of prohibition. In her opinion, the government had no business telling people what they could eat or drink. She just hadn't had much occasion to go to speakeasies or booze parties. But her friends had insisted, and she didn't want to appear snobbish. She spent the evening sipping slowly on a concoction of gin and an unrecognizable sickly-sweet syrup. Her former classmates got progressively spiflicated and idiotic, while she wondered what she was doing there. What did she have in common with these small-town kids anyway? Most of them had decided to work in the local mills, either as foremen or in sales. Steve Koch had been given an executive job at his father's insurance company, and Bobby decided to goof off for a year before getting on with his life. Frances looked at the good-looking crowd of mostly blonde eighteen-year-olds. The girls had been her best friends. Every couple of years she would exchange one best friend for another, as she did with her beaux. Now she realized that they really were interchangeable, and they shared the same small dreams and limited view on life. Nothing outside of Reading really mattered to most of them. Was she a snob? No, she had just changed. It occurred to her that if the strapping Steve Koch had been born a few years earlier, he might have gone to war and perhaps he would have died at the battle of the Somme. But instead of being buried in France, he was whooping it up with the old crowd, drinking his father's gin.

FRANCES

BRYN MAWR, SPRING TERM, 1923

The first week in February, Edna Parker invited Frances to a party at her brother's frat at Penn. And by the way, would she mind asking a few of her friends if they might want to go. She specifically mentioned Caroline and Mary, since she knew that they were her close friends, and besides being cute, they had class. Her brother liked college girls with class. Of course, sometimes he enjoyed the company of the local flappers from the neighborhood speakeasy. Frances couldn't promise that her friends could come, what with their debuts coming up in a month. But she was pretty sure that they would jump at the chance to meet some boys from Penn.

Edna's brother had sent one of his fraternity brothers over with a large car. The girls were waiting near the gate when he drove up and slammed the brakes to a screeching halt. Frances piled in with the girls, jammed in between Caroline and Mary. Edna sat in the front with the driver, an overweight and balding senior at Penn named Waldo. He jammed his foot on the accelerator, speeding down the hills of the Main Line. Caroline squealed with panic, while Mary laughed nervously and squeezed Frances' hand so tightly, she left nail impressions.

Arriving on the campus of the University of Pennsylvania, the girls asked Waldo to show them to a lady's room to repair the damage of their windblown hair. None of the girls had bobbed hair, so there was a lot of brushing, twisting, and pinning of long curls. Caroline brought out a tiny jar of rouge and began to apply it to her lips and cheeks.

"Can I have some rouge?" asked Mary. "I forgot mine."

"Of course, just give me a minute to finish. It would be so much easier if they allowed us to wear makeup on campus. I hate these rush jobs and the light in here is not helping. How do I look?"

"You look gorgeous," said Mary as she took the rouge and began to dab it on her lips.

"How about you Frances? You want some?"

"I'm not adept at applying makeup. Girls never wore it in Reading, so I am afraid I have no experience."

Caroline grabbed the jar from Mary. "Give it here. Come closer, Frances. I think you just need the tiniest hint of color on your lips. With your coloring, less is more. Anyway, it's a shame to mess with perfection. Although, I would show a little bit more leg. Here let me help you," she said, while she pinned the shoulders of Frances' dress, shortening it by two inches.

"That's enough, Caroline," scolded Edna. "Don't forget that my brother specifically wanted classy Bryn Mawr girls. They could go down the block if they wanted low-class flappers."

"Alright, alright," said Caroline. "Let's go. I assume you know some of the boys, Edna.

We prefer eastern boys, none of those corn-fed guys from Iowa or Minnesota. Not that it matters, since Mary and I have steadies who are escorting us to our debuts. But I don't want to see Frances stuck with a dud."

The girls walked into the fraternity house's large living room. Clearly, the boys had made a cursory effort to tidy up. There was a nice fire burning in the large fireplace and sofas and armchairs were arranged in a semicircle so that everyone could enjoy the warmth. Waldo and Sam Parker ambled over to greet the girls. Sam's eyes narrowed with scrutiny when he saw Frances. He took a quick inventory of her attributes: her lissome figure, natural blonde hair, and luminous blue eyes. But as he sidled up to her, she dropped her small purse. She bent down to pick it up and as she lifted her head, her gaze locked onto the most attractive man that she had ever seen. As she straightened up, she lost her balance and grabbed Edna's hand. She saw him staring as he made a straight line to her. And there he was standing at her side, boldly taking her hand.

Turning to Sam, he chided, "You're out of your league with this one, old man. But you might introduce us."

Sam glowered, "I don't know what you're doing here, Jim. You graduated two years ago. Ask Edna to introduce you."

Edna flushing with embarrassment turned to the young man. "This is Frances Austin. She's at Bryn Mawr with us. You're James Whitman, I believe."

"Yes. I am Robert's older brother. He's a senior. I was president here three years ago. I'm in Wharton doing grad work."

Edna, awkward under normal circumstances, was tongue-tied. She excused herself and joined her brother, who was brooding in front of the fire.

Frances froze, her eyes cast down. He still had hold of her hand, and it seemed he had no intention of releasing it or her. She realized that she was holding her breath and not wanting to give him the satisfaction of recognizing the effect he had on her, she turned her head and exhaled.

"Do you think that I might have my hand back?" she teased.

"Well, I guess so," he acquiesced with mock expression of distress. "But I insist on the right to reclaim it at any time."

Frances did not know what to make of him. Putting aside the fact that he was the best-looking man that she had ever seen, outside of a magazine cover or a movie screen, she experienced a physical magnetism that she had only read about in novels. His hair, which was a reddish blond, was parted down the middle and rather long, his eyes were dark green. She remembered that she once had a cat with eyes that color. His features were classic, straight nose, full lips, and high cheekbones. But what really made her pulse quicken was his athletic body. Tall and broad-shouldered, he had a long, lean body. Even with his thick woolen jacket, she could see that his arms were strong and muscular. Oh, wouldn't it be lovely to be squeezed by those arms?

"I had the impression that tonight was to be a frat mixer. But you don't really want me to mix, do you?" she asked with a coy smile.

"No, I forbid any mixing," he chided. "Now, I do have some gin in my car. If we find some tonic, then we can do our own mixing."

"I'm not much of a drinker," she said. "I'm from Reading, and it's as dry as the desert."

"Well, we will have to change that," he said. "Not that I approve of girls that get blotto. I always say just enough to keep us gay."

"I guess I wouldn't mind a drink. Edna said that they have some gin and beer in the basement."

"I would rather take you home right now than subject you to the basement and the lousy frat booze. I have my car outside and I know of a speakeasy that's real class, imported gin and champagne. What do you say?"

For almost a minute she said nothing. She didn't know what to do. If she didn't go, she might never see him again. But what would he think of her if she went so willingly with someone that she had just met?

"Look, James, is it?"

"Jim" he said.

"Jim, I might consider going with you, but just for a glass of champagne and then back to Bryn Mawr by midnight. I am not a crazy flapper out for a night of booze and necking.

So, if you're up for some conversation and a nice evening, I'm your girl."

"Frances, the minute I saw you I knew that you were my girl. I don't intend to let you be anybody else's girl."

Her face reddened and she felt a warm tingling throughout her body. "We'll see about that. Let's start with a drink."

In the weeks that followed, Frances saw Jim Whitman every Saturday night. After a month they spent Friday and Saturday nights together. He told her about his family that lived on the Main Line, just two towns away from Bryn Mawr. His parents owned Whitman's Furniture, an old manufacturing company that was founded in the 1800s. Since he was the older brother, he would take the reins when his father retired. His younger brother planned to take up the law. Jim had one semester left to finish his graduate degree in Business at Wharton.

She didn't tell him much about herself. Instinctively, she knew that if he discovered that she was Jewish, that would be the kiss of death. She told him that her father was a doctor in Reading. She made no mention of her mother's family in Philadelphia. For if she mentioned her Uncle David Cohen, that would be that. She never invited him to her campus, not that he had any interest in spending time at Bryn Mawr. Mary and Caroline knew that she was Jewish, but they would not betray her. But Rachael could be a problem. She had made some snide comments about her late nights and chided her about the fact that she was spending less and less time studying. It was true that her grades were slipping, but she honestly didn't care.

Frances was in love. Moreover, she knew that Jim was crazy about her. But her situation was precarious. If he found out that she was a Jew, would he still want to be with her? Even worse, if his parents knew, she could imagine their reaction. If Mary or Caroline told anyone about her relationship with Jim, even without malice, she knew the gossip would spread like wildfire.

It occurred to her that she had one course open to her,

and the first step was to plan to spend the night with Jim. If she could entice him into making love to her, she knew that he would marry her. She felt her face burning with shame. Scheming to entrap a man that she adored was not in her nature. At the same time, her pulse quickened, and her body stirred as she imagined caressing his body. And though she was conflicted, she knew that she had no choice but to go ahead with her plan.

The plan, however, needed some honing. How could she convince him to spend the night with her without appearing brazen? Where could they go? Bryn Mawr did not allow the students to spend weekends away without a letter of permission from their family or an invitation from a fellow student's parents. It suddenly occurred to her that Caroline had invited her to her debut in March. She had been surprised and pleased to receive the engraved invitation. Mary was the only other girl that she had invited from school. There was to be a dinner on Friday night and the ball was on Saturday. So, she would have an entire weekend in New York. At first, she had wanted to decline because she was not allowed to bring her own escort. Frances had no desire to be paired off with a boy she didn't know. She was sure that Jim would protest.

But now she could use the debut as pretext to spend a weekend in New York. Neither her parents nor the school would object. Perhaps Caroline would give in and allow her to bring Jim as her escort, if not she would leave the ball early.

It was a blustery afternoon when they arrived in New York. Frances had borrowed a beaver coat from Edna, as well as a formal dress for the ball. They entered the lobby of the Biltmore, where an entire floor had been reserved for the Pierson's guests. Frances had been given a small single room. Caroline's mother did not allow any uninvited escorts to attend, so she had decided to skip the Friday night dinner.

While she checked in, Jim stood discreetly near the revolving doors. The hotel was a beehive of activity, with groups of gay girls flirting with well-dressed men. There was hardly an older couple in sight. Her head was swimming with the bustle of the crowds. The women's heady perfume and chic dresses dazzled her. 'What a city!' she thought. 'I see myself here.'

She approached Jim, who was talking to a middle-aged man. "Hello," she said with a wink. "What a surprise to see you here. I didn't know that you were in the city."

Jim smiled and shook the gentleman's hand. "Nice to have met you, Mr. Norton. This is an acquaintance of mine from Philly. It's Frances, I believe."

"Nice to meet you, young lady," he said, tipping his hat and then walking away.

"Yes, it's Frances," she said with a titter. "How nice of you to remember."

"Just passing the time while you checked in. He's an out-of-town businessman. Says he stops here once a month. He claims he likes the hubbub, not to mention a good gawk at the girls' knees. He thinks that the Fitzgerald's have a suite on the top floor. Maybe we'll bump into them in the elevator."

"Now that would be swell. I just adored *This Side of Paradise*," she said. "Darling, I need to go up. The bellboy is taking up my suitcase. I'll be down in a jiffy. I want to get a feel for the city. Then we can take a walk in Central Park before it gets dark."

They returned to the hotel around seven, their cheeks flushed from brisk wind. Giddy and distracted, she floated into the lobby without a care. The warmth and radiance of the room enhanced the couple's emotions. They rushed towards the elevator and minutes later Frances opened the door to her small room. She was surprised to find a bottle of champagne and two glasses on a small table, along with some sandwiches.

"How did you ever manage this?" she gushed.

"Nothing five bucks can't fix," he said.

"Open the champagne and I'll get changed," she said,

taking her small bag into the bathroom.

His eyes widened when she came out. Even though they had done a lot of serious petting, he had never seen her breasts or her legs. Frances had saved her money and bought a silk nightgown, cut high at the hem and low at the bust. Taking the glass of champagne from his hand, she drank it down and asked for more.

"Slow down, Frances. We have all night. And I really want to know if you're sure about this. It's a big step and to be honest, it puts me on the spot. I've never slept with an innocent before."

Her eyes began to fill with tears. "I thought that you loved me. You said so. Have your feelings changed?"

"No, I adore you. And I would like nothing more than to make love to you."

She wiped the tears from her face and wrapped her arms around his neck. Pulling him to her, she kissed him, first lightly, then more passionately. She opened her mouth to his tongue. He tore at his shirt and undid his pants. But he hesitated.

"Jim, I want this," she said. "I want you. You are the only man that I will ever want."

Unable to contain himself he caressed her breasts and stroked her legs. She had no experience beyond kissing in cars, but her instinct and desire took over. Just when she thought she couldn't wait a moment longer, he stopped.

"No, Frances," he flared. He pushed her away, almost brutally.

She could see that he wanted her by the way his body responded. So, why did he push her away? She began to sob and shake uncontrollably and turned her face away.

"Why are you doing this?" she asked, her voice raspy from crying.

"I am stopping because I love you and I want to marry you. We can wait."

"I can wait, but not too long," she said. "If we don't marry soon, I don't know what I am capable of."

On a Wednesday evening in the second week of May, Frances closed her small suitcase.

Nervously looking at the door and hoping that she could leave the campus before her roommate returned from dinner. She had been vigilant in keeping her plan secret from Rachael, and she had no knowledge of the planned elopement. Frances had mentioned that Jim had proposed, and that they might marry when he graduated.

Jim knew almost nothing about her family. She did tell him that her father was a doctor in Reading, and that she was an only child. When he probed her further, she changed the subject.

But when they decided to marry, he pressured her for an explanation for her insistence on an elopement. Lying did not come easy to Frances, but she had no choice. She simply said that her father would be disappointed if she did not finish her studies. She hinted that her parents had tried to arrange a marriage with the son of their best friends and still held hope that it would come off.

Jim didn't understand France's feelings of urgency. He was beginning to vacillate, so she gave him a stark choice; either they marry now, or they go their separate ways. She knew that he loved her too much to refuse her.

A week ago, they had crafted their plan. He had found a justice of the peace in Maryland, who would marry them, even though she was not yet eighteen. They would drive down on Friday, marry and be back in time to go to their classes on Monday. As far as Bryn Mawr was concerned, she was spending the weekend in the Poconos with family.

Unfortunately, Rachael had overheard her speaking to Caroline. Frances and her roommate had reached the point where they barely spoke. But Rachael listened and she didn't hesitate to rifle through Frances' desk. She had found letters from Jim. A bright girl, she had figured out what Frances was planning. She had asked her friend Beth to eavesdrop whenever her roommate spoke on the hall phone, and she had managed to hear enough to reconstruct the couple's plan.

Earlier that day, Beth rushed up to Rachael after class. "Rachael, it's on for tonight. I heard her say something about an eight o'clock train at Broad Street Station."

"Fantastic. Beth you really should think about becoming a private investigator. You have a real talent."

Beth snickered. "Yeah, my parents would love that. So, what are you going to do?"

"I am going to ruin her plans. I'll report her to the dean, but not until she's already left the campus. I want her to be caught in the act."

"You really despise her, don't you?"

"You would too if you had to live with her," she said. "Anyone who would try to pass for something that she is not is beyond contempt."

"I assume that he's not Jewish. I have never known any Jews named Whitman. Then again, Austin isn't common among our people either."

"Exactly. I am convinced that she hasn't told him that she is Jewish. Really, I don't give a damn about him and his snooty Main Line parents. But I think it's really low of Frances to pull such a trick. I personally feel like it's a slap in the face. She needs a good lesson."

At seven-thirty Frances stepped out of a taxi expecting to meet Jim at the ticket booth in the Broad Street Station. To her horror, she realized that something had gone terribly wrong. He was surrounded by a group of people, one whom she recognized as the dean of students from Bryn Mawr. She advanced towards them with trepidation, suffering under their withering stares.

What could she possibly say? Looking to Jim for support, Frances met his eyes which narrowed into a steely stare. A sudden sinking sensation overcame her. He knew the truth about her, and he despised her.

The dean spoke first. "These are James's parents, Mr. and Mrs. Whitman. They have told me that I may speak for them."

Frances glanced warily at the tall, stern man and his plump wife. She stood close to her son; her arm entwined with his. His father's austere face was frozen into an expression of pure loathing.

"What you have attempted to do is not only immoral and hurtful, but it also flies in the face of everything that our school stands for. A Bryn Mawr girl should be honest, pure, and true to herself. You have proven to be none of these."

Frances felt her heart constricting in her chest. Her face burned with shame and anger.

"Could I please speak to Jim?" she begged.

"I don't think that we have anything to say to each other," he said. "You are not the girl that I loved. You've played me for a fool. That's all I'll say, because if I speak what's in my heart, I feel that I would go beyond the bounds of decency."

The dean took Frances firmly by the arm and led her outside where a car was waiting. They rode for a few minutes in silence. Tears streamed down Frances' face, mixing with the rouge that she had carefully applied earlier. Finally, the dean spoke in a low, stern voice.

"You will be allowed to finish the term, so that you may say that you have attended Bryn Mawr for one year. However, you will not be invited back for your sophomore year. Since what you have done has no relation to your academic performance, we will not write it on your school record. We will just say that we are having an amicable parting of the ways. I do not intend to communicate with your parents. I'll leave it up to you whether you will be honest and open with them. Since honesty does not seem to be one of your attributes – well, I'll say no more about that. I would just add one thing. I am disappointed in you, Frances. When we admitted you to our school, we knew that you were Jewish. In the past, it was our policy not to admit any Jews.

But we are a modern, progressive school, so each year we choose a few promising girls of your faith. If we are open about this, we expected you to be equally honest about your background. We find the fact that you hid your background from the Whitman boy distressing. A scandal was averted tonight. You should thank Rachael for being your conscience."

For the first time in her life, Frances did feel ashamed, not of her background, or even for her deception. She felt ashamed that she let a man blind her judgment. She made a solemn oath to herself that she would never let that happen again.

From now on her focus would be on her career. Her dream had always been to be a writer and there were few opportunities in Reading or even in Philadelphia to reach that goal. She was determined not to waste time and energy on futile love affairs. She might find a good man someday. Of course, he would be someone quite different from Jim. Independence and strength were the qualities that she would require, if and when she decided to squander her time looking for love.

ADDIE

NEW YORK CITY, FALL 1922

Dina Del Vecchio had invited Addie to a celebratory dinner at her parent's restaurant. It was the week before she was to start her year of courses at Smith College of Business. It had always been Addie's dream to go to college and study literature and foreign languages.

But life had delivered a terrific blow last month when her adoptive father Barry Lutz had announced that he was leaving Rose for another woman. It had been a shock when she ran into the woman as she waited in the car outside the house as he gathered his last belongings. She had expected a younger, flashy tart, someone in her late twenties or early thirties. But when she peeked into the car, she caught a glimpse of a stout and rather plain woman in her late forties.

Suddenly it occurred to her that Barry, who was a compassionate and patient man, was not leaving her mother for another woman. He was simply leaving her mother. Why should it come as a surprise? For several years, Rose had become impossible to live with. She hounded him for money yet complained when he left for the long sales trips that were essential to his work.

All the while he had been a wonderful father to her, encouraging her to study and make something of her life.

When she took everything into account, she could not blame him. Her mother had become a bitter angry woman. He deserved better.

On an unseasonably warm day in September, Addie approached an ugly grey ten-story building on West Seventeenth Street. The school occupied the entire eighth floor, and was made up of ten classrooms, including a room with ten long tables for the typewriters, a study hall, and of course, the administrative office of Miss Alice Smith. Half the classrooms were interior with no windows, so the lighting was inadequate to say the least. The windows were crepuscular, making for a dreary atmosphere to the classroom despite the electric overhead lighting. The walls were painted in various pastel colors, most likely in a futile attempt to brighten the place up.

The students filed into the large study hall, settling into the stiff, uncomfortable chairs.

Addie noticed that the student body consisted of approximately thirty young women and five men. She was surprised to see any men at all. But as she would later learn, they were pursuing a different course of studies than the girls. After much shifting, murmuring, and giggling, the students fell silent as the faculty filed in and sat at a long table in the front of the room.

Each in turn stood and introduced themselves. Mr. Babson, pompous and unattractive with a sad, shaggy mustache, spoke briefly about his career as teacher of writing and composition in various institutions, and what he expected of his students of Business English.

A frumpy, gray-haired woman introduced herself as the instructor of stenography, or more precisely, the Gregg Method of Shorthand. Her voice was barely audible, and she spoke with downcast eyes. Several other teachers rose to introduce themselves: Mrs. Wright, typing teacher, Mr. Adkins, dull and businesslike, teacher of accounting, and a young, attractive blonde woman, a bookkeeping instructor named Miss Branson.

It was Miss Branson, who introduced Miss Alice Smith, the founder, and head of the school. The directress, a slender, middle-aged woman, stood erect and proceeded to welcome the new students to their year's course at her business college. She went on to expound upon their course of studies and what was expected of them as students.

"Ladies, I will tell you that if you are diligent in your studies and practice, you will be proficient in typing, shorthand, and the composition of business letters. We also offer a course in bookkeeping for those of you who have an interest. Of course, accounting, and basic business law classes are reserved for our male students. However, for an extra fee young ladies may enroll in accounting.

Upon graduation, we offer career counseling. We do have many contacts in the city, so we may be able to find positions for many of you, if you are flexible regarding terms of employment.

Now, as to what I expect of my students. Young ladies should dress conservatively. By this I mean, no high hems or rolled stockings. No sleeveless dresses will be permitted. Shoes should have relatively low heels. You are encouraged to wear gloves and hats when coming and going to school. And of course, make-up is not allowed. If I see rouged cheeks or lipstick, I will send you to the lady's room to wash. And if a girl is reprimanded more than three times, she will be asked to leave.

Young men, you will watch your language while on the premises. Although friendship between all students is encouraged, there will be no dating among the student body. I hope that I have made myself clear." Miss Smith attempted a feeble smile, trying to make herself relatable to the students. But the gesture fell flat.

During the first week of class, Addie fell in with a nice circle of friends. A jolly, young woman from Newark, Dottie Banks, sat next to her in typing class and they began eating lunch together, trying out local restaurants and luncheonettes. There was a petite blonde girl named Esme in her shorthand class. She came from a small farm outside of Lancaster, Pennsylvania. Addie mentioned that she was also from Pennsylvania, from Philly. Esme was shy and somewhat overwhelmed, so she felt it her duty to help guide the girl through life in the big city. She lived in a boardinghouse not far from the school and was very unhappy. She complained of male boarders who had been harassing her. One, a fat disagreeable man of forty, had started knocking on her bedroom door late in the evenings.

One of the school's male students, who was friendly with everyone, approached Addie and Esme to try out a new restaurant. Sandford Todd, an aimable sort, was studying accounting with hope of one day opening his own firm. He was not particularly attractive, but he had a warm and friendly manner that put the young women at ease.

Addie's closest friend in the school was an attractive dark-haired girl from Brooklyn. Evie Segal was extremely bright and lively, with a great sense of humor. She commuted back and forth to school because she couldn't afford an apartment or a boarding hotel. One day over lunch she complained to Addie.

"I love my family, but you have no idea what it's like living with an old-fashioned Jewish mother and an overprotective father. My brother Sam is still at home, thank God. He keeps me sane," she said.

"It's just me and my mother," said Addie. "I'm up in Washington Heights. No brothers or sisters. I really wanted a sister when I was little. In fact, I made up an imaginary friend. The strangest thing is that she looked just like me. I guess I just didn't have the imagination to make up a completely different girl."

Evie smiled. "A sister would have been nice. But I adore my brother. I would love for you to meet him. Maybe on a Sunday you could come over to Brooklyn. The two of us could show you around."

"That would be just fine," said Addie. "Or maybe we could go out on a Friday or Saturday night?"

"Friday nights are out. My parents are very traditional. Everybody must be home for Shabbat."

"Oh, I understand. I had lots of Jewish friends in high school in Washington Heights. I even dated a Jewish boy for a few months," she added.

"Well, that's verboten in our family. Not that I'm happy about it. But Sam and I just accept it. We will marry in the religion."

Addie nodded her head. "I guess I can understand that, but kids in my school pretty much mixed it up. Some of them were wild, especially the popular flapper girls. The Jewish boys loved them, especially the ones that bobbed and lightened their hair. I had a Jewish beau last year. He was always after me to get a bob and to put on some makeup. Finally, I told him I was no flapper and if he wanted one, then I'd break it off. I guess things are different in Brooklyn.

In my neighborhood we were all mixed together, especially the Italians and the Jews."

Evie sighed. "I suppose it depends on the family. I guess your parents aren't very strict if they let you date a Jewish boy."

Addie shrugged. "It's just me and my mother now. My stepfather left us recently. To be perfectly honest, my mother never talks to me about boys. I know that she has had a sketchy past, so she doesn't dare moralize. Anyway, these days she has become impossible. We can't get along for five minutes. She does nothing but criticize."

"Well, I honestly don't know which is worse an overbearing Jewish mother or a mother like yours, who is distant."

"Me neither," said Addie. "As soon as I can afford it, I plan on finding my own place."

"I wish!" said Evie. "Maybe someday we can get a place together."

"One can only dream," said Addie with a sad smile.

The second week in October on a Sunday afternoon, Addie stepped off the subway in Greenwich Village. She had arranged to meet Evie at a restaurant and then go on to meet Evie's brother, Sam, who was giving a talk about rights for the poor immigrant population who worked in factories. Evie had mentioned that he was in his last year of law school at NYU. His parents were proud that their son was going to be a lawyer. But they did not approve of his choice of specialization. Sam Segal was going to fight for the underdog and work towards equal justice for people who had no connections or power. Apparently, Mama wanted him to go into business law.

After the girls finished lunch, they walked over to Christopher Street and into a large room used for concerts and political gatherings.

"There he is," said Evie, waving to get his attention.

Addie watched as he crossed the room. Her breath quickened, and she realized that she was staring, and her mouth was open. She had not expected him to be so attractive. Perhaps she should have guessed, given Evie's good looks, that her brother would have the same striking features and coloring. He was tall and slender, but well-built. His eyes were the same shape as Evie's, but the color, a deep velvet brown, were different. He had a generous, well-shaped mouth when he smiled, and perfectly formed white teeth. She tried her best to pull herself together and smile pleasantly.

"Sam, this is my friend Addie Lutz," said Evie. "Addie, my meshuga brother Sam."

"Nice to meet you, Addie," he said, taking her in from top to bottom. His gaze came back to her beautiful blue eyes. "Evie, you didn't tell me she was a looker."

Addie blushed. "I never thought of myself as a "looker" but thank you."

"That's my brother. He's got a mouth on him," said Evie. "You're about to hear an example of it. I'm sure it will serve him well in the courthouse."

He fixed his eyes on Addie again, and then turned to step onto the small stage. The small crowd gathered in the restaurant did not quiet down at first and he had to almost shout to be heard.

He spoke for about twenty minutes about labor strikes and anarchists. Although he did not defend their actions, he described in detail the terrible working conditions that drove men and women to strike.

"I am not an Anarchist by any means, I can understand why men and women all over the world might feel that violence and nihilism are their only options. Let me stress that I don't believe that violence is justified, except in self-defense. As an attorney, I will defend any man or woman who has committed a crime of violence if it were a matter of self-defense."

She had followed the news of the railroad strikes that affected much of the country and felt sympathy for the workers whose wages were cut. Sam spoke eloquently in defense of the union members and criticized the bosses and the strikebreakers. As she listened to him, she realized that he was unlike any man that she had ever known. She had had crushes on young men, and she had even fooled herself that she loved one or two of her beaux. But what she was experiencing now was quite different. She looked at him and imagined that he might be a creature from another planet, so beautiful and so bright.

She noticed that Evie was looking at her with a sad smile. She blushed and turned her head.

"Don't bother trying to hide it," said Evie. "I know the signs. I can't tell you how many of my friends have fallen for Sam, especially when they first meet him. But I must say you look as if you got it bad."

"Really Evie, I was just enthralled by his speech. How can you say that?"

"I can say it because I have seen it so often. I consider you my friend, and I admire you. So, I am warning you to take care. He never stays with any girl very long. And remember what I said about our family. He will only marry a Jew. So, there is no future for you with him, except perhaps as a good friend."

Addie smiled. "I am not looking for a love affair at the moment. But I like Sam. He is brilliant and I like to surround myself with smart people. Why do you think I like to be with you?"

"Fine," said Evie. "I can see the three of us having some great times. Just be careful not to let yourself fall for him."

"I will be careful," said Addie, knowing that it would not be easy.

FRANCES

NEW YORK CITY, FALL 1923 TO SPRING 1924

Katherine Gibb's School, which was established in Providence, Rhode Island, had opened a branch in New York City in an elegant brownstone on Park Avenue. As she waits for her interview with the school director, Frances mulls over the events of the summer she spent in Reading after her departure from Bryn Mawr.

The months of July and August had been long and dull. She felt guilty lying to her parents, telling them that she didn't fit in with the girls at the school and that the courses were not challenging. If they had known the real reason, she was certain that they would never forgive her. Her mother still held fast to the illusion that she would find a Jewish boy, either in Reading or in Philadelphia. Minnie had practically exhausted the supply of Jewish men in Reading. She had lined up a string of eligible young men, but most of them knew that Frances would never be interested, so they all came up with last minute excuses to bow out. She did agree to dinner with one man who was a recent arrival to Reading.

Jonathan Morgenstern was attractive and witty, and she thought that he had some potential. But by the end of the evening, he admitted that he was not much of a ladies' man.

In fact, he only accepted these fix ups to keep up

appearances. The evening ended on a cheerful note with Frances agreeing that they could be friends. She offered to accompany him to various dinners and parties over the summer.

Her father's reaction to her decision to leave college was an entirely different matter. When she first told him that she would not be going back, his eyes filled with tears.

"I'm sorry to hear that you won't go back. Is there anything I can say to change your mind?"

"No, Daddy. I adore you for always wanting the best for me and I know that you worked hard to save for the tuition. I just didn't fit in, socially, I mean. You saw my grades and I am truly up to snuff academically. But I'm not willing to spend three more years studying subjects that won't help me to get where I want to be in life."

"Where exactly is that?" asked Mike patiently. "I had hoped you might want to go on and study law. Your professors praised your writing ability. If you could just stick it out, so many avenues would be open to you."

"I am sorry. I just can't do it." She was unflappable and she knew that she could bring him around. "I do have dreams, and I have a plan, if you will hear me out."

"Of course, I'll listen and if your dreams are within our reach, I will do all I can to help you."

"Well, to start with, you are right. I am a capable writer. However, to be successful in publishing, you need to know people, important people."

"Couldn't you meet important people at Bryn Mawr?" he asked.

"Not really. The school is full of girls from wealthy and influential families. But frankly, they are not interested in helping a Jewish girl from Reading." She tried to keep her composure. She knew that he would be hurt to learn that other students had been cruel to her because she was Jewish. "But all that doesn't matter, Daddy. I was thinking that I would look for work in advertising. There are so many magazines and so many new products that need to be promoted.

Eventually, I might make my way into publishing. I could eventually write a column in a magazine. Who knows? The sky is the limit."

Mike appeared wary. "All this sounds ambitious. This is the dream. Now, what is the plan?"

"I have it all worked out, Daddy," she clarified. "First of all, I can't make a dent in the publishing world in Reading, Pennsylvania. So, I did my research. I found a school in New York. They have a special program for college girls and even though I did not graduate from Bryn Mawr, they have admitted me for the fall term."

"I don't understand," said Mike, perplexed and frustrated. "You just told me that you don't want to waste three more years at Bryn Mawr. Why would you be so willing to waste them at this school?"

"It's only a one-year program, where I can learn skills that will help me find a job in the business world, the New York City business world. They groom you for positions as executive secretaries in all the prestigious firms. They have contacts with publishing houses, insurance companies, Wall Street firms and just about any field you can imagine."

"So, I am to understand that you want to leave Reading to go live in New York?"

"Daddy, you must have always known that I would never be happy living in Reading. What would you have me do?"

"I don't know. You could run my office, or you could teach high school. I hoped to see you marry a nice boy and have children. You would live close by, and your mother and I would …"

"I'm sorry, Daddy," she interrupted. "I would never be happy with that kind of life. I'm not saying that I will not marry. But I can't imagine being happy with a man from Reading." She took his hand. "You do understand?"

Mike knew when to admit defeat. "Where will you live?"

"There are hotels for women. They are quite reasonable and safe. I have some brochures that you can look over with

Mother." And with that, she knew it was settled.

Miss Tierney, an attractive, impeccably dressed women in her early forties, opened the door and ushered her into her office. Frances was captivated by the décor. It was clear that the office had once been a drawing room or perhaps a library. She could see that the school director had added her own touches, floral drapes, and overstuffed chairs. But the lustrous wood paneling and elaborate ceiling evoked a room from the Victorian age.

"I see that you are admiring the décor of my office. As you know, the school was once the private residence of a very influential family. This was the library. The upper floor bedrooms have been converted into classrooms. Downstairs we have a functioning kitchen and a dining room, so girls can, for an extra fee, have luncheon in the building. Although, most girls prefer to eat at some of the fine local restaurants."

Miss Tierney looked over Frances' file. "I see that you completed a year at Bryn Mawr. We do prefer to enroll college graduates in the program, but your grades and evaluations were superb. And now that I have met you, I am glad that we made an exception. A bright girl with your looks will go far."

Frances blushed and lowered her eyes. Although she was well aware that she was a pretty girl, it always embarrassed her when strangers referred to it. "Thank you, Miss Tierney. But I will do my best to show you that there is a brain in this pretty head."

Miss Tierney smiled. "Yes, indeed. Just work hard and apply yourself. Now, allow me to tell you a little more about the College Program at Katherine Gibbs. Of course, we teach typing and shorthand. But we offer so much more, elocution classes, basic business law, and accounting. Yet even with these skills, there is much more required of the modern young woman to make her way in New York. We can help you make the right connections, advise you on what kind of friends to cultivate, as well as what kind of people to avoid. Of course, our placement office is unrivaled in the entire country. Our alumni are loyal and will always hire a Katherine Gibbs graduate before another equally qualified candidate. We have placed our graduates in the best companies in all domains, publishing, insurance, fashion houses, even real estate. So, the sooner the gals in placement know your field of interest, the better."

"Now, as to accommodations," she said, abruptly changing the topic. "We gave you some recommendations in the packet we sent. What have you decided?"

"Thank you so much. The packet was helpful. My mother wanted me to stop at The Allerton. But I convinced her that The Martha Washington would be a better fit."

"Quite so," said Miss Tierney. "I believe that they have only single rooms. So, you prefer not to have a roommate?"

"For the time being, I would prefer living alone," said Frances. "Perhaps later I would consider living with another student."

"Consider it," she said. "You will find that Gibbs girls often become lifelong friends. You will meet many lovely young women from fine families. And of course, in your program, they will be highly intelligent."

Frances approached The Martha Washington Hotel on East Thirtieth Street. It was a twelve-story, Renaissance style building. She had preferred the hotel because men were allowed to dine in the restaurant, and she did not want to be restricted.

She was shocked when she entered the elevator and found that the operator was a young woman. She smiled and the girl winked. Frances was relieved when she opened the door to her small room and saw that her trunk had been delivered. She laughed when she saw that the room was a quarter of the size of the dorm room at Bryn Mawr. But at least she would be alone.

The next day she reported for her first day of class. There was a brief morning assembly, where the girls were scrutinized. The rules of acceptable attire were explained, and they were exacting: white gloves and hats were to be worn on the street and dresses must cover the knees. Makeup was allowed only if it was discreet. This meant only light rouge and no lipstick.

A Miss Clark prepared to address the incoming class, made up of twenty well-groomed young women. Frances heard a few of the students discussing their last semester at Vassar. She was relieved to see that there were no Bryn Mawr girls in the group, at least none that had known her. She breathed a mental sigh of relief. She had a clean slate, and she had every intention of making the most of the opportunity to carve out a career and a new life in New York.

The students filed out of the large lobby, that had once been a living room and climbed the stairs to begin their day of classes. Frances entered a bright room with large windows where rows of single desks, each with a typewriter, a pile of paper, carbon paper and pencils. As there seemed to be no assigned seats, she made her way to a desk near a window. But as she was about to sit down, a dark beauty slid into the seat.

Frances smiled amiably, "It's quite alright, I'll take this one."

"Sorry," said the young woman. "I didn't mean to be rude. I have a little difficulty with my vision. You really don't mind?"

"Not at all. By the way, I'm Frances Austin, Bryn Mawr."

"Okay, now please don't laugh. I am not trying to put one over on anybody. But my name is Katherine Gibbs. God's honest truth."

Frances looked at her askance with a quizzical expression. "Oh, come on. You're joking, right?"

"No, I am afraid it's true. Of course, I am no relation to Mrs. Gibbs. But just for a lark, I'm allowing the rumor to circulate that I am her daughter. You'll play along, won't you?"

"Maybe you can come up with a rich or famous relation for me," laughed Frances.

"I can be extremely creative. Give me some time and I'll come up with something. By the way, call me Kay, not Katherine."

Frances and Kay ate lunch together almost every day, trying out various restaurants before settling on a little French bistro that they recommended to some of the other students. They had several classes together: typing, shorthand, and elocution. Frances noticed that Kay made minimal effort in her secretarial courses but outshined the other students in elocution. She had an enchanting speaking voice and could memorize long passages. When she recited, the students and the teacher were entranced.

One evening in early spring of 1924, Frances and Kay went for an early dinner at their bistro. As they were leaving, Kay asked her if she would like to come by her apartment and meet her roommate, Lois Long.

Frances discreetly studied Kay's features. She was without a doubt one of the most attractive girls in the school, but she had an odd, exotic sort of beauty. Her features were striking, but slightly large for her delicate face. Her mouth was wide, but well formed. She had an enchanting smile. Frances decided that her nose was not aquiline but nor was it the sweet, uptilted nose of an adorable flapper. Yet it seemed to balance out her other features, particularly her large eyes, which were framed by long dark lashes. What Frances admired the most about Kay's looks were her dark complexion and jet-black hair, which highlighted her olive-green eyes. Her beauty was as mystifying as her character. She considered herself fortunate to have fallen in with such a fascinating girl. Things were looking up.

They arrived at the apartment, which was in a fashionable East Side neighborhood. The building was very elegant and well-situated near chic restaurants and even a few discreet speakeasies. Unfortunately, the apartment itself was miniscule. It consisted of two small rooms and a tiny bath.

As Kay unlocked the door, she said, "Lois pays the lion's share of the rent, so she has the bedroom." She pointed to a sofa in the combination living room and kitchenette.

"That's my bed."

A few minutes later, Lois stumbles into the living room, having just woken up.

"I'm sorry we interrupted your nap," Frances said meekly.

"Don't make me laugh," said Kay. "Lois doesn't nap. The afternoon is the only time she can sleep. She is a theater critic for *Vanity Fair*. Her day begins at seven. After the theaters let out, she's off to the clubs and speakeasies."

"Who's this sweet thing?" Lois asked, stretching her long arms over her head.

"Lois, this is Frances Austin. She's with me at Katherine Gibbs. She's a Bryn Mawr girl."

"How do you do?" she yawned. "Vassar, class of '22."

Frances' face reddened. It wounded her amour propre to be a fraud, which is what she was when she passed herself off as a college graduate. She studied the lovely girl as she slipped into her evening clothes. She had jet black hair that was bobbed quite short, which accentuated her long, graceful neck. She had a large mouth that was not unattractive, especially when she expertly applied her bright red lipstick. She had chosen a black, clingy dress, cut above the knee. As an afterthought she threw on a thin strand of pearls. She was the perfect flapper, but a flapper with class.

"What's the plan for tonight?" Kay asked Lois.

"A very dull play. Unfortunately, it's not a musical. But I plan to make up for it afterwards. Do you two want to come with?"

"Sure!" said Kay. "How about it, Frances? You haven't lived until you've made the round of the speakeasies with Lois."

She hesitated, but then said, "Sure, why not? It's Friday night and I have never been to a New York speakeasy."

"Lois knows all the trendy places with the hottest jazz and the best-looking men."

"I'll just have to go back to my place to change," said

Frances.

"Why bother?" Lois interrupted, looking through her closet. "Kay and I will set you up. I have just the dress for you," she said, handing her a royal blue lamé dress encrusted with beads. "Kay will do your makeup. She is a wiz. It will serve her well when she starts her stage career."

Frances looked at Kay in astonishment. "The stage? I had no idea, Kay."

"It's a well-guarded secret. I haven't even told my mother yet. Of course, she won't mind. After all, she was a fairly successful actress in her day. She dragged me across the country from San Diego to Denver. She never found success on the New York stage, but her little girl will. I have some auditions lined up. If things go well, I'll be a Katy Gibbs dropout."

"I wish you oodles of luck. You won't forget me when you're a famous Broadway star?" said Frances with a mock rueful expression.

"Don't be absurd. You will have front row tickets to all my shows."

The crowds teemed out of the theaters and swarmed the taxi stands to be spirited away to restaurants and clubs. The chic "21" was always the first stop for the well-heeled New Yorker. Because it closed at two, it was considered a private club and thus skirted the curfew law. As planned, Lois met her friends at the door. She introduced them to Charlie Berns who was one of the owners. They swept past the crowded bar and were ushered to a large table in the middle of the crowded room. Kay looked stunning in a figure-hugging sequined dress, which was cut extremely low in the front. This accentuated her flat chest, which was the look all young women strove to achieve. Frances, although fashionably thin, had a shapely bust, which she sometimes would bind when wearing snugger dresses. As they walked through the restaurant, not only did all the men's eyes follow the three lissome beauties, but the women stared at them as well, with palpable envy.

As they took their seats, Lois introduced the girls to the other guests seated at the table. "Kay, Frances, I would like you to meet Herman Mankiewicz. He is also a theater critic, but he's at *The New York Times.* We see each other several nights a week since they often seat the critics together at the shows on Broadway."

Herman smiled amiably, "Nice to meet you ladies. These are my friends Harold Ross and his wife, Jane."

A large, homely man stood briefly and smiled. His demeanor was stiff and awkward, and his pompadour hairstyle made him look slightly ridiculous. His wife, on the other hand, was slim and modestly attractive.

Herman continued, "Harold hails from Colorado of all places. But he's been just about everywhere. He has years of experience in publishing. He and Jane are working on a new project, a magazine that caters to the sophisticated, tony crowd. Do you have a name yet, Harold?"

Jane interrupted. "We've been at loggerheads about that. But I think we've come to a decision. What do you think, Lois? *The New Yorker.*"

"It's brilliant," beamed Lois. I'm so sorry. I haven't properly introduced my friends. This is my roommate Kay Gibbs and her friend Frances Austin. Do keep them in mind when you publish your magazine."

"Oh yes, please do," Frances blurted out, before she realized what she was doing.

"As for me," said Kay. "I am destined for the theater. I do hope your future theater critic will give me a good review, as will you, Mr. Mankiewicz," she said with a wink.

"Of course," said Harold. "Since we are speaking in the future tense, Jane and I hope that Lois will consider leaving *Vanity Fair* once we are up and running."

Lois smiled wryly. "Will I get my own column?"

"Certainly," said Jane. "You could be our theater critic or whatever you choose."

The waiter appeared at the table. Lois whispered to her friends that they should order brandy. "The booze is pretty good here. They have champagne and gin. But you always know that with brandy, it's not doctored. They can't fake the taste of cognac."

After dinner, Lois suggested a change of tempo. "I feel like dancing. Jane, would you mind terribly if these two jazz girls and I went Uptown?"

"Of course not," said Jane. "We have a full day tomorrow and we need our sleep.

You young gals go ahead."

They piled into a taxi. It was already one in the morning. "Driver, 142nd and Lenox Avenue," Lois said, slurring her words slightly.

Frances, trying her best not to sound naïve, asked, "Why are we going so far uptown at this time of night?"

Kay and Lois turned to her and chimed in unison, "The Cotton Club, of course."

"Oh my, you are a little bit of a greenhorn," said Lois. "But with your looks, you will be on easy street soon enough. What a girl needs in this town are looks and talent.

Without both, a woman, or a man for that matter, is just a flash in the pan. Look at my darling Kay. Yes, she is gorgeous, in a dark and exotic way. Come to think of it, she's the polar opposite of you. You're blonde and ethereal, and a natural blonde at that. Anyway, our Kay has talent. I know that for a fact because I've seen her audition. She will be a great actress. Someday we may see her in Hollywood. But you, Frances, do you have a dream, and do you have talent?"

Frances' breath caught in her throat. "I believe that I do. I can write. I had thought of going into advertising and perhaps use that as a steppingstone to a career in publishing."

"A noble dream. Maybe once I have made a name for myself, I could help you. It's still a man's world and I believe that we women must support each other."

They arrived at The Cotton Club, where the stage show was just beginning. Beautiful Negro men and women, wearing almost no clothing, were dancing suggestively.

Frances felt uncomfortable. She found the show

somehow demeaning to the performers, especially since the audience was completely white.

"What's wrong, Frances," asked Kay. "Doesn't look like you're enjoying the show."

"Frankly, I'm not," she grumbled. "It's humiliating. I mean, up there you have all these beautiful and gifted colored men and women performing for a white audience. It's bizarre."

Lois looked at her with an ironic smile. "Don't get up on your soapbox just yet, Frances. If you are a proponent of race relations, we can go to another club. It's not far. They have the best jazz, and everyone is welcome. Zelda and Scott go there almost every night when they are in New York."

"Sounds ducky," said Kay, trying to smooth things over. "I want to dance, don't you, Frances?"

So, the three women walked down the block to a speakeasy with a fabulous jazz band. Men and women of both races mingled and danced the latest steps. Lois bought a bottle of gin, which she drank almost entirely by herself. They stepped onto the packed dance floor and imitated the Negro dancers who had invented the Charleston in Harlem.

At first, Frances felt awkward, but eventually, after watching the dancers, she let go. She danced with anyone who asked. By the time they left, she felt that she had mastered the Charleston and the Black Bottom. It had started to rain, and they had to wait twenty minutes for a taxi. Frances was horrified when Lois threw up in the car.

"It happens all the time," said Kay, rolling her eyes. "She just gives the driver an extra two dollars. It's almost a ritual with her."

When she got back to The Martha Washington Hotel, Frances tiptoed by the night attendant at the front desk and smiled sheepishly at the elevator girl. She struggled with her key to open the door to her room and finally fell into bed exhausted, not bothering to undress.

ADDIE

NEW YORK CITY, FEBRUARY 1924

Esme sat in a corner of the lobby of the school building, brushing the snow off her dull wool coat and wiping her eyes with a sopping handkerchief. Addie almost didn't recognize her as she rushed to get on an elevator. She slid on the slippery floor as she abruptly turned to see what was wrong with her friend.

"Esme, what on earth is the matter? Is everything alright at home? I have never seen you this upset."

"No," she sobbed, with distraught expression. "It's not anything like that."

"Well, what on earth happened?" fired back Addie, impatient to know what had put Esme in such a state.

"You remember I told you about a certain Mr. Schultz, who would knock on my door late at night?"

"Yes, but I thought you said he moved to Cleveland."

"He did," said Esme with a pained expression. "But he came back a few weeks ago. Then he started up again, knocking at my door. Only it's worse, because now he's drunk every night, even sometimes during the day."

"Have you told the manager? Surely, that would be grounds for eviction."

"Mrs. Bradley knows he drinks. But his rent is paid up

for the month, so she won't do anything."

"My advice is to keep complaining and…"

"Addie, please let me tell you what happened, what he did!" Esme said, her sobs becoming fiercer. "Last night when I was coming back from the bathroom, he pushed passed me and came into my room."

Addie stammered. "You're not telling me that he assaulted you?"

Esme led Addie into the lavatory and unbuttoned her coat and pulled up her blouse. Addie gasped. Her friend's shoulders, chest, and arms were badly bruised and there were welts on her upper back. Then she saw horrible bruises on Esme's neck.

"My God!" she cried. "He's a monster. He beat you? Why on earth would he hurt you?"

"He hurt me because I tried to fight him off," she groaned. "He wouldn't stop. I told him to stop, really, I did. I tried to scream, but he put his hand over my mouth. Then he, he…" She struggled for her breath to continue. "He tore off my nightgown and pushed hard down onto the bed."

Addie's expression transformed from concern to horror. "The monster raped you? I can't believe what I am hearing. Did you report him or call the police?"

"I told Mrs. Crane, the landlady, but she didn't want any trouble. She refused to call the police. She did finally kick him out. He hardly had time to pack up his clothes. I begged her to get a policeman. She kept saying she didn't want any trouble and that it would give her place a bad name. But what about me, Addie? What about my good name?"

Addie felt her face burning with anger. "Don't say such things. You are blameless. No one needs to know about this unless you tell them."

"But one day," she whispered, "one day the man I marry will know. What am I supposed to tell him?"

"My dear, there are plenty of things that you can tell him. Girls have bicycle accidents and all kinds of mishaps. But I would suggest that you tell him the truth before you agree to marry him, this future husband. That way you'll know what kind of man he is."

Esme stopped crying and looked at Addie as if she were seeing her for the first time. "I never realized what a wise girl you are. But in the meantime, I can't go back to that boardinghouse."

Addie stood pensively and mumbled as she tried to gather her thoughts.

"This afternoon we are going to look for a new boardinghouse or apartment for you."

"Oh, all the boardinghouses are the same," Esme complained. "And besides, I can't afford an apartment."

"Yes, you can," said Addie. "Because we are going to live together, whether it be in a clean, safe boardinghouse or an apartment. I think I can even get Dottie to join us. She has been saying for ages that she wants to get out of Newark."

Esme's face brightened, and she smiled for the first time that morning. "You mean it?"

"Yes," said Addie. "It's time I moved out too. If I don't, I might end up hating my mother."

Boardinghouses, or as they were sometimes called, boarding hotels ranged from well-furnished establishments with private bathrooms to more modest hotels, with communal facilities, usually one per floor. Addie took charge of compiling a list of places that they would visit. Her process was to eliminate establishments by location: the neighborhood had to be safe and convenient to the subway. Then she categorized the remaining possibilities by rent, placing the most expensive at the top of the list. She saw no need to move Esme from one ghastly situation to another. Dottie had saved quite a bit of money by living at home, so she could afford a higher rent. And though Esme had meager resources, she had told her that she would help her out until they all got jobs in a few months.

The three friends moved into a lovely building on 59th Street between 9th and 10th Avenue. They had managed to secure three rooms on the same floor that was reserved for women. There were two bathrooms on the floor, each with showers and tubs. The clientele was made up mostly of single women, some with children and a few couples. Breakfast and dinners were included with the rent. And so, Addie, Dottie, and Esme settled quietly and securely into the remaining three months of their studies at Smith Business College.

As was the case with most of her classmates, Addie didn't know what kind of work she would find when she graduated. But she soon discovered that moving in with Esme and Dottie, had been a wise decision. She escaped the dismal reality of living with her mother. Ever since Barry had left, Rose complained that she was lonely and bored. Addie tried to convince her to make friends with the Jewish widow that lived next door, but Rose insisted that she wanted nothing to do with Jews. She even began complaining about the Italian families on the block, complaining that they were too loud and boisterous.

Barry had given her mother a generous divorce settlement, so she didn't have to work. Addie noticed that she spent a great deal of time reading trashy magazines and novels. Her only friend on the block was a carbon copy of Rose, a bitter woman who spent her time gossiping about the neighbors.

Moving out was a relief. She was free to pursue a career and didn't have to constantly account her comings and goings to her mother.

ADDIE

NEW YORK CITY, JUNE 1924

The graduates and their friends gathered in a speakeasy downtown. Evie had asked her brother to recommend a classy, yet moderately priced place with a hot jazz band. Sam knew quite a few bars, but he was careful. The booze had to be imported and safe, no bathtub gin or other concoctions. So, on the last weekend in June, the gang of friends from Smith's Business College met at the door of what appeared to be a small Italian restaurant. The attendant looked them over carefully and then waved them through a small inner door.

They found a large table so that they could sit together. Evie and Addie had invited Esme and Dottie, of course. It took some convincing to get Esme on board. She was nervous about breaking the law, and besides, she had never had a drink in her life. Dottie, on the other hand, was gung-ho and had spent a week finding the right dress to transform herself into the picture-perfect flapper.

Sam had invited a friend named Donald Seligman to come along so the girls would have an extra man if they wanted to dance. Donald and Sam had met as children. Donald's family lived in Brooklyn, and they went to the same synagogue. They had remained good friends, even though they saw less of each other as the years went on. Their lives had taken different paths. Whereas Sam was finishing his last year of law school at NYU, Donald had attended Columbia University for two years before he had to drop out when his father died suddenly, leaving a pile of debts. Not one to be defeated, Donald joined a prestigious real estate firm. With his wits and a lot of charm, he had worked his way up the hierarchy to the position of junior partner.

Addie followed her friends' gaze, which repeatedly returned to Sam. Esme would sneak an occasional glimpse through her lowered eyelids. But Dottie was more obvious. She let the strap of her dress slip several times to show off her breasts. 'Poor Donald,' Evie mused. 'He hasn't a chance with the girls as long as Sam is around.'

He didn't have the exotic dark coloring of Sam, and he was on the short side. He did have broad shoulders and a nice build. Strands of auburn hair constantly fell into his eyes, which were expressive, almost soulful. His face was long and angular, his jaw too sharp.

There was a great deal of flirting and staring going on at the table. Once the drinks arrived, Dottie didn't waste time. She gulped down two glasses of champagne and grabbing Sam by the arm, pulled him onto the dance floor. After dancing the Charleston, a Foxtrot, and an awkward attempt at the Black Bottom, Sam excused himself and returned to the table. When he saw Addie and Donald sitting close together in deep conversation, he felt a jolt of jealousy, and his spine stiffened. This reaction came as a surprise, for he had considered Addie as a friend, and nothing more. They had never been alone but always were accompanied by Evie. Yet now, he felt a great desire to separate the two. As he walked to the table, he studied his sister's friend and realized that she was gorgeous. Perhaps her easy and unpretentious manner hid her beauty. But tonight, seeing her in a slinky blue dress that intensified the color of her eyes and noticing her decolletage, which offered a hint of her round, firm breasts, he realized what he had let slip through his fingers. He wondered if she would be willing to be his lover.

Sliding into the chair next to her, he said, "What's the big secret? You two look like you're planning to join an anarchist plot or maybe you have a plan to make a killing on Wall Street."

Donald smirked. "Typical of you, old man. How do you know that I wasn't proposing marriage?"

"Anything is possible with you, Donald," he said with a sardonic smile.

Addie interrupted, "For your information, he was telling me about his work in real estate, which I find fascinating."

Sam almost winced. "I guess if all you care about is padding your bank account, it's not a bad business."

Donald smiled and feigned patience. "I know what it means to be broke. I was a good student at Columbia, and I had to give it up because we lost all our money."

"I'm sorry," said Sam. "That was a stupid remark. Real estate can be a noble profession, if practiced honestly."

"I haven't made any decisions. I only know that I don't want to be a secretary all my life. I prefer to work in a field where there is a possibility for advancement. Since I don't have money to study, I have no intention of working as a legal secretary for my whole life. Some of the girls are going to work in advertising, but I've been told that it's almost impossible to get out of the secretarial pool. I hadn't even thought about real estate until I spoke with Donald."

"And I am glad that we discussed it," Donald smiled broadly. "I have known several agents that started as secretaries. To become an agent, you need only take a correspondence course and pass a test. That is exactly what I did. I can see that you're a smart girl, Addie. You will pass the test easily, and I will be more than happy to help you study."

Addie blushed at the compliment, making her even more appealing. Sam tried his best to hide his jealousy, adapting an indifferent air. Then he suddenly stood up and grabbed her hand. "How about a dance?"

"Sure, why not. I've been dying for someone to ask me," she said.

Dottie glared at her, obviously put out that she had managed to snag the best-looking man in the speakeasy. But she wanted to dance, so she smiled at Donald and pushed him onto the dance floor.

Addie walked slowly up from the subway; she was nervous about the interview. Donald had put in a word with one of the firm's partners. He was looking for a private secretary with skills and some smarts. As she exited the elevator on the fifteenth floor, the operator pointed to the beautiful Art Deco doors with the sign that read, "Butler and Brown Real Estate." "There she be," he said with a big grin.

Addie entered the office and handed her resume to the attractive receptionist.

The two pages had the list of her courses and grades from Smith Business College, names of teachers who offered to give her references, and her address. But at the top of the first page, she had made a significant alteration: She changed her name from Adelaide Lutz to Adelaide Stanford. She had always admired the first name of her friend, Sanford Dodd. It had the cachet of a well-bred person, born and raised in Connecticut. So, she made the slight modification by adding the "t." She had told her teachers and the administrators about the change and had taken care of the legalities. Thus began the reinvention of Adelaide Stanford, soon to be private secretary to Robert Butler, at Butler and Brown, and Associates.

FRANCES

NEW YORK CITY, FEBRUARY 1925

The Broadway theater was overheated, and when she walked onto the street the February cold air felt like a slap across Frances' face. If only she had worn a less flimsy dress and a more sensible coat. And where was Lois? They were supposed to meet in the lobby after the show, but the rush of the exiting crowd had pushed Frances outside. She huddled in a corner to keep warm as she wondered at her friend's performance. She realized that Kay's small role in a modern version of Hamlet would mark the beginning of a successful acting career. Frances was pleasantly surprised to see that her friend had talent.

Kay's life had been a whirlwind in the past two years. She left Katherine Gibbs without ever learning to type. With her dark good looks and reputation as a fast girl, she drew the attention of several Broadway producers who offered her minor roles. She somehow managed to avoid scandal, while bedding agents and directors. After all she was an actress, and she projected the aura of a young woman of good breeding. Even though people in the theater industry joked about her numerous love affairs, it did not diminish her standing in society. She carefully cultivated friends among the old money set. Then suddenly, she interrupted her career before it ever launched and married a wealthy man from Massachusetts named Jim Francis. So, she dropped the Gibbs and rechristened herself, Kay Francis. Though the marriage was wrought with conflict from the beginning, she was happy to keep his name and some of his money. Kay Francis was a name that fit her and would take her far, perhaps all the way to Hollywood.

When Kay moved out, Lois invited Frances to move into the small apartment and slept on the living room sofa. The two young women had much in common, a love of writing, an ambition to carve out careers, and an overwhelming desire to have fun.

Finally, Frances caught sight of Lois, wrapped in a luxurious mink. She was talking with Harold Ross and Dorothy Parker. As she waved to get her friends attention, she saw Lois hug Harold. She looked elated as she pushed her way through the crowd.

"Franny, you'll never guess what happened. Come on, guess," she said, bubbling with excitement. "Let's get some coffee," she said as she practically pushed Frances into a nearby coffee shop.

"I have no idea," she said. "And don't call me Franny. You know I hate that name."

"Spoiled sport," she said as she dug into her purse looking for cigarettes. "Never mind, I'll tell you anyway," she said as she lit a cigarette with an elegant silver lighter and inhaled deeply, blowing the smoke upward. "Ross offered me a job at *The New Yorker*, and he wants me to start next week."

"How fabulous! So does this mean you're going to be a theater critic?"

"Nope," she said with a furtive smile. "He wants me to write a column. Imagine me, Lois Long, a columnist. And he is giving me free reign to write about the places to go and the people to know in New York."

Frances creased her brow and appeared perplexed. "Well, that's kind of vague, isn't it? You mean he wants you to write about the chic restaurants and posh parties?"

"He said I can write about whatever I want. Mainly, he wants me to prowl around as I usually do, go to the speakeasies, the clubs, and well, just spill."

"He wants you to write about speakeasies?" said Frances, incredulous and concerned. "Isn't that risky for you and for him?"

"Have you ever seen me nervous in a speakeasy or a club?"

Frances thought about it briefly and realized that not only was Lois at ease when drinking and dancing in clubs, she was at her best.

"Once I was caught in a raid. It was a little unnerving at first, but then it was a real hoot.

A cop grabbed me and helped me climb out a window and onto a fire escape." She stopped speaking, suddenly deep in thought. Then she took a pencil from her purse and began writing on a napkin.

"What are you doing?" asked Frances.

"I'm taking notes for a column before I forget the details. Anyway, I did ask Harold if there would be any trouble if we published articles about booze. He explained that it was no crime to drink alcohol or to write about other people drinking. It is only illegal to produce it or sell it. So, relax. I may get into trouble, but it won't be with the police."

"I can't believe your luck. Rub a little bit of it off on me. Do you think you can find a job for me?"

"Give me time and I'll see what I can do. We mustn't let you get stuck in a rut at that advertising firm. What's the name, again?"

"Hoffman, Brown, Eckhardt and Associates," she said, imitating her best secretarial intonation. "I am so tired of answering phones and typing letters and proposals. Mr. Eckhardt wants to take me on as his private secretary, but I don't like the way he looks at me. His current girl, a pretty brunette, gave her notice quite abruptly. I ran into her crying in the ladies' room a few days before the news got out that she was leaving. So, I plan to tell Mr. Eckhardt, 'Thanks, but no thanks.'"

"That pretty much ends any chance of advancement for you at Hoffman, Brown, Eckhardt and Associates," she chided.

"Exactly. That's why I need your help. You will keep your eyes and ears open, won't you?" she pleaded.

"Of course. I'm certain I can find something for you in the advertising department. It might be low-level. But you won't have to worry about men harassing you. There are so many women at the magazine in important positions. They would never let them get away with it."

"I would be eternally grateful," said Frances dramatically. "I will clean the apartment and bring you coffee and cigarettes when you wake up."

"Please Lois," she said. "This will be a way to get my foot in the door. I am dying to write and maybe I can circulate a few articles among the different departments. I know that you'll help me," she said giving her a quick hug. "I'm fashioning myself after you. Now don't get nervous. I'm not interested in society or the speakeasies and clubs. But I do want to be an investigative reporter. I am fascinated by how this city is run, how the country is run. No topic is too insignificant. But I like to read about the big fish in the pond, particularly the corrupt ones. City officials, business tycoons and even society swells are of particular interest. I know it's not exactly what *The New Yorker* is covering now. But the magazine has to evolve.

"Oh, I've been meaning to talk to you about the apartment.," said Lois. "Since I will be making more money, I have decided to move. I want a place in a building with a doorman and an elevator. I think I found just what I'm looking for and I want to move in before I start work.

I know it's short notice, but I will pay my part of the rent for next month. Please tell me that you're not furious with me."

"Not at all. If you help me find a job at *The New Yorker*

or another magazine, I should be able to afford the rent. My father still helps me out now and then with a check."

On a rainy, windy April day, Frances started her job in the advertising department of *The New Yorker.* Her title was Assistant Account Manager, a position requiring her to contact department stores, manufacturers of soap and beauty articles; basically, any product or service that would appeal to the sophisticated reader of the magazine. The work was not as challenging as she had hoped, but at least there was an opportunity for advancement. Her supervisor, a stylish woman, who had worked in some very tony advertising agencies, encouraged her to practice writing her own copy. Meanwhile, two nights a week she attended a writer's workshop to hone her skills.

B. Altman & Co., located in midtown, encompassed much of 34th and 35th Streets. Frances had heard through the office grapevine that the publicity office of Altman's had decided to dedicate a substantial portion of its budget for ads in magazines. She took the initiative to arrange a meeting with an acquaintance who worked in a midlevel position to see if she could persuade the store to advertise in the magazine.

She walked through the 34th Street entrance of the eight-story Italian Renaissance building. Crossing through the men's department and then passing the ladies' handbag counter without so much as a quick glance, she caught the elevator just before the operator closed the door. Standing before the double doors that led to the administrative office, she took a deep breath and squared her shoulders. The receptionist indicated the small cubbyhole office occupied by Susan Davidson, assistant to the director of publicity.

"Please have a seat," she said pleasantly. "I'm a big fan of *The New Yorker.* I just adore the *Lipstick* column. I never plan a night out without consulting it."

Frances smiled and marveled at her luck. "What would you say if I told you that I am a very close friend of the woman who writes the column?"

"I would say that you are trying very hard to get this account," said Susan laughing.

"Now, I can't prove it to you. *Lipstick* is, of course, a pseudonym and we are forbidden from disclosing her identity to anyone outside the magazine. But what I can do is get you a scoop on the hottest clubs and speakeasies before the column is published."

"Any chance of meeting her?" Susan asked meekly.

"Doubtful. But if you and I were to go out on the town, we might run into her. I am not making any promises though," Frances taunted, knowing that she would never divulge the truth about Lois being *Lipstick*.

"So, tell me more about yourself," Susan said, changing the subject. I assume you have some experience, although you seem to be on the young side."

"I worked my way up in the usual way," said Frances. I went to Katherine Gibbs and then…"

"A Katy Gibbs girl!" she interrupted. "Me too. So obviously, you have all the necessary secretarial skills and some bookkeeping. But what about experience in advertising?"

"Of course, I had to start out in the secretarial pool. I was at Hoffman, Brown, and Eckhardt."

"And?" said Susan with a quizzical look.

"And my friend at *The New Yorker*, who shall remain nameless, put in a word. I've been there for a few months, and I have brought in tons of accounts. Oh, I forgot to mention that I attended Bryn Mawr for a year. I had to leave because of financial reasons. Now I'm in a writing workshop. I realize that you prefer to supply your own photographs and drawings, but I could write copy and save you time and expense."

"I must say, Frances, that you make it hard to say no. Of course, I'll have to run it by my boss. You'll be hearing from me in a few days. But don't forget what you said about letting me in on *Lipstick's* latest haunts."

Frances stood up and shook Susan's hand. She felt like skipping down the hall to the elevator. If things worked out, and she was sure they would, not only had she just landed a big account, but she had made her first step into writing advertising copy for *The New Yorker.* Her dream of writing articles was still hazy, but it was there on the horizon.

At the end of May, Frances was surprised to hear from Caroline Pierson. Somehow, she had learned that she was working at *The New Yorker.* Wasn't that just like Caroline? Not a word from her since she had left Bryn Mawr three years ago, and now she was proffering an invitation to spend a weekend with her in Connecticut. At first, she thought about snubbing her. She would make up a feeble excuse to beg off. Then she thought, *why not?* It would be nice to get out of the city, especially since it had been unseasonably hot during the past two weeks. Caroline had included her telephone number in the letter, so she picked up the phone and called.

"Frances, dearie," said Caroline a little too enthusiastically. "I'm so glad that you called. Wasn't it clever of me to track you down?"

"It sure was. How did you know that I was at *The New Yorker*?"

"I have an uncle who knows Harold Ross. They were out to lunch at The Algonquin, of all places. And yes, before you ask, at The Round Table. Anyway, Uncle Paul was talking about me. He has no children of his own, so I'm like a surrogate daughter. He started talking about my graduation from Bryn Mawr and what a fine institution it is. Then Mr. Ross said that the magazine had a girl in the advertising department who was at Bryn Mawr, a young woman named Frances Austin. The buzz is that she is making a splash, bringing in big accounts and even writing her own copy. Uncle Paul was impressed. He imagines himself to be literary, even though he runs a chain of hardware stores. He couldn't wait to ask me if I knew you while we were at college."

"That's the long and short of it, eh?" said Frances with just a hint of sarcasm. "If it hadn't been for Uncle Paul, we might never have spoken again."

"Come on, Frances. Don't pile on the guilt. After all, you have always known my address. You could have written."

"After the embarrassing way that I left Bryn Mawr. I don't think so."

"Never mind. That's all in the past. I don't care what happened between you and James. To be honest, I think that he acted like a real cad. You know that I have always liked you. Mary will be here, and she is dying to see you. How about it? Come out for the weekend. We are invited to three parties in Greenwich and there will be oodles of men. And by men, I don't mean students. There'll be a bunch of lawyers, some brokers from Wall Street, and maybe a doctor or two."

"It sounds promising. But let me ask you something. How do you know that I don't have a steady guy?"

"Gosh, I hadn't even considered. Of course, if you do, you must bring him along," she said with some embarrassment.

"Actually, I'm in between boyfriends right now. Just promise me that you will not push me on anybody. Let me do my own hunting."

"I'll leave it up to you. But it is a bit of a shame. I have a cousin who is dreamy. I won't introduce you unless you ask me."

Caroline jerked the steering wheel of her car, swerving to avoid a group of pedestrians leaving the train station. She was running late because she had stopped off to pick up Mary, thinking it would be nice to have a sort of Bryn Mawr reunion. The girls rushed out to the platform just as the train was pulling in. Mary was a simple, kind-hearted girl and she was tickled to be seeing Frances after three years. Caroline, on the other hand, had ulterior motives. Having a friend who worked at *The New Yorker* could open doors in Manhattan. She had been stuck in Connecticut since graduation and life was becoming tedious. Many of her friends were married and settled in their cozy starter homes in Darien and Greenwich. She hadn't rushed into marriage, though she had several offers. The idea of a career in publishing appealed to her. She had landed a job as the society writer for the local Stamford paper. How much more exciting it would be to write for a New York magazine or perhaps work at a publishing house. Frances had already gotten her foot in the door, and she imagined that her old friend could help her launch a career in the city. New York had captivated her since she was a little girl and she would spend the weekend with her parents, always staying at The Plaza, shopping on Fifth Avenue. She longed to live in a glamorous apartment and cultivate an exciting circle of acquaintances. None of her friends had ventured into the city. But now that she had tracked down Frances, things were looking up.

Gathering her suitcase and makeup bag, Frances glanced at herself in the mirror of the train compartment. She almost didn't recognize the reflection of the girl looking back at her. Everything was different: The hair that she once wore in a sleek chignon was bobbed, her eyebrows had been plucked into the form of a high arch, and her mouth, with the help of expertly applied lipstick, was bow-shaped. The most dramatic transformation was in her choice of clothes. Although she had always dressed tastefully, whether it be for work or a night out at a club, she had never owned an outfit like the one she was wearing today. It was Lois who helped her upgrade her wardrobe.

The *Lipstick* column that covered the nightlife of New York City had been expanded to include observations on fashion. A few months ago, the magazine sent Lois to Paris to report on the fashion shows. A few weeks after her return, she invited Frances to her apartment to look at some of the outfits that she had bought on the magazine's dime.

She threw open her closet door, pulling out dresses, coats, and lingerie, scattering them on the bed and rug. "What do you think? No more prêt-à-porter for this girl."

"Stunning," Frances exulted, not knowing where to look

first. "Can I try something on?"

"Sure, let's see what we can do to jazz you up. Here's a little number I literally grabbed out of the hands of a buyer from Bergdorf's. It's like a battlefield at these shows. It's a Patou, a classic suit, but with a flare. I love the drop waist and the pleats. Wait, I think I bought a matching toque. Yes, here it is," she said placing the hat on Frances' head.

"It's adorable," she said. "But it doesn't fit over all my hair."

"Of course, it doesn't. But don't blame the hat or Patou. You're the problem. You should have bobbed your hair ages ago. I'm sorry to point out the glaring truth. I am by nature kind and diplomatic," she said with an ironic smirk. "Listen. Here's the deal. I will be more than happy to loan you several outfits, hats included. However, first you must change your hairstyle."

She glanced at her reflection in the mirror, running her hands through her long, blonde hair. "I have wanted to bob my hair for years, but my mother says that it would kill my father. I really think that he couldn't give a damn. She's the one stuck back in 1900."

"She'll have to catch up. We're in the 1920s and every teenager from Brooklyn to farm towns in Iowa has cut her hair."

The next day Frances walked out of a barbershop with short hair. Lois had mentioned that the barbers were more adept than women's hairstylists, who were late to the game. They were reticent to cut off a woman's glorious mane. Barbers had been bobbing hair since Irene Castle took the plunge during the Ragtime craze. Looking in a shop window, she noticed a sweet brown felt cloche. The salesgirl shot her a sly smile and came to the door.

"Just bobbed it, didn't you?"

"How can you tell?" asked Frances with a giggle.

"We just know. We see a girl looking at her reflection in the window and we know we are going to sell a cloche. Besides, I saw you come out of the barbershop. Let me show you a few of the latest."

As she stepped off the train, Frances pushed her long bangs to the side and adjusted her hat. She waved enthusiastically when she saw that Caroline had brought Mary with her. The three friends jumped with excitement and then hugged.

"Goodness, Frances," said Mary breathlessly. "We all thought you were the prettiest girl on campus, but you look like a Hollywood star. They could put you on the cover of your magazine."

"They never put photographs on the cover of *The New Yorker*. We have artists for that."

Caroline stepped back and took her in. "You look like you're straight off the boat from Paris. Don't tell me that's a real Chanel."

"No, actually, it's a real Patou. Though I did pack a Chanel for tomorrow, if we do something sporty."

"Gee," said Mary, mooning over the clothes. "My parents won't spring for a Patou or Chanel. How on earth can you afford it?"

Frances winked. "Girls, that is a deep dark secret. I will just tell you that it is through the generosity of a woman, not a man"

Caroline wrinkled her brow and bit her lip. "You are interested in meeting some men this weekend?"

"Really, Caroline," she said, exasperated and trying not to roll her eyes. "Try to be more imaginative. It's possible to have generous friends. Besides, you know I never felt that way about girls. If I had, Bryn Mawr would have been a totally different experience. For one thing, I wouldn't have met James and I might well have graduated."

Caroline lowered her eyes in embarrassment. "Sorry, that really was a dumb thing to say."

Mary tried to lighten the mood. "Come on girls. Let's pile into Caroline's two-year-old car and get this weekend started.

The bedroom was strewn with dresses, feathers,

bandeaus, and shoes. It was not an easy time for Caroline to decide what to wear. It was unfathomable to her that she had nothing in her closet that compared to Frances' dress. The little number that she had bought at Lord & Taylor seemed to have lost the pizzaz it had in the dressing room mirror. She had bought it especially for tonight's dance at the Indian Harbor Yacht Club. There was never any question that she could outshine Frances, who was prettier than she was, but the idea was for the two of them to make a splash when they walked in together. Holding up two heavily beaded dresses, she shrugged her shoulders and cocked her head.

"Which one?" she asked. The red might be a tad garish, but it makes me look thinner than the pink."

"Why are you so obsessed with looking thin?" Frances said with a slightly irritated tone. "You haven't changed since college, always on a diet. I think you have a delightful figure. Men like curves, you know."

"It's easy for you to talk, no hips, long legs and a bust just large enough to keep a man interested. Why anyone would think that the Chanel and Patou designed their creations using you as a model. I bet you never dieted a day in your life."

Frances blushed. It was true that she never worried about her figure. Her looks, she had often mused, were a gift from a woman that she would never meet. She had known since childhood that she had been adopted and therefore resembled neither her father nor her mother. Throughout her teenage years, she would look through magazines and combine features of beautiful women to conjure up an image of her real mother.

"I think that you should wear the red. It's not garish at all and it compliments your curves. You need to play up your assets." She reached into her suitcase. "I have a gorgeous rhinestone bandeau. It's just what that dress needs."

Caroline smiled and gave her a hug. "I forgot what a sweet girl you are. I apologize for not tracking you down sooner."

A brand-new daffodil yellow Cadillac V-63 pulled up in front of the Pierson's front door.

Sitting next to Mary in the driver's seat was a rather plain-looking young man sporting a flat cap, which presented a ridiculous contrast with his formal black tails. As Frances lifted herself into the back seat, Mary made the introductions.

"I'd like you to meet my fiancé, Wallace Freemont. Wallace, this is Frances Austin, the girl that I've been raving about."

Frances smiled and held out her hand. "It's nice to meet you. Mary hadn't mentioned that she was engaged. How wonderful! And you didn't say a word, Caroline."

"Don't blame me," she said defensively. "Mary wanted to surprise you. We are all so pleased for her, and you too, Wallace. You're a lucky guy."

"I consider myself lucky too," said Mary, beaming. "The wedding isn't until next June. Wallace has another year of law school at Penn. I wouldn't have accepted his proposal if I knew that I would have to wait so long. But when he told me that he was going to practice law in Greenwich and not in the city, I just had to say yes. I prefer a man who works close to home. I've heard too many stories about pretty secretaries and salesgirls, and how distracting they can be to men, especially when the wives are busy keeping house and raising kids in Connecticut."

Frances smiled sweetly and tried not to laugh, finding it hard to imagine the pretty young secretaries that she knew chasing after a pie-faced, awkward young man like Wallace.

They drove up to the Indian Harbor Yacht Club, a Mediterranean-style building, constructed after the old club burned down a few years ago. Frances could see that the members took their boating seriously. There were dozens and dozens of sailboats and quite a few motorboats at the docks outside and the décor inside was distinctly nautical, with pictures of boats and their owners lining most of the walls.

Upon entering, a pack of elegant, energetic men drifted across the room and surrounded Caroline. Having been brought up in the area, she knew everyone, and everyone knew her. But tonight, she was more sought out than usual, for word had gotten around that she was bringing a gorgeous houseguest to the party. After a quick attempt to make introductions, Caroline was whisked away onto the dance floor, leaving Frances in the uncomfortable position of deciding which of the five men facing her she should accept. She was spared the necessity of choosing when a young man, who couldn't have been more than eighteen, put his arm around her waist and led her around the floor in an extremely uncoordinated rending of the Foxtrot.

The band took a break and Frances caught a glimpse of Caroline on the terrace speaking to a dreamy man. He was tall with broad shoulders. He had the kind of golden blond hair that one normally finds on young children. His features were fine, but what really captivated her were his eyes. They were a beautiful emerald green. She realized that she had been staring for an inordinately long time, and blushed when she realized that both he and Caroline were looking at her. At that moment, Caroline waved and beckoned her to come join them.

Her emotions were in a jumble; magnetism towards the handsome man, countered by envy of her friend for having snared him. However, the clouds of disillusionment were blown away when Frances began to speak.

"Frances, I would like you to meet my cousin, Theodore Pierson, Teddy to all of us who love him dearly. Teddy, this is Frances Austin. I think I might have mentioned her."

Teddy flashed an entrancing smile and she felt herself flush. "Yes, you have spoken of her." He held out his hand firmly and took hers. "So nice to finally meet you, Frances."

She turned to her friend with a discreet expression of gratitude. Remembering that she had categorically refused to be fixed up with Caroline's cousin, Frances had to suppress a laugh.

"I'll leave you two alone to get acquainted. But first let me brag a little about my cousin, because I know he won't blow his own horn. I might have mentioned that he comes from the wealthier side of the Pierson family. But they owe it all to the son who is a wizard at finance. It's true that the family bank was prosperous, but nothing compared to what it has become since Teddy took the helm." She chuckled, "What a fitting expression to use at the Yacht Club. Sometimes I astonish myself. Have fun you two. Don't forget, Cinderella, that we have a house party to go to after this."

She left them standing face to face, and for a few moments Frances was tongue-tied. He quickly put her at ease, asking about her work and her life in the city. "Ross has certainly put together a top-notch band of writers," he said. "James Thurber is brilliant, and of course Dorothy Parker. What a wit! What's the name of the illustrator who does the covers?"

"Peter Arno," she said. It occurred to her that he was impressed with the fact that she worked with such talented colleagues, and she felt proud that he believed that she was somehow on their level.

"Yes, his work is excellent," he said. "I usually read the magazine from cover to cover, except for that fluff written by what's her name, *Lipstick*. I guess that appeals to people living in the city with too much time and money on their hands."

"You know," she said smiling with downcast eyes. "If you like Arno, you might want to know that he's married to Lois Long, who writes the *Lipstick* column. Not only is she clever, well-informed, but she is a good friend of mine. We used to be roommates before she started writing for *The New Yorker*."

"In that case, I will have to give her column a chance," he said contritely. "As a matter of fact, let's make a deal."

She nodded, ready to agree to anything he might propose.

"I will start reading the column. Then we can use it as a sort of Baedeker, and you can be my tour guide. What do you say? I'll come in Saturday nights, and we can try out Lois's latest haunts."

"I don't know if I have the energy to be your guide every Saturday. I am a working girl, and I take classes two nights a week. But let's give it a go."

"Classes?" he asked, looking at her mystified.

"Yes, I am in a writer's workshop. We're an offbeat group of struggling scribblers with very mundane day jobs."

"What do you write, poetry, novels or car repair manuals?"

"Actually, I would like to write investigative pieces for the magazine. Right now, I am limited to advertising copy. You know, 'Use this soap and he won't be able to resist touching your skin,' that sort of thing. But I am always watching and listening when I'm at the office. Everyone is connected and everyone talks. One day I will convince Mr. Ross to let me write an article."

"If you have the drive and are willing to work hard, I know you will get there. In the meantime, I would like to see more of you, if that's okay."

Exultant, she tried to hide her fervor with a shy smile. Caroline and Mary rushed in, flushed and in a hurry.

"Come on kids, we've got to go if we want to make it to the Frye party. I promised we would be there, and I want everyone to meet Frances. You are welcome too, Teddy."

That was the night that Frances began to open herself up again. She refused to fall in love ever again since James had obliterated her heart. She had had plenty of boyfriends, whom she allowed to kiss her once or twice. If a fellow was especially good-looking, she might sit in his car and let him caress her. But now she felt her defenses crumbling.

ADDIE

NEW YORK CITY, FEBRUARY 1925

Working for Mr. Butler at Butler and Brown Real Estate had been frenetic, but not intellectually challenging. Aside from the standard secretarial duties of typing, stenography, and answering her boss's private line, there were myriad errands, as well as the arranging of lunch and dinner reservations. On occasion, Mr. Butler required her to buy birthday presents for his wife and children. But at least he was harmless. He had not once made a pass or spoken inappropriately to her.

Several evenings a week Donald Seligman came over to the boarding house on 59th Street and sat with Addie in a quiet corner of the living room. He had encouraged her to take the real estate exam as soon as possible. Chances were she might not pass it the first time, and he didn't want her to be a secretary forever. Mrs. Strickland, the landlady, had provided them with a small table so that they could lay out their books and papers. As the two studied, sitting side by side, their heads practically touching, they gave the residents the impression that they were in love.

Unfortunately, that was only half the truth. Donald had fallen for her the first night they met. But to Addie, he was a dear friend, nothing more. She never led him on. He knew that he hadn't a chance if Sam Segal was single and available. Tenacity was one of Donald's key characteristics. He saw no reason to give up on Addie. In fact, he felt sorry for her. He knew that she was wasting her time and tears on Sam. Unlike himself, he was not truly broadminded. Sam would never marry outside the faith.

On this particular night, as they were filling out the application for the test, he noticed the name she had filled in. "Why did you change your name from Lutz to Stanford? There's nothing wrong with Lutz."

"There are many reasons," she said. "But to be completely frank, I never liked the sound of it. Somehow it lacks class. There are other reasons. If you're interested and have the time, I'll explain. But let's take a little stroll. It's kind of private."

There was a biting wind as they walked down 59th Street and she intertwined her arm with his and drew closer. A few light snowflakes began to fall, a few landed on her long lashes. Trying to quell his feelings, Donald looked away and took a pack of cigarettes from his coat pocket.

"Do you want one?" he asked.

"Donald, you know I don't smoke," she said with a frown.

"Sorry, I forgot. So, tell me again, why Stanford and not Lutz?"

"As I said, Stanford will look better on a business card when I get my license and it has a better ring to it when I answer the phone."

"And? What's the other deeper reason?"

"There's a lot that you don't know about my background. I haven't told anyone, even Evie. It's not easy for me to talk about my childhood, but I feel that I can trust you, like the brother that I never had."

Those words stabbed at his heart. He felt that she meant them as a compliment, but they had quite the opposite effect.

"Barry Lutz was my mother's husband, my stepfather.

When they married, he adopted me and gave me his name. My mother's maiden name was Strauss, Rose Strauss. I have no idea who my real father is or was. Who knows if he is still alive? I gave up hope of finding him years ago. When I was thirteen, I asked my mother to tell me about him. You won't believe this, but she slapped me and told me never to speak of him again."

His throat tightened, as he put his arms around her. She started crying softly, then her shoulders began to shake. He held her until her tears subsided. Then he lifted her chin and kissed her.

She gently pushed him away. "I'm sorry, Donald. I know that you care for me. I just don't feel the same way about you. Like I said, you are like a brother to me. Please, don't let that put you off. I don't know what I would do without you in my life."

Trying to sound nonchalant, he replied, "I would rather be your friend than be a stranger to you. Let's pretend this never happened."

"Yes, let's," she said. "But just for your own future reference, you are a fine smoocher."

"Is it alright if I ask you about your father?"

"It's alright, but I'm afraid I don't have any answers."

"Now that you're a grown woman, why don't you ask your mother again? I think she owes you the truth."

"My mother has become a bitter woman. My stepfather was good to me, so generous.

But he couldn't put up with her temper and her greed. He left when I finished high school. Now, she hates all men and I suppose that she hates my father the most. There is no way that she will tell me the truth. And I need to know. It's as if there was a piece torn out of my soul. I feel incomplete. It's hard to admit that I have given up hope."

"No, don't do that," he said, wishing he could tell her that he would never give up hope that she would love him one day."

"I'm not sure I want to let you go," said Thomas Butler,

teasing Addie. "You have been quite an asset. Don't let this go to your head, but I don't think that I have ever had such an efficient and bright secretary."

"Thank you for the compliment, Mr. Butler," said Addie reddening slightly. "It's been a pleasure working for you. I have learned so much."

"Yes, perhaps too much," he said gruffly, but with a smile. "You passed the real estate exam with an almost perfect score. I suppose Seligman had a lot to do with that?"

Again, she blushed, and stumbled over her words. "Oh, you knew about Donald?"

"Of course. Not much this old man doesn't know. He's an honest man, not to mention a tremendous salesman. I can't afford to lose him. I even gave him some of the books you used to study. But I gave him the go ahead on one condition."

"What would that be, Mr. Butler?" she said hesitantly.

"He promised that he would stay with our firm and take you on as his assistant agent."

"How can I ever thank you?" she said, a wave of relief mixed with elation washed over her. I really do enjoy working here, and I wasn't relishing the idea of job hunting."

He stood up and walked from behind his desk to shake her hand, but instead gave her a paternal hug and a pat on the back. "Good luck, Miss Stanford."

ADDIE

NEW YORK CITY, JUNE 1925

The apartment house was not far from Addie's boardinghouse on 59th Street. It was a four-story red brick structure that had been recently totally remodeled. Originally, each floor had six small apartments, but a developer had knocked down walls and torn out some floors, resulting in a building with eight spacious duplexes with all the latest accoutrements in plumbing and lighting. The kitchens were completely outfitted with the most modern appliances. Donald had been lucky to grab the listing when the agent from a competing firm had a falling out with the developer. He asked Addie to be the co-listing agent for the sale. She had, after all, proven herself since she became an agent in March. In the four months that they had been working together, she had closed dozens of sales. Last month, he began to step back and encourage her to work alone, only conferring with her if she ran into difficulties.

"These duplexes will sell themselves," he said, looking around wide-eyed. And it won't hurt business to have an attractive young woman show the place."

"Are you trying to disparage my salesmanship skills?" she said with a sarcastic smile.

"Never!"

In ten days, they had sold all but one of the duplexes. The partners had a small celebration after the closing, with champagne. After the other agents left, Mr. Butler handed them each a small envelope.

Outside the office, Addie exulted, "Fifty dollars!"

"We deserve it," said Donald. "And I think we also deserve a little celebration. How about I take you out on the town?"

"Sure, but I really want to invite Evie. And I should invite Esme. She is leaving New York soon. She misses her friends and family in Lancaster. You don't mind, do you?"

"Of course not," he lied.

Donald barely knew Esme and Frances had never told him about what had happened to her. Esme had made it clear that she never wanted anyone to know about the rape. But she knew that the assault had changed her friend in a fundamental way. She had become withdrawn and tense. What saddened Frances the most was that she had lost the wide-eyed wonder and brightness that she had when they first met. So, it was probably for the best that she was leaving New York for the relative security of the small town of Lancaster.

The Pirate's Den was one of *Lipstick's* favorite haunts. She had raved about it in her column in *The New Yorker*. Owned by Don Dickerman, a famous nightclub impresario, it's nautical décor and swashbuckler atmosphere transported the guests to the Caribbean and the Barbary Coast. Waiters, dressed as pirates, enacted scenes from Treasure Island. All the while, a large jazz band played the latest tunes, as the patrons danced and guzzled down beer and rum.

Of course, the champagne was always iced and in great supply.

Evie had reserved a table and whispered the password at the door. She had always wanted to visit this speakeasy and when Addie told her that she and Donald would be picking up the bill, she quickly volunteered to make the arrangements. Addie had specifically asked that Sam be included in the party. Once Evie confirmed that he would be coming, Addie treated herself to a new dress, the shortest that she had ever worn in her life. Her long blonde hair was swept up in a chignon and secured with a large velvet bandeau, adorned with a white ostrich feather. She had carefully applied a small amount of mascara to intensify her luminous blue eyes, as well as a light veneer of pale lipstick.

Esme sat down next to Addie. She was shocked when she noticed that she had bobbed her hair and was wearing a little too much mascara. Addie immediately realized that her friend was using her drastic physical transformation as a shield. By projecting the image of the modern liberated woman, she was doing her best to bury her soul, the soul of a damaged sweet girl.

"Esme you look beautiful!" said Evie. "What will they make of you in Lancaster?"

"They'll have to get used to it," she said. "Anyway, most of my friends back home wear makeup and bob their hair. Life does exist outside of Manhattan, you know."

Evie smiled. "Of course, sometimes we New Yorkers forget that there is a world outside the five boroughs."

Sam walked up to the table and pulled up a chair, his gaze furtively taking in Addie from head to toe. "Sorry I'm late." In a teasing, flirtatious tone, he complimented her on her outfit.

"That's quite a dress, Addie. Have you been reading Vogue?"

She blushed but answered defiantly. "A girl is allowed to put on the Ritz just like a man. I spend my days in brown and gray suits with unfashionably long hems, and tonight I wanted a change."

"Please, don't get me wrong," he said. "You are a beautiful girl. It's just a pleasant surprise because normally you seem to play down your looks."

"It's not as if you haven't known your share of beautiful girls, Sam," Donald said dryly.

"Addie has more to offer than most girls that I know, present company excluded," he said smiling politely at Evie and Esme. "Besides being a sincerely nice person, she is as sharp as a tack. There is no way I would have sold those duplexes so quickly without her. I don't know how to describe it, but she has a gift for reading people and knowing exactly what to say."

Addie smiled broadly, showing her beautiful white teeth. "Donald, you exaggerate. You taught me everything I know about real estate and sales. We were lucky to get the listing. You said yourself that the apartments would sell themselves."

"Hogwash!" he protested. "I have listed plenty of duplexes, but I have never sold them in ten days, and at asking price. You have to learn to accept a compliment, my girl."

Sam's eyes went back and forth between Donald and Addie, and he wondered if they were more than friends. The possibility shocked and worried him. Even though he hadn't seen Addie in months, Evie often talked about her success in business, never mentioning her romantic life. So, he assumed that she was not seriously involved with anyone. Moreover, he and Donald were still close, and he never spoke of Addie as anyone more than a friend and business associate. The possibility that they were involved disturbed him. So, he decided to find out the truth tonight, and if the path was clear, he would make his move.

Donald ordered a bottle of champagne for the table, and they all drank to each other's success: To Addie's first big sale, to Esme's job in Lancaster, and to Evie's new job as advertising assistant at the New York branch of Lord and Thomas.

Addie turned to Sam and inquired, "What about you? Are you still representing garment strikers and anarchists? I haven't heard your name tied to any big cases."

Sam looked at his sister. "I guess Evie hasn't told you about my move to the federal government?"

Everyone laughed but stopped abruptly when they

realized that he was serious.

Donald knew, but obviously hadn't shared the news.

"You're joking, right?" said Addie, covering her mouth and trying not to laugh.

"No, I'm quite serious. I am working in a division of the government that deals with fraud, fiscal and otherwise. They seem to think that I am a wiz at running investigations. I have already brought down my first big shot corporate tax cheat."

"But what happened to helping the poor immigrants, the little guys?" asked Esme meekly.

"To be honest, I couldn't make a living out of it," he said. "Besides, most of the cases never made it to court. So, I figured I would do the opposite and go after the big, crooked fish. In the end, if they pay their taxes and stop perpetrating frauds on the public, that also helps the little guy."

"I think it's wonderful," exclaimed Addie. "Maybe someday you'll bring down some of those Tammany Hall types. I can't stand corrupt politicians."

He winked and took her hand. "I'll do my best. Look, the band is back. How about a dance?"

Donald glared as they glided onto the dance floor. Sam was holding her extremely close as they danced a Foxtrot. It was obvious to him from the way she looked at him that she was in love. Life could be so unfair. Addie would never be more than a short-lived love interest to Sam. For in the end, he would marry a Jewish girl and he would break her heart. He on the other hand, did not care about religion. His gaze drifted to Evie, and he pondered why he had never asked her out. She looked stunning in a short sheath dress that accentuated her curvy figure. Her makeup highlighted her large brown eyes and bronze complexion.

She noticed him giving her the once over and stretched out her leg. She was wearing rolled silk stockings. She winked at him as she took a small silver flask from her purse and stuck it into her garter. "Don't worry, Donald. It's not gin, just perfume."

He laughed as he answered his own question. Evie would always be Sam's kid sister and even though most people would call her pretty, she didn't hold a candle to Addie.

Sam and Addie walked down Amsterdam Avenue near the West Seventies. They had slipped out of the Pirates Den when the others were all on the dance floor. Somehow, he had managed to talk her into coming back to his apartment. He had finally moved out of his parents' home in Brooklyn and rented a studio in a doorman building. He was living the life of the single professional man about town.

"Art Deco. Somehow that surprises me," said Addie, her eyes scanning the small apartment. "I would have expected 1910 Folk Art style or perhaps Greenwich Village Bohemian."

"The place came furnished," he said, shrugging his shoulders. "It serves my needs, small and uncluttered. I am expecting to be doing a lot of traveling with my job. I'll be in Washington a lot." He stood up suddenly, opening cabinet doors in the corner of the apartment that served as a miniscule kitchenette. "I have a bottle of wine somewhere. Ah, here it is, a Chianti that was offered to me by a Mafiosi as a bribe. I took it, but he will still be indicted."

"I'm glad that you're staying honest," she said laughing.

He poured out two glasses and taking her hand led her to a beige leather sofa. They sat together, silently finishing off the bottle. Then he put his arm around her shoulder and gently kissed her.

"That was nice," she whispered. Her pulse was racing. He kissed her again, this time with passion. She exhaled, "It's obvious that you have had a lot of experience. My limited experience is confined to petting in parked cars. So, suppose you tell me what you have in mind for tonight."

He seemed embarrassed and surprised by her candor. Most girls were either eager to let things progress, or they brought things to an abrupt end, either with an indignant comment or a slap.

He drew back slightly and looked at her quizzically. "You're a strange one. I was hoping that you would spend the night. I'm not comparing myself to Rudolph Valentino, but if you give me a chance, I don't think you'll be disappointed."

"Sam Segal! Would you make the same proposition if I were a nice Jewish girl from Brooklyn? Or is it because I am a shiksa from Washington Heights that you assume that I am ready to jump into bed with you?"

He frowned. "First of all, there are plenty of Jewish girls in Brooklyn and elsewhere who would sleep with me. I don't categorize my conquests, but whether a girl sleeps around or not seems to be a matter of choice. And you should know that I don't judge a girl either way. If we both can find some mutual pleasure in each other's arms, I find that we are both happier for it."

"I'm sorry if I seem angry, but this is all new to me. I have never gone alone to a man's apartment, and I have only done so now because I have strong feelings for you. You can't tell me that you don't know that I have been crazy about you since we first met."

"I admit that I guessed as much, and I can't deny my attraction to you. It's more than physical. I truly admire you. If we were to take this step, I mean, become lovers, it would not be a fling. If things go well, we could see each other exclusively."

"It's certainly a tempting offer, but I am afraid I need time to think it over. Are you willing to wait?"

"I am a patient man, especially if it's someone worth waiting for."

"In the meantime, I suppose that you will be inviting other girls up for Chianti?" she said with sarcasm.

"It depends on how long you make me wait."

"And that depends on how often you see me, and also how you treat me," said Addie.

"Now, would you mind walking me out and finding me a taxi?"

Sam felt his face flush with shame and disappointment. Girls rarely turned him down, even well brought up Jewish girls and the occasional debutante. So not only did Addie's rebuke hurt his pride, but it also shook his self-confidence to the core. Yet, he could not help admiring her honesty and self-assurance. This was a girl with character. It also meant that if he were to start a serious love affair with her, he wouldn't have to worry about her straying. But mostly he was captivated by her beauty. His physical desire only increased with her rejection. He had to have her. So, he would have to play by her rules.

FRANCES

NEW YORK CITY, NOVEMBER 1925

The New Yorker had been open for over seven months and things were not going well.

Frances had been hoping for a small raise, but circulation was not picking up and even the writers were not making much money. Lois, of course, had all her nightly club expenses covered, and now she had a husband to help pay the bills.

Having a father to supplement her income with monthly checks, helped Frances cover her rent. But there was little left over for new clothes or theater tickets. The clothes that Lois had given her helped and she mixed and matched skirts and blouses to stretch her wardrobe. It was important to her to look presentable when she and Teddy went out to restaurants in the city or to parties in Connecticut and Long Island.

Tonight, Lois had invited her and Teddy to a party at the home of Harold Ross and his wife Jane. They opened their home in Hell's Kitchen to writers, musicians, and entertainers. On any given weekend, a guest might see Dorothy Parker with her latest lover, Edna Ferber arguing with George Kaufman over their latest play, or even Harpo Marx bantering and just being ridiculous as he ran through the living room. The parties were always the main subject of conversation on Monday mornings at the office. Frances had never been officially invited, but much like parties of the fictitious Gatsby, people were rarely invited, they simply showed up.

"Just stick with me," said Lois, as they all threw their coats onto a chair in the bedroom.

"Of course, I might lose track of you if I have too much to drink, in that case, all bets are off."

Teddy and Frances stood discretely in a corner pretending to drink glasses of disgusting bathtub gin, while Lois prattled on about the other guests.

"Oh look. There's Dottie Parker. She puts her name down as an editor but hardly ever contributes a piece to the magazine. What a bitter woman, thrown over by one man after another. She puts on airs, playing the upper-class Protestant. But everyone knows she's a Jew. For God's sake, her maiden name was Rothchild!"

Frances flushed. She had never heard Lois speak ill of Jews before and it made her uncomfortable.

"Not that I really have anything against Jews," she qualified. "It's just that when they hide it. I mean look around. George Kaufman, Edna Ferber, and Groucho Marx are all here tonight. Most of Broadway is run by Jews, not to mention Hollywood. But I always say that people should be authentic. Don't hide who you really are. I certainly don't," she said, smiling demurely.

Frances smirked. "Now, that's the truth. You certainly have no qualms about coming into the office at four in the morning to write your column, still drunk and disheveled from your nightly carousing. I heard that you and Peter were caught naked on the office sofa last week."

It wasn't easy to shock the staff of *The New Yorker*. But when a shy secretary had discovered them intertwined and naked, she let out a scream. At least a dozen employees ran to see what was wrong. The couple struggled to regain consciousness and kissed each other good morning, ignoring the onlookers.

"Yes," Lois laughed, not the least embarrassed. "We were blotto and thought we were in our apartment. So, we made love on the sofa and fell asleep. So what? We're married after all."

Teddy had his arm around her waist and gave it a little squeeze. Frances would have expected him to be shocked, but he didn't react. He was relaxed as he took in the scene. Thinking back on Lois's comments about Dorothy Parker, she began to worry. Her face reddened as she felt the full force of the rebukes. She was overcome with shame for she was no different than Mrs. Parker. In fact, she was worse for she was hiding the truth from the man she loved. It struck her that ever since she was a child, she had tried to obscure her Jewish identity. Of course, everyone in Reading knew. But she had always preferred her Gentile friends and had resented her mother for trying to make her mix with her own kind. Then there was Bryn Mawr and the fiasco with James Whitman. And why? What if she had married Jim. Would she have lived a lie for her entire life? Would it have been even possible or desirable to erase her past and cut off her relationship with her own family? For the first time Frances saw herself for who she was, inauthentic and weak.

She was in a quandary. She looked at Teddy. He had not reacted to Lois's comments about Jews, so obviously he had no idea that she was Jewish. She would have to ask Caroline if she had told him. The time had come to reveal the truth to him and to Lois.

Lois glanced across the room. "Listen kids. Take care of yourselves if you don't mind.

I want to talk to Harpo about getting some tickets for his new musical. It's called *Cocoanuts*, of all things. It's set in in a hotel in Florida. I'm told that it's hilarious."

"No problem," said Frances. "But speaking of theater, did you hear about Kay?"

"No," said Lois. "I haven't heard a peep out of her, and she hasn't been on Broadway for months."

"I got a call from her. I'm surprised she didn't call you.

Are you two on the outs?"

"Not, particularly," said Lois.

"Well, she has remarried an extremely handsome and successful lawyer and banker. It was a secret marriage in her apartment. Don't ask me why. True to form, it's complicated. He lives and works in Boston, and she is staying in New York. She'll probably go back to the stage."

"That's our Kay," said Lois, looking back as she strode across the room to talk to Harpo.

A few weeks later Frances had lunch with Caroline at a restaurant near her office. She had spoken with some Katherine Gibbs friends that worked at *Vogue*, who helped Caroline find a job as a copywriter. She was grateful and happy to be living and working in the city.

It was a difficult subject to broach, but she had to know if she had said anything to Teddy.

"Caroline, I need to know if you said anything to Teddy about me, I mean about the fact that I'm Jewish. I would not hold a grudge if you had, because I plan to tell him anyway. But if he already knows…"

"Don't be such a little fool!" Caroline practically shouted, realizing that people in the restaurant were looking at her. "Of course, I didn't tell him. I never discussed it with anyone, even when we were at Bryn Mawr. It was your horrible roommate who advertised it. Besides, I could care less, and neither would Teddy. He's not antisemitic. You mustn't judge everyone by the standards of that spoiled, weak James Whitman. Maybe I shouldn't tell you this, but I know for a fact that Teddy is crazy in love with you. I have known him all my life and I have never seen him like this with any other girl."

Tears spilled from her eyes, and she grabbed Caroline's hand. "Thank you. I have been idiotic. I don't know why I am so afraid of people judging me. There has always been something deep inside, almost like a missing piece to my soul, that has stopped me from completely opening my heart. I hope that will change."

"You know Frances, I can actually see a change. You look, I can't explain it. You look lighter."

"I am. I plan to tell Teddy when I see him on Christmas Eve. I hope that you are right about him. I couldn't bear to lose him."

The original plan was to spend Christmas Eve with Teddy in Greenwich. He wanted her to meet some of his childhood friends. Caroline was to be there with her new boyfriend, and of course, Mary and Wallace. But Frances felt uncomfortable and duplicitous meeting his closest friends while she hid the truth about herself. To confess to Teddy, she wanted to be on her own turf, so she invited him to her apartment. This came as quite a surprise to him, and he wondered what she had in mind.

With little experience in cooking anything more than eggs and chicken soup, she spent an entire week shopping and experimenting with recipes. In the end, a simple steak and fried potatoes made up Christmas Eve's dinner. She had managed to find a decent red wine from Lois's bootlegger. For dessert there was a chocolate cake from a nearby bakery.

Teddy appeared at her door around five thirty with a bottle of imported champagne.

"Wherever did you find that?" she asked smiling with delight.

"A gift from a client. I did very well by him this year."

"Come in," she said, brushing off his dark coat. "I didn't realize that it had started to snow."

"Yes, it's coming down hard and steady. Between the snow and it's being Christmas Eve, I'll never get a taxi to the station. The folks will be disappointed. We always spend Christmas morning together."

"Let's not worry about that now," she murmured, her eyes downcast. "I'll put your coat on the radiator so it will dry."

"Do you have any champagne glasses?" he asked.

"You're kidding!" she laughed with a tinge of sarcasm.

"You realize that Lois Long lived here? I have a cupboard full of wine and highball glasses."

Pouring out two glasses, he took her hand and led her to the sofa. "So why the change in plans, Frances? Everyone was looking forward to seeing you."

"I need to talk to you about something. It's serious, and frankly, it's extremely personal."

She started to speak but her throat suddenly constricted, and her mouth was dry.

"I had hoped that it was something personal," he said, wrapping his arm around her waist and pulling her close. "I have never been to your apartment, and well, I was hoping that we could sort of jump ahead to the next level in our relationship."

Her breath caught in her throat. "That's not the reason that I invited you here, at least not consciously. I admit that I do want us to be closer. But first, I must tell you something. And what I'm about to say may change the way you feel about me. That's why I didn't want to come up to Connecticut. I wanted to avoid a scene. It's best that we talk here."

She considered what she was about to confess. Suddenly waves of shame washed over her. She had been false not only to Teddy, but to her parents and her friends. Suddenly she was overtaken by feelings of guilt for treating her childhood friend Sonia with derision. It wasn't that she had to shout out to the world that she was Jewish, but neither should she hide it, especially from the man that she adored.

"Well, what is this earth-shattering revelation?" he asked, a little exasperated.

"We have never spoken about my childhood and my people. I want you to know the truth."

"Fine. I would love to hear about your family. I know you're from Pennsylvania."

"Yes, Reading, Pennsylvania. I am the only child of Dr. Michael Austin and his wife, Minnie."

"Your father is a doctor. Now, that's an honorable

profession. So far, I am not shocked or disappointed in any way."

"Yes. But there are two facts that you might find objectionable. First, I am adopted. So, I will never know who my true parents were. I mean one can only imagine. I have never had the courage to ask my parents about the details."

"So, what! A lot of people are adopted. It's how you are raised that matters. I think that your parents did a fine job. You are a beautiful and intelligent young woman."

"Yes, as you say, it is how you are raised that matters. Teddy, I was raised as a Jew.

My parents are Jewish, and my mother is deeply religious. Frankly, she would never approve of my going with a Gentile." She took a deep breath and exhaled. "So, there it is. I'm Jewish. I regret not telling you sooner."

His eyes were intensely focused on her, and he said nothing for almost a minute.

She could feel her heart beating wildly, as panic set in.

But unexpectedly, he took her face in his hands and kissed her tenderly. Then he released her and shook his head, smiling sweetly. He reprimanded her, as if she were a child.

"You silly thing. What do I care about religion? You could be a Catholic, a Muslim, or a Jain, and I wouldn't care."

Sobbing with relief, words failed her. She had misjudged him, and it was she who was unfair and small-minded.

"There are some people who care about religion, even among my friends," he said. "But it just doesn't matter to me, never has. What matters is character. You, my lovely girl, have plenty of that. I can see that you have had a rough time in the past. If you want to tell me about it someday, I will listen and I will never judge you. I realize that your admission shows that you must really care for me, and that is a great relief."

"Care for you? You idiot, I adore you. Otherwise, I don't think I would have had the courage to tell you. I couldn't go on hiding the truth."

"Thank God that you said it first. I was going to tell you that I loved you tonight, whether we made love or not."

She wiped away her tears with a napkin from the dinner table. Flashing a seductive smile, she asked, "Do you want to eat dinner before or after we make love?"

He took her hand, and she led him to the bedroom. They made love quickly and passionately, regretting that they had held back for so long. He poured them each another glass of champagne, which they didn't finish. They made love three times before they sat down, famished, and elated, to a cold steak dinner.

FRANCES

NEW YORK CITY, JANUARY 1926

By January, Teddy and Frances were seeing each other almost every day. He had rented a small apartment on 46th Street off 5th Avenue. To keep up appearances, they would meet discretely at his place if she planned to spend the night. Most of their friends in Stamford and Greenwich knew they were an item. Caroline was thrilled that her fix up had been a success.

While her private life was going along swimmingly, Frances' professional life was shaky. *The New Yorker* had not taken off as expected, and she had still not obtained a raise. So, she regretfully began to hunt for a new job. She wanted to write, but unfortunately for the time being that would have to be a hobby. She lined up several interviews with department stores and with a few small magazines. Happily, she ran into a bit of luck when Caroline helped arranged for her to interview at the Lord and Thomas branch of the Chicago firm. Someone at *Vogue* knew the top executive at the agency. Exactly what the job entailed was a bit vague but would be explained during the interview.

An attractive and impeccably dressed woman in her late thirties sat behind a large desk in a large, oak-paneled office. Frances had expected an older woman, after all she held the highest position in the New York branch of the top advertising agency in the country. But Mrs. Roberts wore a fashionable knit suit. Her curly, blonde hair was styled into a longer bob that had lately become the rage.

"Please have a seat," she said pointing to a beautifully carved Art Deco chair. "I'm Mrs. Dore Roberts, but please call me Dore."

"How do you do? Thank you so much for seeing me."

"I'll be honest with you, Frances. At first, I wasn't sure that I wanted to interview you. But when I saw on your resume that you worked at *The New Yorker*, I was intrigued. I see that you mainly handled accounts, but that you also write copy."

"Yes, Mrs. Roberts, I mean Dore. I prefer the writing aspect of the business. However, to be perfectly frank, things aren't going so well at the magazine and a girl has to pay the bills."

"You have no idea how well I understand your situation. I had to work my way up from the ground floor. And I am speaking literally. I started as a cash girl at Wanamaker's when I was fifteen. You should have seen me then, a naïve girl, terrified of my father. You see we were immigrants, Russian Jews escaping the pogroms. I grew up in the tenements and my father insisted that I quit school at fourteen to help the family. I won't give you all the gory details, but it was a struggle. I was lucky to have several mentors who guided and encouraged me. I worked at Wanamaker's during the day and went to school at night. It takes hard work and dedication for a woman to succeed in the advertising world. Do you think you have what it takes Frances?"

Frances' eyes widened. "How admirable! My journey has not been nearly as arduous.

But I take my work seriously and I am willing to learn."

"Good. We are looking for copywriters, particularly in the fields of fashion, makeup, and soaps. But I hope you wouldn't object to calling on our clients. You are so attractive, and that always is an advantage with men, but even more so with women."

"Really? One wouldn't think that it would matter to female clients."

"Oh, it does. They see you as their public. They may even get ideas for their products while examining your clothes and your makeup."

"I hadn't thought of that. I already have quite a few clients. My biggest is B. Altman's. Of course, they do their own creative work in-house."

"Yes, I know. So, I may assume that you wouldn't mind handling accounts as well as writing copy?"

"Not in the least."

"Very well, we will let you know as soon as we have finished interviewing."

"May I ask when that might be? I am anxious to give my notice at the magazine. I have had several offers, but I would prefer to work here."

"Very well. You are a smart girl. You can give your notice and start with us next week."

ADDIE

FOREST HILLS, JANUARY 1926

As Donald and Addie exited the train at Forest Hills, they were pleasantly surprised. The station itself was opened in 1911. The Forest Hills community was built in 1909, but with the arrival of the train linking Queens to Manhattan, new houses were going up at a fast pace.

There were also apartments, churches, and parks. It was being transformed into a garden city. They walked out to the entry plaza at Station Square, which was built in the style of a manor house. The structure was adorned with patterned brickwork and there was a domed tower, surrounded by arched walkways.

It was Donald's idea to investigate the possibility of working with a group of developers. Last summer he had met a group of locals at a tennis match at the Forest Hills Stadium. He heard them talking about plans to extend the subway out to Queens. They were enthusiastic about the coming changes, claiming that Queens Boulevard would be transformed into a new Park Avenue.

"Yes, indeed," said a stocky balding man named Rudy. "Queens is on its way up." He looked at Donald inquisitively. "Are you thinking of moving?"

"Perhaps," he answered cautiously.

"Well, if you have a family, it's a great little neighborhood," said a tall, athletic-looking, middle-aged man. "I'm sure you have noticed the parks and gardens. And there is talk of a neighborhood of new houses going up soon."

This piqued Donald's interest. "Do you know what company is doing the construction?"

"As a matter of fact, I do," he answered. "I work at the bank, and I'm involved with the financing. The architect's name is Atterbury. He's a dependable chap with a good track record.

His buildings are sturdy and stylish. Also, he puts them up fast using prefabricated concrete walls. Word is that he is planning a development of rowhouses. He's working with a fellow named Tappan, who will be building smaller homes. I've seen some drawings, Neo-Tudor exteriors with Arts and Crafts interiors."

"Do you think that I could call on you at your bank?" Donald asked, trying to sound as casual as possible.

"I don't quite understand," said the banker. The homes won't be completed for almost a year. I don't think they will be on the market for months."

"I apologize for not being completely honest with you," said Donald. "You see, I'm a realtor with a top Manhattan agency. We might be interested in representing the developer in the city."

"Oh, I understand. I can't make any guarantees, but I'll see what I can do. Give me your card if you don't mind. Here's mine."

A week later they met Mr. Tappan at the station at ten and then went on to the building site, so that they might see a model home. Donald saw him approaching and waved to get his attention.

"Mr. Tappan, this is Miss Addie Stanford," said Donald.

Tappan gave the impression of a congenial and confident man. "It is very encouraging indeed to take a meeting with agents from Butler and Brown."

"Thank you, Sir," said Donald. "I will be honest with

you. Our agency doesn't normally take listings in Queens. As a matter of fact, this is the first time. Miss Stanford and I had to work hard to convince Mr. Butler to let us even take this meeting."

"Yes, I realize that the Forest Close and Forest Arbor developments are unconventional.

However, if you consider the fact that the railway already connects us to the city and that we will have a subway stop in a few years, I am sure you will agree that there is money to be made for people with vision."

"I agree," said Addie. "I realize that we are young, and perhaps you might think that we lack experience. But please feel free to check our sales history."

Tappan flashed an officious smile. "I have. Very impressive. Ah, here's my car."

A driver jumped out and opened the door for Addie and Donald. Then he opened the front door for his boss.

They drove up to the building site, where large slabs of concrete were being erected. "As you see, we use prefabricated walls. This saves time and money. We embrace the concept of mass production, as long as it does not compromise the integrity of the homes."

"They certainly look solid," said Addie. "I imagine it leaves you more time to work on architectural detail."

"It does. We are looking for a certain style," he said, pointing to the solitary completed home. It was a model of the rowhouses that were to make up a large part of the community."

The exterior of the home was Neo-Tudor, with wooden lattice patterns, pointed gables, and windows with multiple panes. This style was complemented by sections of decoratively patterned brickwork. Men were busy planting trees and gardens to surround the homes.

"What we will have here is affordable housing, surrounded by gardens with easy access to Manhattan."

"What are your thoughts on pricing?" asked Donald.

I'm working that out with the bank. But we see this

neighborhood as an escape for the New Yorker of means. I'm not saying it's for the rich, mind you, but we would like to attract professionals, who make a good living."

Once they returned to the office, they spoke with Mr. Butler at length. The decision was made that Donald and Addie should work with the developers on a commission basis. If Tappan agreed, they would sell the homes on speculation, but only if the agency had an exclusive contract.

They spoke with Tappan a few days later. He said that the investors were hesitant to draw up a contract that agreed to exclusive representation.

"I don't like this, not one bit," said Donald. "It's true we have the advantage of getting in on the ground floor. But there is nothing to stop them from opening up sales to other agencies."

Addie seemed nervous and uncertain. She felt a little shaky. "I don't know, Donald. I don't know if we can trust Tappan. But on the other hand, people change agencies all the time.

That's how we got our duplexes."

"But does your gut tell you to go ahead? Please excuse the expression," he said, slightly embarrassed.

"Yes, my instincts are telling me that we stand to make a great deal of money. Of course, that depends on what is expected of us; money for advertising, open houses, and other promotional expenditures."

"We need to try to keep the expenses down. The other partners are on the war path about the agency's budget," he said. "But it looks like Queens is going to be the new frontier. We wouldn't want to miss out on that."

"So, what date have you fixed?" asked Addie. "I can't believe it. I knew that you were seeing Aaron exclusively, but I had no idea that you were even considering marriage. I haven't even met the young man. I mean, what are you hiding?"

"Don't be ridiculous," said Evie. "I'm not hiding anything. He's busy finishing up his doctoral thesis. He wants to finish in May so that he can start work in June right after the wedding."

It was a blustery day, the freezing wind, mixed with sleet cut into their skin. They ducked into a crowded coffee shop and found a table at the very back, next to the kitchen.

"I forgot. What is he studying?" asked Addie, taking off her heavy coat.

"He's studying physics and engineering. He will work as an electrical engineer for a large industrial concern. He was offered the job a few weeks ago and the salary is tremendous. That's why he wants to finish his thesis and get married quickly. He wants to start his new job without any distractions."

"I imagine that you will be quite a distraction," Addie giggled. "Your mother must be terribly busy making the arrangements. Are you going to have bridesmaids? Is that part of the tradition at a Jewish wedding."

"The wedding will be fairly small. My cousin is the maid of honor and two other friends from the neighborhood will be bridesmaids. I hope you are not offended. My mother is controlling everything, the ceremony, the guest list, even the menu. In our culture, even in 1926, the Jewish mother rules."

"I understand completely," said Addie, trying to hide her disappointment. "It's odd that Sam hasn't mentioned the wedding. I will have to ask him to educate me about the traditions and advise me on what to wear."

"Oh, I asked Sam not to mention it until I told you." Evie avoided looking her in the eye and Addie knew that she was lying. "I think that you should talk to Sam yourself.

It's delicate. I know how you feel about him, and I can tell that he's crazy about you. But please don't expect too much from him. A wedding is a big deal for a Jewish family. And, well…"

Addie could feel the blood rushing to her face when she understood what Evie was trying so hard to tell her. "I see. As far as your parents are concerned, Addie Stanford doesn't exist."

"Look, I adore my brother. But when it comes to confronting my parents, he's a coward. His romantic life is never a topic of conversation when we gather on Friday for Shabbat. My father sometimes jokes with him. You know the sort of thing: A wink and how's your love life? My mother has a growing list of aging Jewish spinsters from good families. Addie, I'm worried that he's going to hurt you. Don't get in too deep."

Later that evening, Addie was clearing the table at Sam's apartment. He adored her lasagna. She had learned a lot about Italian cooking from her friends in Washington Heights. When she was growing up, she often spent entire weekends with the Del Vecchio family, and she would watch how the meals were prepared.

Sam placed the last plates in the sink. "That was delicious," he said, pulling her down onto the sofa. "A guy gets tired of brisket and kugel, not to mention Chinese takeout." He kissed her and began to caress her breasts. When they were first together, he took things slowly, testing her limits. But he was becoming impatient, and he could see that each time they were together she became more responsive to his touch. He took hold of her garter and began to unroll her silk stockings and stroke her leg.

His touch aroused her; a tremor ran over her skin. Her breath quickened. Normally, at this point she would have curtly put a stop to his lovemaking, but she felt her body taking over and her resistance waning. He began to moan, and she realized that if she didn't resist at once, she would lose control of her own desire. She brushed his hand away and pushed him forcefully.

He protested loudly, his face contorted with a mixture of hurt and anger. She hadn't meant to push him so violently, but it was an involuntary reaction.

"What's wrong with you, Addie? I wasn't forcing myself on you," he said, crossing his legs to hide the evidence of his arousal. "I know you wanted me. It's not fair of you to lead me on like that."

Her guilt for hurting him disappeared in an instant, and anger filled the void.

"How dare you accuse me of leading you on! I love you and a few days ago I decided that I would let you make love to me. Tonight, you saw how my body responded to you. But after speaking to Evie today, it finally struck me that you see me as just one more girl in a long line of lovers, serious lovers, but no more significant than the others."

"What are you talking about? What did Evie say?"

"Don't play the innocent. Your sister and I are close friends. Why would she hide the fact that she is getting married? It's obvious. She held out the vain hope that you would tell me yourself. You haven't mentioned it. I don't blame her for staying silent. She didn't come out and say as much, but she was testing you. And you failed miserably. I know why you kept me in the dark, but I want to hear you say the words."

Flustered and bewildered, his shoulders slumped, and he could not meet her gaze. He tried to call up the words to try to justify his behavior, but he remained mute.

"I understand," she said, her eyes filling with tears. "I guess that I have always known that I would not be the exception to the rule. It just baffles me that Evie and you speak so often and so eloquently about antisemitism. Yet, you have no problem judging me because I am a Gentile. It's absurd that you don't see it!"

"I know it is," he stammered. "But family is everything to us. It's the way I was raised. Evie wants you to come to the wedding. But I told her that I would feel like a hypocrite if you came, and I had to hide our relationship. Of course, you can come if you like. But we can't go as a couple."

She stood up and straightened her hose and dress. Don't bother to come down with me. I will talk to Evie. Obviously, I won't be attending the wedding. However, I will not give up my friendship with her."

"And us?" he said.

"I don't think that we should go on seeing each other," she said as she walked toward the door. "You have no idea what you have lost in letting me go. I must be honest. I love you and it will take a long time for me to get over it. But I will."

FRANCES

NEW YORK CITY, FEBRUARY 1926

In 1926 magazines and newspapers were full of advertisements for products from cosmetics to girdles. A new mouthwash named Listerine was on the market. Frances noticed that many of the goods that were being pushed on the American public played on people's insecurities, particularly the insecurities of women. Clear skin and cheeks made rosy by rouge were de rigueur for women of all ages. New salons were opening every day. Women had their eyebrows plucked and dyed. The beautician had arrived on the American scene and women no longer went to barbers to have their hair bobbed. They met other women at the hairdresser and discussed the latest in fashion and beauty treatments.

Women and men worried about losing their appeal to the opposite sex. "Do you have halitosis?" was a freshly invented condition that appeared in numerous ads, which claimed that your love life and your business relationships could be impaired by bad breath.

The sight of a woman smoking, which ten years earlier would have been considered an abomination, was common in the mid 1920s. Dore asked Frances to write copy to go along with a photograph of thin, stylish young women lighting up after a tennis match. It was not the first time she felt uncomfortable with an assignment, but she knew it was part of her job.

One Monday evening, she met with members of her writing class at the Uptown apartment of Claudia, who was a wealthy Barnard grad. Also present were two other women who were working on short stories, as well as two men, one writing a novel about his experiences during the war. The other, a man in his late thirties named Paul, was writing a novel, a social critique along the lines of Sinclair Lewis's "Babbitt."

"What are you working on, Frances?" asked Claudia.

"I'm thinking about doing a piece on advertising and its effects on women."

"Really?" asked Paul. "Isn't that a bit risky, considering your position at Lord and Thomas?"

"I know," she said. "I doubt that I could ever get it published. I mean what magazine would risk alienating the companies that are their bread and butter? But I need to be passionate about my topic. Even if it isn't published, I will hone my skills."

"What claims do you find the most outrageous?" asked Claudia. "After you tell us, we can go look in my bathroom and see how many I have bought," she said laughing.

"Well, some of the makeup ads are so deceitful. I've seen how they spend hours applying makeup to models who are eighteen and flawless. Then they want the poor forty-year-old secretary to think that she can achieve the same results."

"Yes, I find them absurd," said Claudia, rolling her eyes.

"The worst is advertising cigarettes," said Frances. "I don't believe the ads with doctors claiming how good it is for your health. My father is a doctor and he quit smoking years ago. I have an assignment to write copy for a photo of two young women smoking after a tennis match.

I am to allege that smoking is healthy because it will stop you from eating sweets and therefore help you keep your slim figure. I must also emphasize how glamourous and liberating it is. I'm to use the term 'cigarettes are torches of freedom for the liberated woman.' What rot!"

Frances arrived home later that evening to hear the telephone ringing. It was well after eleven o'clock and her heart was beating wildly with panic. It could only be bad news.

Her father's voice was trembling, and he tripped over his words. "Mother has had a stroke. I can't believe it. I came home and there she was on the floor."

"Oh, Daddy," she said, trying to control her sobbing. "Is she going to be alright?"

"I brought her to the hospital, but she is unresponsive. Please try to come home. There is always a slim chance that she might wake up. If she does, it would mean so much for her to see you."

"I'll take the first train out, Daddy, but I don't imagine I'll get there until morning, unless there is a late train running. I'll call the hospital from the train station. What's the number?"

There was a late train and Frances arrived at four in the morning. Her father picked her up and they drove to the hospital. He was uncharacteristically silent on the ride.

When they arrived and entered the room, Frances could see that it was too late. Her mother was gone.

"What am I going to do without her?" he whispered. "I loved her. She was the only woman that ever meant anything to me."

She was slightly confused by his last statement, but let it go. "Daddy, I'm so sorry. I know how much you loved her, and she adored you. I only wish that I had been a better daughter and spent more time with her."

"Don't say that. You were her pride and joy. She would brag about her beautiful girl, who was carving out a career in New York. She couldn't have been prouder if she had given birth to you herself." Suddenly he began to cry, at first silently and then he began to sob loudly and uncontrollably.

Frances had never seen her father cry. He had always been a model of calm professionalism. In life and death situations, he offered comfort and stability to his patients, his friends and to his family. She wrapped her arms around him and tried to console him. It was as if they had switched roles, and she had become the parent. But it was a role that she couldn't play for long. Suddenly, her body began to shake violently as she allowed the feelings of anguish and heartache to overcome her. To these emotions, she added a sense of guilt for not being respectful and caring towards the woman that had loved her so dearly. It dawned on her that she had never shown true affection to her mother because unconsciously she knew that somewhere out in the world there was another woman who had given birth to her. How could she have been so unspeakably unfair and cruel to the woman that devoted her life to raising her?

Mike bent down and kissed Minnie for the last time. Frances could feel his anguish.

"Let's go home, Daddy. We will make arrangements tomorrow for the funeral."

"Esther Bash has called the rabbi," Mike said as he turned on the living room lights. "Since she passed away so late, we can wait until the day after tomorrow for the funeral. Irving and Esther will take care of everything."

"I'll help too," she said.

"I deal with life and death almost every day. You would think that I could handle this.

But I just can't, I can't."

The next day, Frances called Dore and explained why she hadn't come to work. Dore told her to take as much time as she needed. Then she called Teddy and told him about her mother.

"Darling, is there anything I can do? Can I come to Reading to be with you?"

"No, Teddy. I never told my parents about us because I was so worried about how my mother would react. And now, she's gone. I wish that I had told her and that she could have had the chance to get to know you. She would have liked you."

"My love, don't torture yourself. Life is full of absurdities, and we never know how things will play out. But shall I come down?"

"No, darling. The funeral is tomorrow, and we sit shivah for seven days. It's not a good time to tell Daddy about us. I'll call you in a few days."

Two days before she was to leave, Frances heard her father in a heated argument with Irving Bash. It was a shock, as her father hardly ever raised his voice, especially not to Irving, who was his best friend. They were outside the house, hoping, in vain, that she wouldn't hear them. Esther was there, doing her best to deescalate the situation, but they ignored her. She opened the door and stepped out. They immediately stopped arguing.

"What on earth is going on between you two? If you must raise your voices, please come into the house. It's unseemly. We are still sitting shivah."

"Never mind," said Irving. "Your father will explain things to you. Oy, let's go, Esther. What a mess."

Her father stood looking out the front window as Irving walked away. He was shaking with anger. She had never seen her father this furious, but she also noticed fear in his eyes.

"Daddy please tell me what happened. It doesn't have anything to do with mother. I can't imagine…"

"No, it's me," he interrupted. "I am a fool; a careless fool and I am not worthy of your love and admiration."

"Stop it! You are being absurd. There's nothing that you have done or could do that would make you unworthy of my love."

"No, there's quite a bit. I don't know where to start. But I guess I should begin with Irving, although the entire scheme was my idea. But he certainly made it worse."

"Please try to make sense," she said, with an exasperated tone.

"Come sit down. It's a long story. Last year, the Golds and the Abrams went to Miami and stayed in Coral Gables.

Max Gold went on and on about the money that people were making in real estate. I didn't believe him at first. You know Max, everything with a grain of salt. But I bought some magazines and there were full-page ads, in color no less."

"Yes, I have seen them," she said. My agency even helped place a few. 'Coral Gables, the Stuff Dreams Are Made Of' was one of the titles. And what does that have to do with you and Irving?"

"Irving got it into his head to go down and see if he could buy a little piece of paradise. He wanted me to go along, but I was too busy with the practice and Mother was against it. But when he got down there, he kept calling and cabling. He said that we had to act quickly. There's this fellow, George Merrick, who was developing Coral Gables, dividing it into neighborhoods, what he called villages: French Village, Normandy Village, Italian Village, and so on."

"So, Irving bought a house?" Frances was becoming impatient and worried, waiting for the bombshell.

"No, it doesn't work like that. You buy from a plan. It's a map with the lots marked out.

The problem is, Irving was so naïve. You would think being an accountant, he would have been more cautious."

"Irving has always been cautious," she said. Her father had trusted him with his money for years. It suddenly occurred to her that she had read an article in *The New York Times* that described in some detail the frauds that were perpetrated on naïve tourists in Florida.

"This time, he lost his head. They are all going crazy down there. He didn't go to a reputable realtor. He used one of those fellows they call binders."

"Binders? I have never heard that term," she said.

"These are rooky realtors, some licensed, some not. They stand on the curb and sell lots from a plan. The buyer can purchase a lot paying ten percent down. The balance is due when the papers are filed, and he is presented with the deed."

"Don't tell me he gave his money to a crook on the street!" She gasped.

"Binders are supposed to be legitimate representatives of reality companies. Unfortunately, some of them run their own private scams. They sell you a lot, taking your money, then they resell it to someone else the next day. Or they have another swindle where they hold on to your contract and never file for the deed. Since the values of properties are skyrocketing, the buyer finds that the new value is out of his range. The binder pockets the ten percent."

"Poor Irving. Did he lose much?" She truly felt bad for him. The Bashes were not wealthy, and he was not young enough to earn enough to recoup his lost savings. "Thank God, you didn't go down there," she murmured.

"He didn't have much to put in, but he lost what he had, about $8,000," said her father, lowering his head and trying to avoid her stare. "Frances, I didn't go to Florida, but I gave him a large sum to invest. I should have listened to your mother. She was dead set against it. I never did tell her that I gave him the money. At least she's not here to witness my ruin."

"Ruin?" she cried; a chill ran through her body. "Daddy, how much money did you invest?"

"Everything, $15,000. That was all our savings. Irving said the investment was rock solid. He didn't invest my money with a binder. He used a realtor, Horace Bronson, who turned out to be an even bigger shyster."

He seemed to fold in on himself, and Frances realized how much her father had aged. He was in his early sixties, but he looked eighty. The dapper, carefree man she remembered had changed. She searched for words of comfort but found none.

"I'm so sorry. It's so unfair, not to mention illegal. Maybe we can hire a lawyer."

"I don't want to throw good money after bad," he said, sounding completely defeated. "So many people have been robbed. I don't trust lawyers any more than realtors at this point. I'll just have to keep working for another decade, maybe more." He tried to go on, but he was overcome with shame. Then he lowered his head. "I'm afraid I won't be able to send you anymore checks, at least not for a while."

"Don't worry about me," she reassured him. "I'm fine. I have a good job now. But I think that something needs to be done about what they did to you. It's outright fraud. If you don't want to hire a lawyer, perhaps we can investigate the realtor."

"Investigate? I don't know any detectives in Florida."

"No, Daddy, but you know a writer here who wants to specialize in investigative articles."

"I do?" he asked, completely baffled.

"Yes, you do. I haven't been published, but I have been taking writing courses for a couple of years. I have been searching for a case that would be personally meaningful and consequential. Well, this is personal!"

"What is going on in that pretty head? I don't want you to get into any trouble. You said yourself, you have a good job. I don't want you to lose it."

"I'm not worried. The woman I work for is supportive. She has encouraged my writing. I think that she will give me a leave of absence or perhaps some vacation time. Daddy, I'm going to Florida to check into this."

"What's the point," he said, sounding completely defeated.

"I doubt that I can recover your money, but I will do my best to expose the crook who stole your life savings."

Mike Austin beamed with pride. He could see that she was determined, his beautiful, brave daughter. But for a moment his smile disappeared, a wistful expression transformed his face. Perhaps it was Minnie's death or another loss that he had experienced in his life.

Frances returned to New York at the end of the first week in February. She wanted to spend as much time as possible with Teddy before she left for Florida. They were together many evenings during the week and every weekend. When she was alone in her apartment, she spent her free time reading articles about Florida. There was a long piece in *Forbes* which investigated bank fraud related to the real estate craze. She learned as much as possible about the situation, so that she could have a roadmap to run a coherent investigation.

Teddy encouraged her to go out to clubs and theater and to have some fun. Lois had presented her with two tickets to the Marx Brothers' musical, *Cocoanuts*. She and Teddy attended a Saturday night performance. The theater was packed. The play was a hit, with music by Irving Berlin. The fact that the lyrics were written by George Kaufman surprised Frances, for up until now he had written plays with Edna and a few Hollywood screenplays. She found it incongruous that he was writing for the Marx Brothers. They tended towards slapstick, where George's plays were more sophisticated. The setting for the play was a hotel in Florida, and in fact that is why she had wanted to see it. In one scene Groucho was trying to bamboozle a group of tourists into buying some real estate in Miami. The line, "*You can have any kind of home you want. You can even get stucco. Ho, how you can get stuck-oh.*" was particularly striking. She took it as a sign. Now more than ever, she knew that she was doing the right thing traveling to Florida to write her article, even if she never found a publisher.

That night she told Teddy that she was going to leave for Florida sometime in mid-March. He seemed dismayed.

"I wish you wouldn't leave," he said. "I know that you feel that you owe it to your father."

"It's not just for my father. What's going on down there is criminal and I feel that it needs to be exposed. Perhaps I can stop other people from making the same mistake."

"I admire your passion for justice, but some people will not be dissuaded by articles or any other evidence. I've seen so many investment swindles in my work on Wall Street. People make and lose fortunes all the time."

"Of course, that's true. But this is my father who has lost

his life's savings. If ever a racket needed to be exposed, this is the one that hits closest to home. I know that he will survive. But now he will have to work until he is an old man. But Teddy, there are other people who have lost everything, people who piled into their Tin Lizzies and drove from all over the country. They are not doctors or accountants, but hardworking laborers and farmers. Most are destitute and can't even afford to get home."

"I have read about them and it's reprehensible. On the finance end of it, I have heard that many local banks in Florida will go under. I worry that the situation will have a ripple effect that will touch the whole country."

"Darling, I knew that you would understand. You won't get yourself into any trouble while I'm gone, will you?" She said, pretending to be worried.

"Don't be ridiculous," he whispered before kissing her. "As a matter of fact, I might take a week off to come and join you. I might be able to slip away in April."

"That would be wonderful." Then she looked at him thoughtfully. "Maybe you could help me by scrutinizing how the Florida banks are handling real estate transactions."

"Maybe, but I have to be discreet. I don't want to make any enemies. I see that I can't stop you from going, but I would like to set one condition to give you my full support."

"Condition? You've never placed conditions on our relationship before. What do you mean?"

"My condition is that you agree to marry me." His face glowed and he began to stumble over his words. "You do love me? Please don't tell me that I have exaggerated the extent of your feelings. I'm not out of line, am I?"

Frances leaned into him and kissed him. She had been hoping for it, but never really expected a proposal. "Out of line, how absurd! I love you and I will marry you." Her knees almost gave way with the shock, so she sat down on the couch. "It's ironic," she said sadly. "I am heartbroken that my mother is gone, but in a way I'm relieved that she won't have to face the fact that I'm marrying outside of the religion."

He stroked her hair. "I am sorry. But what about your father?"

"Daddy never really cared about religion, at least I never heard him speak of it. He hardly ever goes to temple, and he has loads of Gentile friends. Reading is a small town and even though there is a sizable Jewish community, as a doctor who is on the hospital board, he and mother often socialized outside their Jewish circle of friends." For a moment, her gaze was distant, and she appeared wistful. "I never wanted to acknowledge it, but my father always had an eye for the ladies. He was always chatting with young women, usually blonde, attractive Gentile women."

"Really?" said Teddy with a sympathetic smile.

"I'm sure that he never did anything untoward. He adored my mother." She tried to summon a casual laugh. "Why, the idea is absurd!"

"Of course, it is," he said. But will he accept me as a son-in-law?"

"How could he not accept you? You're perfect," she whispered and kissed him. "But I think that we should hold off telling him. It's too soon after Mother's death. And I need to get this Florida business over with. As a matter of fact, let's keep it our secret until I come back."

"If you like. That will give me time to shop for a ring."

"Suddenly, clutching his arm, her face darkened. "How will your family react? I know that Caroline will be thrilled. But what about your father?"

"Dad will be delighted. He's been so lonely since Mom died, and he has told me several times about how much he likes you. In his words, "You bring sunshine into his dull life."

"He really doesn't mind about my religion?"

"No, our family has never been like that. I know that there are plenty of bigots in Connecticut, but we have always been above all that. Please don't worry. Let's enjoy our secret for the time being. Perhaps you'll stay the night so we can celebrate?"

It took her several days to work up the courage to tell Dore about her plan to go to Florida. She didn't want to risk losing her job, especially now that her father could no longer help her with the rent. Fortunately, she had enough money saved for the train ticket down. Finding lodgings was another matter.

"I wouldn't blame you if you dismissed me. I haven't been working here for very long, after all. But the fraud that is going on in Florida needs to be exposed and I have never felt so passionate about an issue. It's personal you see. My father and his best friend were sucked into a real estate scheme. Both lost all their savings."

"I'm sorry to hear it," said Dore, with a serious expression. "I don't plan on dismissing you, but I must check with the head office in Chicago about allowing you to take more time off.

Then there is the ethical aspect. Lord and Thomas is one of the biggest advertising firms in the country. If we have an employee investigating other agencies, it might not look good."

"I am going to concentrate on the real estate agencies as much as possible. But I will expose any advertising firms that have been complicit in the fraud. If I manage to get an article published, I could resign. I would never want to do anything to the detriment of Lord and Thomas, and especially of you, Dore."

"Let's not get ahead of ourselves. I have an idea. The president of the agency, Albert Lasker, is a brilliant and principled man. I am going to make the proposition that we finance your trip to Florida."

"Really?" Frances was dumbfounded. "Why would he agree to pay for an investigative article that exposes fraudulent advertising? Doesn't it make the industry look bad?"

"That's the point. When publicity is blatantly false and people suffer as a result, it makes us all look bad. If we are the ones to expose it, we place ourselves above the fray. I will speak to Mr. Lasker about the idea. You will report back to us. Of course, you may write your article, but we will need to read it first."

"I understand. What will Mr. Lasker do if I find that there has been false advertising?"

"He's a very influential man. I suspect that he might create a commission of some kind to go down and look into the legalities and other details."

"When could I leave?" she asked.

"I would like you to wait a week or two to tie up any loose ends with your accounts. I also want you to help with the Wanamaker campaign. Can you wait until the third week in March?"

"Of course," said Frances, secretly overjoyed about the prospect of spending a few more weeks with Teddy.

ADDIE

NEW YORK CITY, FEBRUARY 1926

Addie had kept her resolve and had not seen Sam in over a month. She saw Donald every day as they worked to put together publicity for the Forest Hills project. Even though they had promised Mr. Butler that they would not spend exorbitant amounts of money on advertising, the expenses mounted. They had made up some brochures and paid for advertising in two prominent magazines.

In the beginning of February, Donald spoke to Robert Tappan several times a week. But by the middle of the month, Tappan seemed to be avoiding his calls. Now, he wasn't taking them at all. Donald guided Addie into an empty office and told her that she had better sit down.

"He has a nerve," Donald seethed, his voice had a hard edge. "I never should have trusted the bastard!"

The color drained from her face. In all the time she had known Donald, she had never seen him lose control. "What's going on?" she asked, a sensation of dread crept through her body.

"Tappan finally took my call. He said that they have decided not to use an outside realtor. The bank is going to help them finance their own publicity campaign and they hired a team of realtors to work in the company."

"He is a bastard!" she exclaimed, clasping her hand over her mouth with embarrassment.

"Well, that wasn't very ladylike. But it's true, nevertheless. So, I assume that we are out of the deal?"

"Out of the deal and out over five hundred dollars in expenses," said Donald, trying hard to control his anger.

"Do we have any recourse at all?" she asked, already knowing the response.

"None. And now we have to tell Butler," he said, his mouth twitching with rage.

"Maybe I can tell him. He might go easier on me."

"Why, because you're a woman? I doubt it. He will just use the situation as confirmation that women should not be hired as realtors."

"Well, I'm going with you when you tell him. Do you think he'll fire us?" she asked.

"I don't know," said Donald. "But I can't stay on. Everyone will know what happened, and believe me, there will be plenty of them happy to see me get my comeuppance."

"Really? I always thought that you were well-liked by all the agents."

"Sure, on the surface. But most of them are jealous of my success. I've heard their whispers and I know human nature. They can't stand to see a Jew do well. As far as you're concerned, the men see it as an affront for a woman to grab a top listing. And I'm sure you have realized that the secretaries are just plain jealous."

She was silent for a moment. Then she blurted out, "If you leave, I won't stay."

"That's nice of you. But it won't be easy for you to find a position in another agency because you're a woman. And when word gets out about how we were manipulated by Tappan, well, I don't need to spell it out."

"Donald, what are we going to do?" she asked, close to tears.

"New York is not the only city in the country. I've been thinking about going down to Miami. There's a boom that's been going on for the past few years."

"Florida! I can't imagine you there, wearing a white suit and a straw hat."

"It's an idea that I've been kicking around for a few years. But once I started working with you, I didn't pursue it. I couldn't abandon my business partner. Besides, I always told you that I would wait for you until you finally got over Sam."

Her cheeks flushed and she lowered her gaze. "So, you know that we are not seeing each other?"

"Sure. I'm still his friend, even if he is a cad. He is pretty broken up about it. But not too much. He's been going to the clubs with a different girl every night. He claims it's the only way to get you out of his blood."

"He can do as he likes. I'm trying my best to get over him. Moving out of New York would certainly go a long way to make that easier."

"I don't know," he said, cautiously. "I should warn you. Florida real estate can be risky and there are a lot of crooks. I used to think that I could spot a rotten deal in a minute. But after Tappan, I'm not so sure."

"After this experience, you'll be even more astute. I'm intrigued by the idea, but there's the problem of my mother."

"What's going on with your mother? You haven't mentioned her in months."

"She's extremely ill. It's her heart. I went with her to the doctor last week. She can hardly walk and is practically bed-ridden. He said that it could be a matter of weeks. You know that we're not close, but I don't think I can move from the city before…Well before the end."

"I understand," he said. "Do you really want to go?" He was incredulous.

"I do. If I want to continue to work in real estate, I must get out of New York, at least for the time being. I don't want to move to Ohio or even back to Pennsylvania. Maybe you can go to Miami and scope things out. I'll follow when

I can."

As predicted, Mr. Butler exploded when he learned of the Forest Hills fiasco. He didn't outright fire Donald, but it was obvious that he wouldn't be handing him any good listings. So, he packed a suitcase and took the first train to Miami.

Two weeks later, Addie received a phone call from her mother's neighbor. She rushed to catch the subway to Washington Heights. Upon entering the bedroom, she was shocked to see how thin and pale her mother had become since their visit to the doctor. Her breathing was labored and shallow, but she was still conscious and able to speak. Trying her best to hide her alarm, Addie gently squeezed her hand and stroked her thinning hair. She averted her gaze, and her chin began to tremble, as she fought off tears. There had been a gulf between the two of them in recent years, but the reality that she was about to lose the only family she had hit her hard.

"Mama, I had no idea that things had gotten so serious. I would have come sooner," she whispered.

"Thanks, but it wouldn't have changed a thing. My time has come. It's too bad that I'm not a religious person. Some of the neighbors have been coming over and praying, but I think they were putting on a show. Maybe it makes them feel better."

"I wish I had words of comfort about heaven or an afterlife. But that's one thing we have in common. I can tell you that I love you and that I know that you have always done your best for me."

Rose turned her head and stared at the wall. Addie panicked, afraid that she had died. But then her mother turned her head and her eyes focused intensely on her daughter's face. She began to murmur. Her breathing was shallow, and it was difficult to make out the words. "It's not true. I could have done much more. You could have had much more. I want you to know that before I leave this earth. Your father…"

"My father," Addie said, pleading. "Please tell me before it's too late. It's the biggest gift that you could give me."

"No," said Rose, her voice almost inaudible. "I don't want to give him the satisfaction. He doesn't deserve to know you. He got what he wanted; he got his child."

"Mama, I don't understand what you are saying. He doesn't have his child. Is he alive? Mama, please tell me his name. Please!"

Rose's eyes went blank as she exhaled, and Addie knew it was too late. As she wept, she wondered if the tears streaming down her cheeks were for her mother or for herself. She kissed her mother one last time, but she felt numb. A door had closed and there was not another person on the face of the earth who could help her unlock it.

ADDIE

MIAMI, FLORIDA, MARCH 1926

Sam had been in Florida for several months. His assignment entailed combing through bank records of real estate development financing, as well as keeping a sharp eye out for conflict of interest between bankers, city officials, and big developers. There was no shortage of paper trails, although most deals were made in secret meetings with only a handshake. There was so much speculation going on with depositors' money that a few banks began to fail.

At first only small banks went under, so the pain and shock were limited. But Sam knew that the way things were going, sooner or later, the damage would be widespread. The bankers were acting in a reckless manner. They would lend up to eighty percent of the value of the land purchased. A parcel of land might be bought for $700,000, subdivided and resold at twice the price a month later. Another problem was speculation on hotels that were never built. Bank records were sloppy. In one case, he discovered a bank examiner, hired on to the board of a bank that he was investigating. He was so busy that he had little time to enforce penalties for the irregularities he found.

However, he had recently received a directive from the New York office to drop everything to take up a new case.

A smooth operator, named Charles Ponzi, was in town. He had served five years in New York for a financial pyramid scheme. After completing his prison term, he became involved in another ruse. He was arrested and let out on bail. Having slipped quietly out of New York, agents traced him to Florida. He was staying in a small hotel in Miami Beach. Sam had checked into the hotel in the guise of a gigolo from up north in search of wealthy heiresses. It was a role he liked playing; he enjoyed chasing after girls, especially the more naïve types from the Midwest.

Ponzi was printing up brochures for worthless lots found in swamp land. He seemed to have lost his touch, perhaps because there was so much competition in the real estate fraud business. Still, Sam had all the evidence he needed, so he called in the local federal agents. He later regretted not bringing down the more professional men from Washington. Ponzi gave them the slip. Having shaved his head and grown a mustache as a disguise, he jumped on a freighter for Houston. He was finally caught in New Orleans.

Donald was working for a small agency that sold properties and houses for Carl Fisher the largest developer in Miami and Miami Beach. The owner of the agency, Horace Bronson, was a Florida native and knew all the local bankers and construction company bosses, as well as the union leaders. Lumpish, stoop-shouldered, he, nevertheless, considered himself a ladies' man, stepping out with flappers of all shapes and ages. He did not discriminate as long as his companion offered a good time that ended in a tumble in one of the hotel rooms he rented exclusively for these trysts.

He was impressed with Donald's manner and experience, and especially his willingness to work all hours. And for Donald, working was a more agreeable alternative to spending time in his lodgings, a room that he shared with two young men in a house in a seedy neighborhood in Miami. The cheap rent allowed him to save money while he looked for work and started to build a clientele. The two men who lived in the room with him were two brothers from New Jersey. Franco and Gorgio Bruni, who went by Frank and George Brown, could have been twins. With their dark good looks and smooth manner, they were spectacularly successful binders. Donald had no intention of standing on the street corner or at the train station to entrap hayseed Midwesterners or naïve mechanics from the east coast. He was a licensed realtor and planned to work within the confines of the law in a reputable agency.

But he soon discovered that the business in Florida was not straightforward. Dubious deals and devious practices abounded. "Sell for profit by any means," was the credo. Horace had spelled it out for him the day he started his job. Now Addie had arrived, and he sat in on her interview with his boss, listening to the job expectations that had shocked him when he had first heard them.

He could see Addie's face color; her expression one minute perplexed, the next dubious. Neither of them had operated outside of the norms of the profession in their careers. But Donald had learned that this is the way things were done in Florida in 1926.

Bronson's stare bordered on lewdness causing Addie to shift in her chair and lower her eyes to avoid his gaze. Donald could feel her distress and for a moment regretted bringing her in for the interview.

"As you know, Miss Stanford, we work for Carl Fisher, selling lots in his Miami developments and Miami Beach."

"Yes, Mr. Bronson, Donald has mentioned that. But what are your expectations regarding me? Will I be limited to showings or am I to follow through with each sale to closing?"

"I see Donald hasn't fully explained how things work here in Florida," he said, not hiding his impatience.

"No, Sir," said Donald. I thought I would leave that to you. After all, I am still finding my way around and learning how things are done."

"Alright, Alright, let's not pussyfoot around. The role of

an agent is much broader down here, especially the way things are now. A year ago, we didn't have to be so pushy. Clients would come to us. But now, with the binders and all the advertising, we have to put on a dog and pony show."

Addie glanced at Donald. Her initial impression of the small untidy office should have alerted her to the fact that Bronson was neither principled nor professional. She felt bewildered and disappointed. She had quit her job to travel to Florida, and for what?

"So exactly what are my responsibilities?" she said trying to hide her exasperation.

"We'll start you off on the welcoming committee."

"Welcoming committee? What does that entail?" she asked.

"You go to the station and welcome the tourists, who we consider prospective customers.

Then you help arrange tours on our buses. This is where our agents are expected to show their nettle. And in your case, your looks and charm will be a great asset."

"Now wait just one minute, Mr. Bronson!" she protested, making a move to stand and head for the door.

"Nothing untoward is expected, Miss Stanford. Please calm yourself. I was going to say that I will arrange for you to work with the single women. We have a lot of them, widows, working women with money, and wives and daughters who come down to scout around for the Papa who is busy working."

"So, as I understand it, I am to herd the ladies into the busses that you supply. How exactly am I to proceed?"

"Well, I believe that the women will gravitate to you. I mean they will trust you over a man. Then of course, we offer to help them find lodgings. We have a list of reasonably priced hotels. We have special pricing with them for our clients."

"Kickbacks," said Donald with a smirk.

"Never mind, Seligman." Bronson protested.

"Anyway, don't waste your time with the young flappers

or any of the hicks. Only seek out the more prosperous looking women. Then after you get them settled into their hotel, you take them on the tour of our properties. These will be the neighborhoods that have already been built. Show them the schools, the grocery stores and such. Then take them around a couple of the model homes. Spend at least an hour on that, maybe more. You have to show them the dream."

"So, there are houses that are for sale in these neighborhoods? Do I get any of the listings?"

"No, my dear," he said, stifling a laugh. "At this point we are selling very little from developments that are already built. Our sales are speculative."

"Speculative?" she looked at Donald with a flash of temper.

"Donald and I know a lot about speculation and disappointment."

Bronson grew impatient. "Well, this is how it's done in Miami. Don't forget, I represent Mr. Fisher, who is a reputable businessman. He's building a university now. So, if you find our methods questionable, you are free to go back to New York or to Chicago for all I care."

Addie tried to compose herself. She had made the move to Florida, and now she had to make the best of it. Her throat was dry, and speech was difficult.

"I apologize if I seem reticent. It's just that things are so different here. I'm sure I'll get along. Please continue and explain what happens after the tour."

"The tours should take most of the morning. Then you take the ladies to lunch, on us, of course. Then you show them the plans. I prefer that you bring them back here to the office. It's more discreet and businesslike."

"So, if I understand correctly, they choose a lot, not a home."

"Yes, now she's understanding! Smart girl, Donald. Pretty too. Thanks for bringing her in."

"Can they choose any lot? How much do they put

down?" Addie asked.

"Sure, they can choose any lot. It's usually not a problem because they're all the same size. You explain that they must put down ten percent."

"And the financing of the balance?" She asked.

"We don't get involved in the financing. We tell them that there are plenty of local banks, although to be honest, the banks are skittish about loaning to out of towners. Things have changed after the bad press we got from *The New York Times* and those other magazines."

"I've read some of the articles," said Donald. "This bad press is beginning to affect sales."

Donald had realized from his first meeting with Bronson that his methods were not traditional, perhaps not even kosher. But his frustration and shame for bringing Addie into the venture overwhelmed him. How could he have let himself be duped by this shyster? Now he had been hoodwinked twice, and both times he had dragged Addie into the quandary.

"I know," growled Bronson. "But we have to forge ahead. We are dealing with a new crowd. The buyers that are looking now are not particularly well informed. So, we take their ten percent. And Addie, you will have any easier time of it, dealing with the ladies. They are more trusting if you handle them right. Tell them that they will have to pay the balance when all the formalities have been completed and the deed is issued."

"How long does that usually take in this state?" She asked.

"That's the beauty of our scheme. It takes months, sometimes as many as three. And the market is still hot. The value of the property increases, and the client usually can't afford the higher price. Anyway, it always works out in our favor. If they have the money, they are usually willing to make up the difference. If they can't afford it, then we keep the ten percent down payment. Oh, make sure to tell them that it's nonrefundable when they sign."

Donald's embarrassment was visible to Addie. She realized that he must be uncomfortable with the situation, to say the least. But here they were, and they needed to make a living. She considered turning down the job, but she didn't even have enough money for the fare back to New York.

"A few more details," Bronson continued. "Miami and particularly Miami Beach are restricted. In other words, completely closed to Negros. They have their own neighborhoods on the outskirts. Of course, they are allowed in the city during working hours, but we expect them to clear out after six. Now, as a rule, we don't sell to Jews. But Mr. Fisher has softened his position on this recently."

Donald interrupted politely. "Excuse me, Mr. Bronson. But you do realize that I am Jewish?"

"Of course, I do. I have nothing against Jews. Mr. Fisher is now encouraging us to sell to people of your faith. But he stipulates that he will only sell to a better class of Jews. You know, the ones that look like you, not the greenhorns."

"Oh, the ones like me," Donald said with a slight hint of disdain in his voice.

"By George, it was one of the reasons I hired you in the first place. You can sort them out better than a Christian fellow can. Moreover, they're a hard crowd to fool. Doesn't take much to pull the wool over the eyes of our clients from the small Midwestern towns. I knew right away when you walked into my office that you were clever and could deal with the more cautious buyers."

Donald and Addie looked at each other, without saying a word, they were both remembering the humiliating deception they suffered from Tappan and the failed Forest Hills deal.

"So, I won't be expected to entertain gentlemen tourists? Can we agree on that?" Addie insisted.

"One can never be definitive about these matters," said Bronson. "If a gentleman takes a shine to you, I might ask you to socialize with him. You know, take him to a club or dinner. But you can always make a party of it. Invite Donald here along."

"You can be sure that I will not let her go alone," said Donald defiantly.

As they stood up to leave, Bronson made an awkward bow and shook Addie's hand.

"Oh Donald, before you go. I meant to ask you to recruit one or two binders to work for us on the street. You will handle them. Make sure that they don't cheat us, and I'll make sure you get a cut."

When they got off the elevator in the lobby, Addie was in tears. She wanted to give Donald a piece of her mind, but she knew that it wasn't his fault. He had followed the siren's song to Florida, and she had too.

As for him, he couldn't find the words to express his remorse. He gave her a hug, shrugged his shoulders, and said, "Let's go get a drink."

FRANCES

MIAMI, FLORIDA, MARCH 1926

Dore contacted George Merrick, the developer of Coral Gables, which was the newest area of Miami. Even though it had recently received some negative publicity in the northern press, the lots were still selling well and at a steady price. She told Mr. Merrick that Albert Lasker had interviewed Miss Austin himself and that he highly recommended her for a position as an account executive. She said that Frances had worked for her for several months and had shown herself to be talented and serious. Merrick said that he would be happy to take her on if Mr. Lasker recommended her.

Two days after arriving in Miami, Frances was ascending to the fifteenth floor of the Giralda Tower of the Biltmore Hotel in a beautiful Art Deco elevator. An attractive receptionist greeted her at the front of the Coral Gables administrative office and ushered her into a private office where a good-looking young man motioned for her to have a seat while he finished up a telephone call. She noticed his accent at once, British, but not upper class.

Hanging up the telephone, his gaze ran up and down her, from head to toe. Being accustomed to his reaction, she didn't bat an eye. She did think it was unprofessional behavior for a coworker.

After a moment, he recovered and quickly changed his demeanor. "Sorry to make you wait. I'm Theyre Weigall, but I'm called T. H. I'm told that even though you are new to our agency, we are to be partners. In other words, we are equals, and I'm not the boss. However, I am responsible for training you and explaining your particular duties for the Coral Gables Development Publicity Department."

"It's a pleasure to meet you, T. H. Have you been in Florida long?"

"About a year. I came down from New York. As you can hear, I'm from England, London to be more specific. I worked in advertising over there, but I felt the pull of America, the land of opportunity."

"And has America afforded you opportunity?" she asked with a smile.

"Well, I'm working for George Merrick, the most successful developer in Florida. And Florida has become the new American Mecca of pleasure. You see, Miss Austin, it is our job to keep the dream alive."

Frances flashed a congenial smile. She admired his bravado, even though she felt it was slightly pretentious. In any case, her goal was to gather information for her article about deceptive advertising. It would only complicate things if she befriended one of the targets of her investigation.

Weigall unrolled a large map of a new Coral Gables. "This entire parcel of land belonged to Merrick's father. It was his homestead and he wanted to develop it as a retirement village for people of modest means. After working for other real estate companies and seeing the rapid growth in Miami, George has altered his father's vision. He has 3,000 acres, and he believes that we can fit 50,000 homes into the area. He is also involved in commercial real estate in downtown Miami."

"That is quite impressive," said Frances, looking over the map. "What are we looking at as far as architectural style?" she asked.

Her business acumen impressed him. "We're calling the

style, Mediterranean Revival. Our architect is very particular and insists on approving every detail."

"Doesn't it discourage perspective buyers if there is no variety in style?" she asked.

Again, her insightfulness surprised him. "You're quite right. We have heard comments to that effect. So, we're building spec homes that depart from our usual style. We anticipate the creation of seven new villages in different styles: Chinese, French Normandy, and Dutch to mention a few."

"Have you done much landscaping?" she asked. "It's not indicated on the map."

"Yes, indeed. We have a great landscaping team from Chicago. We have created canals lined with tropical plants. Of course, we left the orange and grapefruit trees intact whenever possible. The landscapers added some flowering plants and tropical trees. I particularly like the jacaranda and the bougainvillea. After lunch and our meeting with Merrick, I'll get my car and give you a tour. After all, you need to see everything before you begin your writing."

"I can't wait," she said, genuinely eager to see more of the city.

"We'll see the Riviera section first. It's the crown jewel of Coral Gables. First lunch and our tour of the Biltmore. It was just completed a couple of months ago. Merrick is immensely proud of it, and that's why our office is in this tower. The Giralda tower was designed to resemble the church in Seville. Did you know that the original Giralda was once a minaret built by the Moors?"

"Yes, I did," she said.

He shrugged and seemed embarrassed. He was the typical undereducated man, who always was surprised to find a working woman who had more culture than he did. They descended to the elegant lobby and T.H. guided her towards a wall of windows that looked out on an enormous swimming pool.

Frances' eyes flashed open wide. Many of the large

estates in the Hamptons that she visited had pools, but none could compare to this.

"Impressive, isn't it?" Said Weigall. It's the largest in the world, at least for the time being. The L-shape was Merrick's inspiration."

They sat down at a shaded table under an awning. As they ate their delicious crab salad, Frances couldn't keep her eyes off a handsome young man, who was surrounded by a flock of flappers wearing the latest revealing bathing costumes. He was diving from the high board and generally putting on a show.

"I see you've noticed our swimming instructor. He's quite a looker. Don't you think?"

Frances blushed. "It's hard not to notice. Look at those silly creatures fawning over him. I'm glad that I am an engaged woman. Even if I wanted to, I couldn't make a fool of myself over a showoff like that."

"Don't be so condescending," he said. "That's Johnny Weissmuller. He's training for the Olympics. But it's true that he can be unruly: He chased a naked coed through the halls on the third-floor last week."

"Shall I mention him in my advertising copy?" she asked sarcastically.

"Just say that we have swimming instruction and spend more time describing the pool and the other amenities. Speaking of amenities, you will need to visit the golf course and speak to the pro. He will give you a breakdown on what to include in the ads. Golf is a big pull. It's the main reason people come down here, next to the girls and booze, of course."

"The booze? I'm sure that you are aware that prohibition has not curtailed the consumption of alcohol in New York. It is available at any number of speakeasies and clubs. So, I don't see that the availability of booze would be a big draw for tourism."

"You're quite right. But here there are no raids. The police and the club owners have an understanding. Besides the quality of the liquor in Florida is superior. We have rum runners from the Bahamas and Cuba. The guests in our clubs and hotels are served champagne, scotch, and gin that is not easy to find up north."

"But T.H., it's illegal to mention alcohol in advertising. So, what are you suggesting?"

"You don't need to mention it. If you describe the clubs and the clientele, people will get the message. Throw in a few names, society girls and celebrities. They adore to see their name in print. Our art department will supply drawings and photos."

"I understand. We allude to the debauchery without mentioning the booze. If that's what you want, I am up to the task," she said with a laugh.

"Also, we need to advertise Tahiti Beach. It's not on the grounds, but we have plans to build a canal connecting it to the hotel."

"Tahiti Beach?" she asked, raising her brows.

"It's the bathing area. You know, Tahitian bath huts thatched with palmetto. They have just put up a band shell, so we can book some big-name orchestras. I'll have one of the assistants take you over."

A waiter served an enticing fruit plate, made up of pineapple, cherries, citrus fruits topped with shredded coconut. "I must dedicate an entire article to the food. It's important to the clientele that doesn't drink alcohol."

"Fine idea, Frances. I'll have the kitchen prepare some dishes and the art department can take the photographs."

"T.H., I usually like to write from 'the what we offer that they don't' angle. Any tips about the competition's shortcomings?"

"Sure. The first thing that comes to mind is The Breakers. I'm sure you read about it in the papers up north."

"You mean the fire?" she asked.

"Yes. Not that Mr. Merrick takes any joy in the misfortune of others. But we can use the fire to illustrate how seriously we take safety precautions in our construction. The exterior of The Breakers was wood. The Biltmore is concrete, which is fireproof. If you write about the fire at The Breakers, be sure to mention how many of the guests' lost jewels and expensive clothing, which were thrown out of windows, only to be stolen by the help and possibly other guests. In contrast, you should mention that we offer safes for our guests. It's just another layer of security."

"Thanks. I will dedicate an article to it entitled 'Hotel Safety.'" Any other suggestions?"

"Speaking of competition, right now we are concerned about Joe Young and his Hollywood by the Sea development. His bathing pavilion is in direct competition with Tahiti Beach. It is much more impressive, with over eight hundred dressing rooms with shower baths. There is also a shopping plaza and an Olympic-size pool, although it is much smaller than ours.

He just opened the Hollywood Beach Hotel with five hundred rooms, each with a private bath.

It doesn't compare to The Biltmore, but they have an amenity that we lack. They offer direct wire connection with Wall Street, so they get a lot of bigshot tycoons and their girls."

"But they don't have the class of The Biltmore or a golf course," she interrupted. "That's what I'll play up in our ads, with tons of beautiful photographs. After all, pictures of overweight businessmen receiving wires will not entice tourists."

"That's the ticket," he said. "Also, Young is building houses and apartments in Hollywood by the Sea. He's trying to make it into a small version of Miami Beach. But he doesn't have the vision of George Merrick, which reminds me. We had better head upstairs to see him. He doesn't like to be kept waiting."

A ruggedly handsome man sat behind an absurdly large mahogany desk. In his mid-thirties, he was square-jawed and blond with steel blue eyes. When he rose and walked around the desk to great her, Frances was taken aback by his height and square shoulders.

Trying her best to convey a confident air, she shook his hand while meeting his gaze.

"I am happy to meet you, Mr. Merrick, and I can't tell you how grateful I am that you are letting me join your advertising team."

"We are happy to have you. Anyone, who comes with Albert Lasker's recommendation can only be an asset to our company. Besides, it's a top-notch idea to have a woman's point of view. Only sorry I didn't come up with the idea myself."

"There are an increasing number of women going into advertising, Mr. Merrick. After all, more women are working outside the home and making decisions regarding how they spend their money."

"Good point. I see from your letter of recommendation from Dore Roberts that you are educated and experienced, Bryn Mawr and Katherine Gibbs. My wife says that's an impressive background and reflects the kind of female client we want to reach. You see we have no trouble attracting the flappers and the gold diggers to Florida. But they seldom buy property. We want to appeal to the heiresses and the society doyennes. First, we get them to stay at the Biltmore and then we plant the notion that they must have a second home in Coral Gables. But it needs to be done subtly and with class, above all class."

"I completely understand what you expect of me," she said with confidence. "However, you do realize that the process is much more complex. One doesn't just sit down and pound out a glowing article or an attention-grabbing advertisement. The buyer, especially the wealthy female buyer, wants to get to know the society here in Florida, the people that count. It is my goal to help them become familiar with exactly who those people are."

"You have a point. What would you suggest?"

"In order to write an article to attract New Yorkers of means, I will need to meet their counterparts in Florida, to see their homes and understand how they entertain." She did her best to exude self-assurance for she was asking for a lot.

"George, she has a point," said T.H. "People will respond to a description of the wealthy Floridian at home and at play. You have to offer them the possibility of mixing with society, even if it is an empty promise."

"Sure, sure. I see your point. We'll get you over to Villa Mizner to meet Addison and his brother Wilson. Everyone ends up there sooner or later," he said, looking at Frances with a broad smile.

"Yes, you'll get to know some interesting people," said T.H. "You'll see the movers and shakers in real estate and mix of celebrities."

"And of course, I must meet the wives. Can you arrange that? In my experience, I have found that it's almost impossible for a stranger to break into the women's inner circle."

"I'll have my wife handle it. She knows everyone. I'll have her arrange a little soiree and invite couples who own homes in Coral Gables and Palm Beach. There's no need to waste invitations on tourists, even if they have money. Oh, of course we must invite Flo Ziegfeld and his wife Billie Burke. I'll see if Joe Kennedy is in Palm Beach."

"How about getting her together with Marjory Stoneman Douglas?" Weigall interjected.

"She's got that silly little house in Coconut Grove. That would make a nice special interest article. She used to write for H.L. Mencken. What was that column called?"

"*The Smart Set*," said Frances. "I used to read it when I was young. I also read several of her short stories when I was in college. And I never miss her articles in *The Saturday Evening Post*."

"She's a fine girl," blustered Merrick. "She wrote a booklet for *The Herald* praising Coral Gables: *America's Finest Suburb*. It was a fine piece of writing with photographs included."

T.H. was enthusiastic. "Yes, I'll arrange an introduction.

It doesn't hurt that her father owns *The Miami Herald*."

"Never mind. I'll give her a call myself," George insisted.

T.H. and Frances descended from a car in front of Villa Mizner, a five-story building that dominated Worth Avenue. Addison Mizner had designed the entire street with its Mediterranean-style architecture and arcades. The winding side streets and small plazas could have been picked up and transported from any of a thousand Mediterranean villages.

Mizner made his home on the second floor of a small tower. It was here in his enormous living room that he held court in the afternoons, after flitting about from one of his many projects to the other. Around four o'clock, he was almost always at home to greet his guests in the Gothic room. In the center of the room, decorated with elaborate furnishings brought over from palaces in Italy and Spain, he appeared languid and slightly amused. Seated in a large throne-like chair, which barely accommodated his corpulence, he surrounded himself with friends, social climbers, and potential investors. The mood was usually jovial and sometimes raucous. Nobody took these afternoon cocktail parties seriously. How could they? For one thing, Addison never entertained without Johnnie Brown, his Capuchin monkey.

Frances wore a sleeveless chiffon dress, with a hem that reached just below her knee. Perhaps it was her perfume that attracted Mr. Mizner's two chow dogs to run and jump on her, scratching her legs with their sharp claws. So, her first interaction with the famous architect was, to say the least, embarrassing and painful.

"Boys, stop that! Leave the young lady alone!" he shouted, not bothering to lift his bulky body from the chair. "Wilson, get a hold of those rascals."

A diminutive version of Addison, unshaven and straggly, lumbered into the room. Frances was shocked when she realized that he was barefoot. He took the two chows by their rhinestone-studded collars, whacked them violently and deposited them at his brother's feet.

"I do apologize, my dear. The boys always overreact

when a pretty girl enters the room," said Mizner. He stretched out his plump hand to welcome her and dropped a piece of embroidery and a spool of thread onto the floor. He was flamboyantly dressed in Chinese silk pajamas.

"Oh, T.H., how are you, old man?" he said when he noticed him standing behind Frances.

"I'm just fine, Addison. May I present Miss Frances Austin, recently transplanted from New York. She's working with me now."

"Oh, recruited by George Merrick, eh? It's a pleasure to meet you, Miss Austin. What kind of work will you be doing?"

"I'm in advertising. I worked for Lord and Thomas. I'm writing advertising copy and articles about Mr. Merrick's real estate success in Miami and Coral Gables."

"Could we possibly get you to mention Palm Beach and Boca Raton in one of your articles?" he asked, his mouth forming a sardonic twist.

"I would love to, but I'm certain Mr. Merrick would not approve. I must admit that I am dazzled by what I have seen of Palm Beach. Why the palaces rival the loveliest homes in New York. And of course, Park Avenue does not have the ocean and the beautiful beach at its doorstep."

"I thank you for the compliment," he said bowing his head almost imperfectively. "We have transformed what was already a paradise into a kind of fairyland. Whatever our clients can imagine, we build."

As Mizner turned to talk to another guest, Frances was surprised to see Anita Loos enter the room. Anita was an acquaintance of Lois and was also a writer. She had just written a play entitled, *Gentlemen Prefer Blondes.* Frances seemed to recall that she was married, and so it surprised her when she saw her discretely embrace Wilson Mizner. She reexamined Addison's younger brother, and on closer study found him extremely unattractive; noticing his sagging shoulders, she realized that he was not young. He had flecks of gray in his hair and his hairline was beginning to recede.

Whatever did Anita see in him?

Suddenly Johnnie Brown, the capuchin monkey, jumped from Addison's chair, swung from a light fixture, and landed in Anita's arms. He grabbed her purse and ran from the room. No one seemed surprised or upset.

T.H. smiled. "Johnnie is always stealing purses and hats. Nobody minds because all the articles are returned before the guests leave."

"He is amusing and clever," said Frances. "I must include this afternoon in one of my articles."

"Oh, it can get riotous," he said. "The cocktails are never in short supply. Although Mizner limits himself to one drink. I think he used to have a serious problem with alcohol, so he is careful. But the same cannot be said of Wilson. He's got a very shady past and he can't be trusted."

"Really? Said Frances. "I know Anita. We're not particularly close, but I know that she is married. Do you think I should warn her?"

"I wouldn't bother. Everyone knows about Wilson. I think that she is just having a little fling. But you might warn her against giving him any money. He's always running one scam or another. He's a real schmoozer. He is known for his aphorisms. 'Easy street is a blind alley' is one of his best."

Frances laughed. After helping herself to a glass of champagne, she approached Anita, who remembered her and gave her an enthusiastic hug.

"It's nice to see you again, Frances," she said, slurring her words a little. "Have you been in contact with Lois recently?"

"I haven't heard from her in ages, said Frances. "I don't work at *The New Yorker* anymore. I thought I would try things out down here. I doubt it will be a permanent move."

"Oh sweetie, nobody is here permanently, with the exception of Addison and Wilson, of course. There's oodles of money to be made, but it's getting a little dicey."

"Really?" said Frances, trying to sound surprised. "I've read articles, but I didn't believe them. The one in *Forbes* sounded absolutely dire."

"Just between the two of us," said Anita, lowering her voice to a whisper and leaning into Frances, "I think there's going to be a lot of trouble, and not just with the developers. The bankers and the politicians are in over their heads. Yes, I think that you are wise not to make your move permanent."

"Thanks for the warning," said Frances, making a mental note of what Anita had revealed. She could hardly believe all the great material that she had gathered for her article by attending an afternoon cocktail party."

Anita pointed at an attractive older man who had just entered the room. "Do you see that fine looking man who just walked in?" She had been drinking a lot and she was getting a little too loud. Frances steered her over to the far corner of the large living room.

"Yes, he is nice looking," she said. "Who is he?"

"That, my dear, is Paris Singer, the sewing machine heir. He's working on some project with Addison. I think it's Boca Raton, but I'm not sure."

"Do you know him well, Anita?"

"Unfortunately, I do not. He was married to Isadora Duncan. You know, the dancer?

So sad. They lost their two young children in an accident in France. Their car went right off a bridge and the nanny and children were lost. I think that it drove Isadora quite mad. Do you know that she is dancing in Russia now, for the Communists? I mean really, what on earth is she trying to accomplish? Meanwhile, Paris is living in an apartment at The Everglades Club."

A few moments later, Anita walked over to greet Paris, who was discussing business with Mizner. Frances discretely moved to stand near them to eavesdrop.

"I think that I've got William K. and Harold Vanderbilt to put up some money for Boca," said Addison.

"What about Rodman Wanamaker?" asked Singer.

Mizner squirmed in his large chair, a frown creased his

forehead. "He wasn't easy. His money is tied up in the store. But he says he's going to try to raise a hundred thousand. Irving is going to put in a small amount. But tell me what you know about this Elizabeth Arden. She seems anxious to invest."

Anita practically leaped with enthusiasm. "Oh Addison, she is a doll. And she is making a fortune in makeup."

Frances walked over casually to join the conversation. "I know her, Mr. Mizner. I worked on her advertising in New York. She is charming and remarkably successful."

The room was beginning to empty, and the men were either talking business or drinking and smoking malodourous cigars. Frances watched Mizner for the better part of two hours. She noticed that he never stopped gorging himself on French pastries and Spanish tapas. She estimated that he must weigh at least three hundred pounds. But he was not a drinker. In fact, he had barely touched his frozen cocktail, which had melted and was now a sickening green color. Frances asked T.H. if they might leave. Anita and Wilson were snuggling on a chaise longue. So, they took their leave without saying goodbye. It had been a fascinating and informative afternoon, and she was in a hurry to get home to put her impressions down on paper.

ADDIE

OVERHEARD

Siting in the lobby of the Flamingo Hotel waiting for Horace Bronson and Donald, Addie was beginning to feel uncomfortable. Horace reserved a table for dinner at eight and after they were to meet clients to take them to a club. It was already eight-thirty and she had been sitting alone for half an hour. It occurred to her that she might be taken for a girl on the prowl, looking for a free dinner or even worse. She was glad that she had chosen a conservative outfit, a black jersey Chanel copy, with a jacket that covered her arms.

A group of people were sitting in a circle of chairs so close to her that she could hear their conversation. She did not intentionally eavesdrop, but she could not help listening. Several people approached them, and she gathered from several rounds of introductions that one of the gentlemen was none other than Carl Fisher, biggest developer in Miami, and the lady his wife, Jane. She decided to take advantage of the situation to learn about the man that Horace spoke of so highly. After all, she too was working for him.

Mrs. Fisher was speaking to a fleshy woman in her forties, elaborately made up and sporting a garish headband with feathers.

"Constance," said Jane. "Do you know Carl's story?"

"No, actually I don't," she responded.

"It's fascinating. He used to be a race car driver. Then he moved here and bought Miami Beach from a farmer. It was absolutely barren. Anyway, Carl was already the master of Ballyhoo and a successful businessman and gambler. But he made his fortune here in Miami Beach."

Constance sighed, "He certainly is impressive. You are a lucky woman."

"Well, it's not a bed of roses," Jane lamented. "He's a drinker and as you can see, he isn't exactly handsome. But I love him, so I put up with his foibles. I also must be pleasant to his business acquaintances and prospective clients. Just look around. What do you see?"

Addie took a moment and scanned the lobby, scrutinizing the crowd.

"It is an absurd mix," said Constance with disdain. "I do recognize a few heiresses."

"Yes, the heiresses," said Jane with a scornful laugh. "They come down on a lark, to drink and strut around in outrageous bathing outfits. But I really abhor the gold diggers. They are prettier than the heiresses, but they talk like mob molls. You know these days; you can't tell the difference between the two groups until they open their mouths."

Addie covered her mouth to stifle a laugh.

"Jane, you are too funny! You should write for a magazine," said Constance.

"As a matter of fact, I am writing an article on society in Florida, if I can find a publisher. Oh, look at that poor soul," she said, pointing to an overweight businessman, exhausted with the effort of trying to look charming. He sat next to a stunning, buxom blonde, who was whispering into his ear. "You see, Constance, that man is the girl's sugar daddy."

Again, Addie tried not to laugh. She was thoroughly enjoying Mrs. Fisher's description of the strata of society.

"Sugar daddy?" exclaimed a perplexed Constance.

"The gold diggers have a sugar daddy to keep them in

new dresses and expensive hotel rooms," Jane Fisher continued, as if giving a lesson to a child. "The heiresses have gigolos. The gigolos pretty much get the same deal as the gold diggers. Some of them actually dare to propose marriage to the heiresses. They are almost always disappointed."

Addie was trying hard to keep her composure. The conversation was so diverting that she was so glad that Horace and Donald were late. At that moment, she saw them enter the lobby.

"Addie, we are so sorry for being late and making you wait," said Donald.

Horace was less apologetic. "Yes, sorry old girl. We got held up with a hesitant client, who wanted to make changes to a contract. You understand."

"Yes, business comes first," she said, trying to hide her aggravation.

Before she could make another complaint, she heard Horace loudly greeting Carl Fisher.

"Well, hello Carl! What a nice surprise to run into you. And Jane," he said, shaking her hand. "You are looking as lovely as ever."

Jane greeted him offhandedly and turned her back to continue her conversation with Constance. Together they walked off to chat with a group of ladies, who were prattling on over a flower arrangement.

"Carl, I would like you to meet two new agents just down from New York. This is Donald Seligman, and the lovely young lady is Addie Stanford."

Carl shook Addie's hand, giving it a perceptible squeeze. "Nice to meet the two of you. Since you're working with Horace, you realize that we are all on one team. You both look up to the job. Things are about to get a little shaky. Horace will explain about the market. But there is still plenty of money to be made, so don't lose heart."

His last statement made Addie flush with worry. She knew that they had to stretch the truth when dealing with clients, but she assumed that the man at the top knew his business. She decided that tomorrow she would have a serious talk with Donald.

They met for breakfast the next day to schedule showings of some Miami Beach cottages. But before Donald said a word, Addie nervously broached the subject of Mr. Fisher's warning about things getting "shaky."

"What do you think he is trying to tell us, or rather, not tell us? I have been uncomfortable since we started working for Horace. His methods are unethical to say the least. I'm afraid we are skirting the law here and I want nothing to do with that."

With downcast eyes, he avoided her gaze. He faltered as he began to speak. "You're right, and I have known that things weren't kosher for a while. But I was making money, especially in the beginning, so I ignored the sordid sales tactics. However, when I realized the grand scale of the corruption, I decided that it was time to get out."

"Yes, it is time to leave. It's so embarrassing to go back to New York after two months. Evie and Sam will have a good laugh at our expense."

"Not at all. I saw Sam a few days ago. You know that he's been down here working for the government."

A sensation of heat radiated from her neck to her face, and she hoped that she wasn't blushing. "I had no idea. What's he investigating?"

"What do you think? He's looking into real estate scams and banks. He also had a run in with the disreputable Charles Ponzi."

"That must have been exciting," she said, trying to sound casual.

"Anyway, we had a long talk. I told him the truth about our business practices. Obviously, he's already clued into much of it, or they wouldn't have sent him here."

"Then it's definitely time to quit," she said. "Not that I feel that I've done anything illegal up to this point, but I refuse to continue to treat naïve people in such a deceitful manner."

"I agree. But Sam convinced me not to quit just yet."

"Are you crazy?" she exclaimed.

"Addie, hear me out. I had the same reaction at first, but Sam has an angle."

She rolled her eyes. "Sam always has an angle."

"Put your personal feelings aside for the moment and listen to what he proposes."

"Alright, Donald," she sighed.

"He wants us to continue working for Horace in his agency and even try to get in tight with Fisher. He suggests that we keep up the appearance of using the ten percent down contracts and all the other tactics to bamboozle the customers. However, we will give him a list of all our clients, and he will warn them before they sign on."

"And to what purpose?" she asked.

"He wants us to act as informants. We will be paid a decent salary, and they won't prosecute us for anything that we have done in the past or may do during the investigation."

"I don't know. I really have no desire to see Sam, never mind working for him."

"You'll have to get over him. I invited him to meet with us this morning."

At that instant, Sam walked into the restaurant.

He was even more attractive than she remembered. His already dark skin was tanned, and his black hair was combed back with a pomade, which was becoming. He shook Donald's hand and bent down to kiss her on the cheek. She didn't want him to see her emotion, so she turned her face.

"How are you, Addie? You are looking fine. Florida agrees with you. His tone seemed put-on, as if he were speaking to a client.

"I'm just wonderful, Sam," she responded, trying to suppress the tone of acrimony that crept into her response. She would not give him the satisfaction of seeing how she was suffering.

"Thanks for meeting us this morning," said Donald. "I

know that this restaurant is out of the way, but I didn't want to risk being recognized meeting with a government man."

"It's not a problem. I've been keeping a low profile. That's part of my job. Now the two of you will have to learn the skills of deception."

"We've sharpened our skills working for Horace Bronson and Carl Fisher," said Donald.

"I am sorry to say that this will be even more difficult because you will have to continue misleading the clients and, at the same time, deceive Bronson. You're playing a double ruse. I know you can pull it off. But what about you, Addie?"

"I'm no actress," she said. "You have personally experienced my unwillingness to compromise when it comes to the truth, but in this case, I feel that I will be working for a higher cause. There is no shame in deceiving crooks who are taking advantage of naïve clients.

I've seen these people arriving in trains and their Tin Lizzies. They're not rich. They are everyday people, some middle class, some poor. They have worked hard and believe that they are buying a dream."

Donald and Sam looked at her with admiration. It was unusual for her to speak so passionately. Anyone watching the scene could surmise that both men were in love with her.

"I know that you will put your whole heart into this assignment," said Sam, his voice full of esteem for her. "It is important that you both believe in what you are doing because it won't be easy."

"Exactly what do you expect of us?" Asked Addie.

Sam spoke softly, looking around at the other clients in the restaurant. "You should continue working for Bronson. Gather information on sales and contracts. We need to know how many people are walking away from contracts and how much money they are losing on down payments. Any information that you can glean through Bronson about Carl Fisher's dealings with banks and city officials would be especially helpful. Oh, and Donald, keep me apprised of what is going on with the binders."

"Most of the binders have given up and gone back home. As you say, people are beginning to wise up and they are no longer signing contracts on the sidewalk. As a matter of fact, my roommates have left, so I'm looking for an inexpensive hotel."

"I'll find you a place," said Sam. "Your new salary will be more than sufficient to pay for decent lodgings. How about you?" he said, looking at Addie.

"Only if my salary will cover it. I am not comfortable in my current room. Would it be possible to put Donald and me up in the same hotel?"

"Of course. It would make things easier. If Bronson asks why you are moving, just tell him that you came into a little family money."

"I can tell him that my mother left me a tidy sum in her will," said Addie, looking at Sam for a reaction.

Sam's faced reddened with embarrassment. "Yes, Donald told me about your mother. I am so sorry. It must have been a difficult time for you."

Addie stiffened. "Not really. We were not close, especially in the past few years. It's only that there were so many things we didn't say, so much unfinished business." She suddenly stopped talking, realizing she was showing her vulnerability.

"In any case, I am sincerely sorry," said Sam.

After breakfast, Donald and Addie headed back to the office to see if there were any leads. They walked for blocks without talking.

Finally, he broke the silence. "You're still in love with him, you little fool."

She didn't respond, but he could tell from her expression that he was right.

As the three began working together on the investigation, Addie made a point of never meeting with Sam alone. She insisted that it would be more efficient for them to be together for their weekly updates. Since she and Donald were staying in the same hotel, they would meet at a local restaurant or sometimes at the beach.

But one evening she received a telephone call from Sam. They had just met that morning, so she thought he had forgotten to give her some instructions. But the tone in his voice was not casual or businesslike.

"Please, Addie, have dinner with me. I know my behavior was inexcusable that last night we were together. I didn't want to let on in front of Donald, but I still love you. Please meet me, so we can talk."

She was on the point of berating him when she realized that it was hopeless. What was the point? She loved him and he knew it.

"I'll meet you. But you'll have to convince me that you have changed. And I will be able to tell if you're lying."

Sam was now staying at the Biltmore to be close to George Merrick's office in the Giralda Tower. He was doing his best to keep an eye on the comings and goings of bankers and politicians, who were visiting with greater frequency. He could only assume that they were increasingly concerned about the bottom falling out of the real estate market and the problems that they were having with the ridiculous low-interest loans that they had made to Merrick.

Addie agreed to have an early dinner at one of the hotel restaurants. Choosing a conservative skirt and blouse ensemble with long sleeves, she hoped to show Sam that dinner was the only thing on her mind. But at the last minute, she changed her blouse and skirt for a little black dress that was sleeveless and close-fitting. She threw on a fringed shawl for a modicum of modesty.

The Biltmore hotel lobby was grand with tall ceilings and frescos. It was made of marble and carved wood. She was so distracted by the splendor of the entry hall that she almost didn't see Sam waiting for her at the door. He approached her, took her arm and they walked slowly toward the restaurant.

Conversation was awkward. It struck her that he was as nervous as she was. This meant for the first time in their relationship, he did not have the advantage. This knowledge gave her the confidence that she could resist his advances. She felt in control of her emotions and refused to play games.

"Sam, please tell me what you want from me," she said after a long uncomfortable silence. "I have come to terms with the reality that we are over. I thought that you had moved on, and I am not sure that I believe that you still love me. Just tell me the truth. Have your parents changed their wish that you marry a Jewish girl?"

He was evasive at first, explaining that traditions were important in Jewish culture and that his mother was tenacious about getting her way. When it was obvious to him that Addie was not interested in his excuses, he admitted that nothing had changed.

"My father might come around, but my mother will never welcome a Gentile into the family."

"Then why are you playing with my emotions?" she asked, baffled. "I can't help it if I was not born Jewish. Religion never mattered to me, and it certainly never mattered to my mother. She never stepped foot inside a church. It's absurd and futile to go on seeing each other. Someday you'll marry someone your mother has chosen for you from the synagogue and that will be that."

Sam was close to tears and when he spoke there was a tremor in his voice. "I can't deny that what you say about my mother is true. But I will not marry to please her. Addie, I have finally grown up. I have seen life for what it is, hypocrisy and corruption. Politicians, philanthropists, and businesses all declare that they are working for the good of the public. All the while, they are using the system to rob hardworking people. Exploitation is the fastest route to success."

What he said moved her, but she still didn't know if she could trust him. "I have come to the same conclusion. It's nothing new to me. People are always quick to compromise when it comes to money. I learned that from my own mother."

Well, I am no longer willing to compromise," he said, grasping her hand. "I have no choice because I love you. I will talk to my mother and tell her that I intend to marry you. That is, if you still want me."

How could he doubt that she still wanted him? But could she believe that he meant what he was saying? Somehow the look on his face told her that it was true.

"I will marry you, Sam. But I warn you that I won't wait long."

"We'll marry as soon we go back to New York, and I face my family. I promise."

After dinner, skipping coffee and dessert, Addie and Sam went up to his room. Slipping out of her little black dress, she allowed him to roll down her stockings. As they fell onto the bed, he kissed her so passionately that she could hardly catch her breath. Without doubt or caution tugging at her heart, she allowed him to caress her breasts and her thighs, and she gave herself permission to respond, fully and ardently. He had much experience, and she had none. It didn't matter because now she didn't doubt that he loved her. Later, exhausted, and amazed, she began to cry.

"He kissed her tenderly. Please don't tell me that you have doubts or regrets."

"Of course not. I have wanted to be with you like this for a long time. I'm crying because we can finally be lovers, knowing that I will be your last."

FRANCES

A CONVERSATION WITH MARJORY IN COCONUT GROVE

"I arranged a meeting with Marjory this afternoon at four o'clock. I told her a little bit about your background and your desire to be a writer," said George Merrick.

"Thank you. I adore her writing. I've read all of her short stories," said Frances. "And I hear that she has led a fascinating life."

"That's a fact said T.H. smiling. She is an independent lady and shies away from controversy."

"Yes, she is starting to get under my skin lately, what with her objection to overbuilding in Florida and carrying on about the Everglades," said Merrick. "But I can't forget all that she did for us in the beginning."

"Quite right," said T.H. "She wrote most of the advertising copy and even some booklets before I came on board. Of course, she needed money back then. Now she has built her little dream house in Coconut Grove, and she has moved out of her father's house."

"Coconut Grove?" asked Frances. "I've heard of it, but it hasn't been fully developed yet, if I'm not mistaken."

"No," said Merrick. "It started out as a Negro community back at the end of the last century. It was an independent city for years, but it was annexed by Miami last year."

"I don't know what interviewing Marjory can do to boost sales, Mr. Merrick," said T.H.

"It won't do a thing for us. But Frances wanted to meet her, and I always like to reward good employees." He looked at Frances and smiled benevolently. "Just consider it a favor."

"I do appreciate it," she said.

Merrick handed her a piece of paper. "Here's the address and directions. It's a small bungalow in an obscure corner of the neighborhood. Better take a taxi."

They were just about to part ways in front of the Biltmore when Carl Fisher walked up to greet Merrick. He gave Frances a quizzical look.

"George, nice to see you. I hope that you don't mind me coming to your hotel for lunch?"

"Of course not, you're always welcome. After all, business is business," said Merrick, shaking his hand cordially.

Fisher looked at Frances in an odd manner. "Have we met before?"

Frances looked at him with a perplexed air. "No, Sir," she said timidly. My name is Frances Austin."

"Well, I swear!" he said, seeming equally bewildered. "Didn't we meet at the Flamingo a few weeks ago? You were with that realtor, Horace, oh what's his name? Darn! I'm terrible with names, but I never forget a face, especially a pretty one."

"I am sorry, but you must be confusing me with another young lady, after all there are so many here in Miami," she answered, trying to sound casual.

"Well, she could have been your sister. But she had long hair. Did you recently cut your hair, Miss Austin?"

"No," she laughed. "I bobbed my hair a few years ago."

"Yes indeed. This other young lady works indirectly for me. I'll have to look her up and see if we can get you two together. You would be amazed."

"Yes," she said. "That would be amusing. Now, if you will excuse me, I have to get ready for an interview."

"By all means. It was a pleasure to meet you," he said, tipping his hat. "Nice to see you, George." He walked into the lobby towards the restaurant, leaving Merrick and T.H. wondering what on earth he was talking about.

However, the incident left Frances with an odd sense of astonishment and curiosity.

She felt slightly dazed. He seemed so certain that she was this other woman.

Then, realizing that she had to dress and find her way to Coconut Grove, she put the conversation out of her mind.

As she rode to Coconut Grove in a taxi, Frances tried to think of a graceful way to resign from her position. She had gathered enough material to write several long articles. She was anxious to share what she had learned with Dore and Mr. Lasker. But most urgently, she missed Teddy. She couldn't imagine surviving another week without being in his arms. She would give her notice in the next day or two.

The taxi drove through a neighborhood rich with vegetation, facing the beautiful turquoise waters of Biscayne Bay. They reached their destination on Stewart Avenue after a ride of only ten minutes. The driver seemed annoyed about the small fare, so Frances gave him a generous tip. The house was a single-story bungalow which seemed patched together; the style half Tudor and half Mediterranean Revival, surrounded by wood frame, was odd. There was no garage or driveway because Marjory didn't drive.

Frances was about to knock, when a petite woman, who couldn't have weighed over a hundred pounds opened the front door. One could not call her attractive. Her long hair was streaked with gray, and her face was oddly shaped. Dressed immaculately and wearing a string of pearls, her floppy straw hat detracted from the lady's attempt at refinement. But her exuberance and warmth made Frances forget all about appearances. She felt at ease. Marjory Stoneman Douglas greeted her as an equal.

"Miss Austin, welcome, welcome. Please come in and make yourself comfortable," she said. "My home is humble, but it's all mine. I can't tell you how much that means after living under my father's roof for so many years."

"I'm delighted to meet you, Mrs. Douglas," said Frances as they shook hands.

"Oh, do please call me Marjory. Even though I was married to Mr. Douglas only briefly and I continue to use his name, my friends rarely utter it. It was, after all, a short and rather unhappy marriage. But I am over it. I live as a free and productive single woman."

"I would be honored to call you Marjory. It is kind of you to let me stop by and speak with you."

"It's my pleasure. When George told me about you, I mean your ambition to be a writer, I couldn't resist. He mentioned that you went to Bryn Mawr. I graduated from Wellesley, so we are sisters from the seven sister schools. I can't imagine why you want to write an article about me. I haven't done anything awe-inspiring, not yet anyway," she said with an enigmatic smile.

"I was thinking about including you in an article about notable people living in South Florida. Your life is such a contrast with the other people who have built Miami and the surrounding cities. I always feel that one should give a broad and inclusive assessment when covering a topic."

"I agree. And I also agree that the path that I have chosen is different from the typical Floridian business tycoon or socialite. As a matter of fact, I am about to become an apostate."

"Really," said Frances, her interest fueled. "How so?"

"My interest in writing short stories is waning and I feel that I must do something meaningful. And I had only to look around me, here in Miami and in Southern Florida. This will be my crusade."

Marjory's declaration was enigmatic, and Frances waited for her to clarify what this crusade was all about. She imagined that she might have an axe to grind with some of the local social doyennes or corrupt businessmen.

"I won't leave you in suspense. First, you see that I believe in living a simple life. You will see that in this bungalow, which is still not quite finished. But be assured, the lack of certain modern conveniences, a stove and air conditioning, is intentional."

"I did notice that there was no stove, but I had no idea about the air conditioning. But being from the north, it's nothing unusual. Very few people have installed it in their homes."

"Yes, I know. But here, most of the new homes have small window units in each room. I refuse. Since I choose to live a natural life, I have decided to do without certain luxuries.

I don't cook. I eat mostly vegetables and fruits. If I want fish, I will go out to a restaurant, but very occasionally. But I do enjoy my sherry. I was just about to indulge. May I offer you a glass?"

"I would like that very much, but just a small glass. I want to stay sharp, so I don't miss a word about your new crusade, as you put it."

Marjory poured two glasses of sherry, her expression becoming serious and then animated. Frances took a small notebook and pen from her purse.

"I hope that you have enough paper in that little book. Once I start talking, I tend to forget myself."

"That suits me fine," said Frances. "Perhaps you can begin by telling me what your new crusade entails."

She began speaking quietly and earnestly. "I have lived in Florida for over ten years, and I have seen how it has changed: The destruction of plant life to build roads and houses. Development is not a bad thing in itself. However, when it alters the natural order, it is devastating. The digging of canals and the modifying of the coastline to create beaches disrupts the balance of nature. We are losing species of birds and altering the flow of our waterways."

Her revelations gripped Frances. She had never seen

Miami or Palm Beach before Mizner, Merrick, and Fisher began their transformation. Moreover, she hadn't realized the effect the development had on the environment.

"First Flagler tried to carve out a trench in the Everglades from Miami to Key West. He had hoped to build a railroad. The men, who helped to pump out the water, worked under atrocious conditions. Over a hundred men were killed and the project was a complete failure. Unfortunately, it has not deterred others from attempting to tamper with nature."

"If you don't mind," said Frances. "Would you mind sharing what projects you think have been the most destructive."

"Of course, I don't mind. I'm working on a book, but that shall take some time to finish. If you write an article, it might bring the situation to the public's consciousness at once."

"I will certainly do my best. I will have to find a publisher."

"I will help you with that," said Marjory. "I feel an urgency to alert the public of the adverse effects of the overdevelopment in Florida. The Tamiami Trail, which is the tail end of the Dixie Highway, is a cautionary tale. Not only did it harm the natural balance of variety of landscapes in the Everglades, but it also had a high cost in human lives. I particularly object to the use of prisoners to complete the project. I suspect that there will be more and more development around the edges of the Everglades. This will not only alter local vegetation and animal life, but it could also create an imbalance that will affect other areas of the state."

"I don't know if you noticed, but all my stories for *The Saturday Evening Post* were set in Florida with a focus on its landscape, as well as its fauna. My aim was to engage the reader in the cause of preserving this beauty. Frances, everyone needs love in their life. I have never truly been in love with a man. But I am in love with the natural world.

Frances spent three hours with Marjory Stoneman

Douglas. When she left, she was glad that she had called for a taxi because it was dark. There was no outdoor lighting since the house was in a newly developed neighborhood with only a few other residents. She was bursting with ideas for several articles. And she realized that she had spent the afternoon with the most amazing woman that she had ever met. Although she lived without romantic love, her heart was brimming with love for the beauty of her surroundings.

The next day the office was humming with gossip and speculation. T.H. had missed an important meeting with Merrick and when his secretary called over to his rooming house, she was told that T.H. Weigall had packed up his meager belongings and left town. No one in the publicity office had the slightest notion of the reason for his hasty departure. But Frances knew that he had been stepping out with one of the stenographers, so she took her to dinner to see what the young woman knew of his whereabouts.

Cecilia, a pretty brunette from Chicago, was reticent at first. But after several cocktails, she divulged that T.H. was nervous about the direction the business was taking. He was uncomfortable about the promises he made in his advertisements. In particular, he had written a press release about a new hospital Merrick's company was building and the claim they were making that "every human need for health would be met in the new construction." He had also told Cecilia that he had made some risky investments in a new arena that the Coliseum Corporation was planning to build.

"He invested a large sum in the arena," said Cecilia, relaxed after her third martini. "He had to leave. He owed money on other deals he made. For someone in the business, he never made the right decision."

"Have you heard from him today?" asked Frances.

"No, he didn't even take me out for a farewell dinner. Can you believe the nerve? He had me type up a release about the development of the Biscayne section while he slipped out of the office. He called me last night to say goodbye. What a gentleman!" she said sarcastically.

Frances had overheard whispers among the company accountants about the skyrocketing expenses for publicity and marketing for the Coral Gables newest project. One young man warned that expenditures would wipe out potential profit for the lots that were sold. She could see the writing on the wall. Soon they would be reducing advertising and marketing staff, and she would probably be among the first to be let go.

So, after lunch the following day, Frances sent a telegram to Dore at Lord and Thomas, telling her that she would be returning to New York in a few days. After all, she gathered enough material for several articles. In addition, Mr. Lasker would have sufficient information about deceitful advertising practices that the developers were employing in South Florida.

She imagined that Lasker would form a commission that would eventually take the Florida real estate moguls and advertisers to task. But she had done her part and felt quite satisfied and proud with the results of her efforts. She was anxious to get back to her life in New York and Teddy. She hadn't realized how much she missed him. She loved him and it was time to make plans for their future.

ADDIE

PULLING UP STAKES, JUNE 1926

The binders had all packed up, leaving unpaid contracts worth eight million dollars.

The stream of potential buyers was drying up. Many agents had either moved to the Tampa area where things were less dicey or had returned up north. Things were changing quickly in Florida.

The free flow of good liquor still attracted the tourists, but now the Coast Guard was chasing down the rumrunners. One afternoon at the Flamingo Hotel, Carl and Jane Fisher were attending a tea dance when shots rang out from a Coast Guard motorboat, which was pursuing a famous bootlegger. This played out in front of the guests who were gathered on a terrace near the beach. The bootlegger was laid out in full view of the public, while a doctor tried to save his life. Although people bragged about being present at the scene, tourists avoided the Flamingo for a few weeks.

Florida's nightlife continued to thrive, for the booze still made its way into the clubs and hotels. New supper clubs and even casinos continued to open. Gambling was allowed for non-residents. But the raucous parties and the casinos were beginning to attract a criminal element.

A famous gangster named Al Capone had recently

bought some property. Still, the tourists seemed to flock to the clubs. The more boisterous the scene, the more they came.

As for buyers, some made the trip to look, most of them wealthy people looking for a second home. Addie and Donald continued to meet the few tourists that were looking to buy.

They made a record of every dishonest transaction and turned everything over to Sam.

In the meantime, he was investigating local banks. More than forty Florida banks had gone under. Bank officials often worked as part-time developers, creating a conflict of interest. Politicians served as bank presidents. Unbridled insider fraud in local banks included speculation with depositors' money.

The three met for lunch at a hotel restaurant the second week of May. Although Addie had never confided in him, Donald could tell that she and Sam had become lovers. All he had to do was look at Addie's face. The constant blushing and the softness around her eyes left no doubt.

He wondered if Sam had finally worked up the nerve to face his parents. He could only hope that he was not playing with her. He pushed the thought away and brought his mind back to the business at hand.

"Well, I think that I have reached the end of the road," he told Sam. "Fisher has overextended himself, what with the hospital and the arena projects that petered out. Only Mizner and Paris Singer are launching new projects. Now they are advertising heavily for the Boca Raton development. The ads imply that the resort is complete and ready to open. But if you go on site, you'll see that the only building that is up is the administrative complex, and it's not quite finished.

"I'm surprised that Mizner is mixed up in the affair. From my research, he's almost broke," said Sam.

"It's mostly Singer's money," Donald interrupted. "And believe it or not, Paris has a new folly. He has bought an island north of Palm Beach. He plans to build a hotel tower, which Mizner is designing."

Addie listened with disbelief. "They're mad. It's as if they want to destroy themselves."

"Seems that way," said Sam. "But for a long time, real estate was a sure thing. Banks would lend eighty percent of the value of the land, even before construction began. The industry is corrupting every type of business. Did you know that the publisher of the Palm Beach Post owns fifteen hundred shares of Boca Raton?"

"That's why the paper is full of ads for the place," said Addie. "I should say full of lies."

"Yes, the tide has definitely turned," said Donald. "Have you noticed the price of food and drink lately? The railroad embargo has made the cost of building materials skyrocket, as a result everything is becoming more expensive."

"And there you have it," said Sam. "My agency has ended the active investigation and recalled me to New York. I hope that you are both ready to head back north."

Addie shot a tender glance at Sam. "I'm ready." Then an expression of concern flashed across her face. "I don't even know where I am going to live or work."

"I have a few leads," said Donald. "I'm sure we will find work. Queens and Brooklyn are growing and there will be plenty of houses to sell."

Addie looked relieved. Sam took her hand and squeezed it to comfort her. Donald averted his eyes and turned his head to hide his distress. Up until now, he thought that he might have a chance to make her love him. Now he could see that he had lost her. His brows turned down and his jaw clenched, for he didn't trust his friend not to break Addie's heart.

"Maybe Donald can find you a place. How about it, old man?"

Donald didn't even try to hide his antagonism. He glowered at Sam. "Addie is capable of finding her own apartment. But I would be happy to help."

Later that night, Donald called Sam at his hotel. He had decided to speak frankly and to hold nothing back.

"Listen, old man," he said with sarcasm. "It's obvious that you and Addie are involved again. She hasn't spoken to me about it, and I have no desire to bring it up with her. But I would like to know what your intentions are. Have you proposed marriage?"

Sam's speech was muffled. He stuttered a bit, and it took him a few seconds to come up with a reply. "I did propose, and she accepted. Now I must convince my parents, especially my mother."

"I respect you for proposing. I certainly hope that you can bring your mother around. If indeed you do, I wish you and Addie happiness."

When he hung up the telephone, Donald cried for the first time in years.

FRANCES

HOME, JULY 1926

Mike Austin met Teddy and Frances at the Reading Railroad station on a muggy July afternoon. She had written her father two weeks before to tell him of her engagement. It had been a struggle to find the words to inform him that she was going to marry a Gentile. Above all, she did not want to sound apologetic. If her mother were still living, she might have found it necessary to act contrite. But she felt sure that her father would not object.

They drove up to the house in suburban Mt. Penn, her childhood home. Built in 1900, it was small and old-fashioned. The only renovations that her mother had allowed were the addition of modern appliances in the kitchen and a washing machine in the detached garage, and even those were outdated. Nothing in the house had been altered since her mother's death. Each framed picture, fruit bowl, and flower vase were in the same position; only there were no flowers or fruit. Perhaps it was a way for Mike to believe that Minnie was still present in the house. After being unfaithful during their marriage, he would try to make amends by being faithful to her memory.

Frances noticed that he looked tired, most likely from overwork, or perhaps it was loneliness. Now without the companionship of her mother, he spent all his time working in the hospital or in his office. He had hired a woman, who came in every day to clean and cook. A plump Pennsylvania Dutch lady with a sour disposition, she did her work and was gone before he returned home. What joy did her father have in his life? He was in his sixties, and she wondered if he had considered remarrying. There was no lack of Jewish widows in Reading. Many of them brought casseroles and offered to accompany him to hospital functions. He joked about this with his daughter, telling her how he avoided going to temple and to the Olympus Club where he was bound to be besieged by the ladies, or sometimes their daughters, asking if there was anything at all that he needed. He just needed to be alone. It distressed her to see him like this. But he was still mourning his Minnie, so the ladies would have to wait.

Frances went to the kitchen and made some coffee, while Teddy chatted casually with his future father-in-law. At first, she didn't want to leave them alone. After all, what could they possibly say to each other? But then she thought that Teddy's charm and warmth would win him over.

She brought in the coffee and the two were chattering away, while her father pointed to pictures in the family album.

"This is Frances at the Old Tower up on Mt. Neversink. Wasn't she a beautiful child?"

"Golly!" said Teddy. "Look at that hair. It's so light. It almost looks white."

"Yes, she was such a lovely child, and a blessing to me and her mother."

"Daddy," interrupted Frances. "Teddy knows that I was adopted. It has never been a secret. In fact, it's a point of pride to me. Out of all the children in the world, you chose me."

Tears filled her eyes, and she hugged her father. Unexpectedly, his body stiffened, and he turned his face away. She couldn't understand his reaction yet dared not ask him about it.

Teddy noticed nothing.

"I am happy for the two of you," said Mike, recovering his composure. Have you decided when and where the marriage will take place?"

"Well, Sir," said Teddy in a respectful tone. "If it is all alright with you, we would like to be married in Connecticut. We don't want to wait too long, just long enough to make the arrangements. We thought perhaps the third week in August. It's convenient for me since most of the people in the financial world take their vacations then. That way it won't disrupt my work."

"Daddy, I hope that you can take some time off from the hospital. We will take care of all the arrangements. You will stay with Teddy's family, of course."

"Don't worry, my dear. I can ask Dr. Farber to cover my practice. May I invite Irving and Esther?"

"Of course," said Frances. "I've made a list of a few of Mother's closest friends. I have a few school friends; Patricia, Betsy, and, of course, Sonia. I have all their addresses, except for Sonia's."

"Her parents are both dead," he said, shaking his head. "Victor died of a coronary last year. I think he never got over Ana's death. She died two years ago in an automobile accident.

I don't have Sonia's address in Bethlehem, but I'm sure you can find her through her company."

"I'll take care of it. Daddy, I'm so sorry to hear about the Goldmans. Why didn't you write?"

"Why should I bother you with such sad news. Besides, a nice young couple bought the house. They have two little boys. It's nice to have all that activity next door, and they were kind when your mother passed away."

"I'm glad to hear it. But if you ever decide to retire, you will always have a room in our home, that is when we buy a home."

"I don't plan on retiring any time soon. But tell me,

where do you plan to settle? I realize Ted's job is in New York. But will you live in the city, or will he commute from Connecticut?"

"We plan to buy an apartment in the city. I will continue working. I enjoy my job. Now that I have found an agent, I might do more writing for magazines, and perhaps I may publish a book."

"That year in Bryn Mawr wasn't wasted," her father said, laughing.

"No, it wasn't. It opened a lot of doors," said Frances. "But it is determination that helped me go farther than I ever dreamed."

Teddy put his arm around her. "I am proud of your daughter, Dr. Austin. She is not only beautiful, but she is intelligent and hard-working. It's not a combination that is easy to find."

Frances noticed a faraway look in her father's eyes, as if he was searching for a long-lost memory. She had seen her father like this before and she always wondered what he was thinking about. But she never had the courage to ask him. After all, she had her secrets, and he was entitled to his.

ADDIE MAKES PLANS

NEW YORK CITY, JULY 1926

Mr. Butler had warmly welcomed Addie back into the fold at Butler and Brown. She had told him a modified version of her real estate work in Florida, leaving out the deceitful methods that she had used on unsuspecting clients. It went against her nature to lie, but she justified her actions by telling herself that in the end she had worked with the government to help expose the corruption that was eating away the core of the real estate establishment in Southern Florida.

She returned to work in July, after settling into a small studio apartment on the Upper West Side. It was convenient to Sam's apartment. She expected that they would be spending a great deal of time together now that they were engaged. But Sam began to travel back and forth between New York and Washington, so they saw each other sporadically. He was working on new cases of corporate fraud, all while tying up the loose ends on his Florida report. He had told her that he might need to make a trip to Florida in September for a special meeting between realtors and federal investigators.

One evening at dinner, Addie subtly asked him if he had told his family about their engagement. She asked when she would be meeting his mother and father.

"Baby, I have been so busy. It's not going to be an easy conversation. I can't just blurt out the fact that I am getting married and then dash off to Washington. It's Evie's birthday next week. I'll tell them then."

"I don't want you to ruin Evie's birthday celebration. I don't understand why you haven't told them. If you had, then I could be there to celebrate as her future sister-in-law.

By the way, what did she say when you told her that you proposed? I'm sure she never expected it. I haven't had a chance to see her, or I would have told her myself, just to see her expression."

"Don't do that!" He barked, visibly in a panic. "I want to discuss it with the family calmly. It will require tact and patience to convince my mother."

"Alright," she said with consternation. "But we need to make plans. Even though I have no family, I have friends that I want to invite to the wedding. Have you considered where we might have the ceremony? I know of several hotels or other venues that we could reserve."

"I think that it's too early to be talking about details. Besides, I'm sure that my parents would not approve of their son getting married in a hotel or hall."

"What do you mean? Would they rather have an intimate ceremony at their home?"

His face clouded and he averted her gaze. "No, my parents will insist that we be married in the temple by our rabbi."

"I didn't think that was possible," she said, in a confused tone with a hint of anger. "I mean from what I understand, a rabbi will only marry Jewish couples."

"Yes, that's right. So, there is only once course to take," he said tentatively. "You will have to convert. That's why I haven't told my parents yet."

The possibility of converting had never even occurred to Addie. Her mother had never joined a church, so she had no religious education to speak of. She hardly ever entered a church of any denomination, except for the confirmation of one of her friends in high school and the occasional wedding. She didn't object on principle to conversion but wondered if she could embrace the Jewish teachings and the complicated traditions.

"So, if I convert, you believe your family will accept our marriage?"

"I can never predict how my mother will react," he said evasively. "But it's our only chance to win her over."

"What does it involve? Will I have to read some books and take classes?"

"I'm afraid that it's much more complicated," Sam sighed. "You will have to study and meet with the rabbi weekly."

"How long will this go on?" She said, trying to hide her exasperation.

"It depends on how fast you learn, how much effort you put into it. You will have to study Hebrew, so that you can read prayers. It's a matter of months, at least six months."

She felt her face burning with rage. "Six months!" she blurted out.

"At least, said Sam, rather meekly. In the meantime, my mother will have time to get to know you and hopefully accept you as her daughter."

"It will be quite an undertaking. But you will have to speak to your parents before I take such a serious step." As they left the restaurant, her mood shifted as she kissed him and took his arm. "In the meantime, let's go back to your apartment. With all your traveling, I've longed to be in your arms. You know that I regret that I missed out on all the years that we could have been making love."

"As do I," said Sam. "But I admire you for your principles. The fact that you refused me until I proposed only increases my passion when we are together."

That night after they made love, Sam stood up and put on his robe. After pouring them both a glass of wine, he sat on the edge of the bed, staring at the floor. Addie could see that he was uneasy. For a moment, her body prickled with fear, for she was never completely sure of his love.

Finally, he spoke. "Addie, I have been meaning to ask you about something. I mean, we have been making love for weeks, and well, frankly, we have never used any means of protection. I suppose I should have taken measures, but I thought that you might be using something. I have heard about devices and methods of contraception that are available."

"Devices, no. Darling, I simply didn't think it mattered since we are engaged. Of course, I always thought that we would be married sooner, so if I were to become pregnant it wouldn't be a problem."

"Yes," he said. "But you must understand that the way things stand, we should use some form of protection. I can buy something for myself, but it diminishes the pleasure for a man.

I know of a midwife who will help you. She doesn't ask embarrassing questions or make judgments."

Addie's heart froze in her chest as a wave of panic surged through her body. The possibility of pregnancy never crossed her mind. She had little experience with men before Sam. It dawned on her that she should have had a period a few days ago. But it was not unusual for her. Her cycle was often irregular. She realized that the way things stood an unplanned pregnancy would spoil their plans.

"If you give me the name and address, I will see her as soon as possible. We do need to be careful. But what if I were pregnant? What would we do?"

"Let's not get ahead of ourselves," he said, reassuring her. "You are probably fine. We will be careful from now on. Anyway, I will be traveling a lot the next few months."

"No," she protested. "So, I am to be left alone with the rabbi and my lessons. Maybe I can get Donald to help me study."

"I wish you wouldn't see so much of Donald. You do know that he is infatuated with you, and he never has approved of our relationship."

"Don't be absurd," she scoffed. "Donald is probably my dearest friend. He's responsible for my career in real estate. As a matter of fact, he has opened his own agency and has offered me a position."

Sam scowled. "Of course, he did. If he weren't one of my best friends, I wouldn't let you work for him."

Addie drew him to her in the bed and kissed him deeply. She fought her feelings of arousal, deciding that they should not make love until she procured protection. But he wouldn't take no for an answer, and they made love until they were wearied and fell asleep. Addie did not return to her apartment. They were both late for work the next day.

Three days later, Addie approached a small brownstone on 76th Street. She had been surprised when she read the address that Sam had given her, expecting that a midwife would be practicing in a more obscure neighborhood. For a brief moment, she was apprehensive. She wondered how Sam had come to know about this midwife. But she tried to chase any suspicion from her mind. That was all in the past. Now that they were engaged, she trusted him completely.

She walked up to the second floor of the brownstone and entered a large anteroom that was tastefully decorated with upholstered chairs, a mahogany table, and several potted palms.

A pleasant receptionist asked if she had an appointment. Blushing because it had not occurred to her that midwives took appointments, she shook her head.

"That's quite alright, dear. As you can see, Mrs. Green's schedule is light today. There are only three ladies before you, so I would imagine that we can fit you in, although you will have to wait about an hour."

Settling into one of the comfortable chairs, she looked around the room. The three women who were waiting had come prepared, two had brought novels and the third was knitting what looked like baby clothing. Discretely observing the women, she wondered if the other two were expecting, or perhaps, like herself, they might be in search of a means of avoiding that condition.

When she finally gained entrance to Mrs. Green's private office, she found herself facing an attractive, middle-aged woman. Slim and elegant with striking features, she reminded her of Evie. She invited her to make herself comfortable in a chair facing a desk where stacks of charts, books and papers looked like they might tumble over onto the floor.

Noticing Addie's reaction, she laughed. "You see, Miss Stanford, I am a little overwhelmed. I keep meticulous records on my patients, and that involves quite a bit of paperwork."

"I understand. I work in real estate, so I am familiar with the burden of paperwork. But may I ask, I mean, does all this remain confidential?"

She took Addie's hand and gave it a reassuring pat. "You may be confident that nothing leaves this office. The only time that I release a patient's record is when they go to a hospital and the case is taken over by a physician. You see, midwives are not allowed to practice in hospitals. The doctors don't like the competition. Occasionally, a woman or more commonly a husband will have a change of heart about giving birth at home. In any case, what is said between myself, and my patients stays in this room. So, what exactly can I do for you today?"

"I would like to acquire some form of contraception," she said, her gaze lowered and her face hot with embarrassment. "I have had a lover for a few months and so far, I have been lucky.

But we discussed it a few nights ago, and although we plan to be married, we decided that a pregnancy, at this time, would be inconvenient."

"I understand," said Mrs. Green, without a hint of judgment. "I can certainly take care of that today. But first I will need to ask a few questions about your menstrual cycle and overall health. After that, we will go next door, where I will examine you and fit you for the device."

"You mean that you can actually give it to me today?"

"Of course. However, we need to keep anything related to contraception within these walls. You do realize that it is illegal for me to dispense any form of contraception or for that matter, even to offer advice on the subject? Therefore, I ask for your complete discretion. Also, whoever referred you should be careful when giving out my name and address."

"Certainly. I will tell no one."

"First, I will need to know the date of the first day of your last period."

Addie held her breath for a moment. "It has been five weeks, so I am a week late. But this is not unusual for me. My cycle has always been irregular. But then, until two months ago, I was a virgin and it never worried me."

"You might have nothing to worry about. But I'll examine you, even though at this point there is no way of confirming a pregnancy without a test. I will fit you for the device and I will teach you how to use it. But I would ask you to come back in three or four weeks for another examination if you have not menstruated."

Addie left the office feeling relieved. The fact that the midwife could not confirm whether she was pregnant or not was encouraging. She would probably get her period soon. In the meantime, she and Sam could resume their lovemaking without risk.

FRANCES AND TEDDY

GREENWICH, CONNECTICUT AUGUST 1926

"I can't believe Lois Long is actually here. She might mention the wedding in *The New Yorker*," Caroline whispered breathlessly. She grabbed Mary's hand. "Come on. We need to help Frances get ready. I think she's upstairs with her father, but she needs to hurry if this wedding is to get started on time."

The guests had started arriving at the home of Teddy's father, Theodore Pierson, Sr. Set up on a hill in Greenwich, with a sweeping view of the Long Island Sound, the large house was surrounded by expansive green lawns, interspersed with oak and pine trees. The flowerbeds were rather sparse because of the August heat. The ceremony was to be held in the conservatory; a large glass enclosed structure built in the Victorian style. Frances and her father were staying in a charming guest house, which was larger than her childhood home in Reading. It was more convenient for her to change into her bridal gown in what had been Mrs. Pierson's bedroom.

She had asked her father to spend a few minutes with her before the ceremony. They had not had much time to talk since his arrival two days ago. There were parties, last minute preparations, and a panic about some lilies that had not arrived on time. She had so many things that she wanted to say to him.

"Daddy, I wanted to see you alone to thank you for everything that you have done for me. You have let me follow my own path, starting with my year at Bryn Mawr and then on to New York. Believe me, I have made mistakes. I will spare you the details. But most of all, I can't tell you how much your understanding and acceptance of my marriage to a Gentile means to me.

It must be difficult for you not to have Mother here with us today. I miss her so much. Perhaps she would not have approved of Teddy. Yet somehow, if she knew him, I think she would welcome him into the family, as you have. He is not religious by any stretch of the imagination. He once offered to convert if it would make things easier for you."

Mike cleared his throat, which was tight with emotion. "Sweetheart, I think that your mother would have loved Teddy. I never told you how she changed, especially in the last year of her life. She was softer, more relaxed. She had given up the temple sisterhood and had even made a few Gentile friends in the neighborhood. After she offered to work as a receptionist at my office, I thanked her but suggested that volunteer work at the hospital might be more fulfilling. Can you imagine your mother as a receptionist?" He said with a chuckle.

"I wish I had known. I should have spent more time with her. But it's not too late for us to be closer. Teddy and I want you to be a big part of our lives, and hopefully one day to be there to spoil our children."

Mike's face was transformed by a sweet, sad smile. His eyes glistened with tears.

"Frances, I hope that you have lots of children. It's better to have more than one. I wish that you had sisters and brothers when you were growing up. But we were lucky to find you."

"I was lucky that you found me," she said, hugging him tightly. "You have been a loving father. And it's funny that you should talk about sisters and brothers. I never told you this, but when I was young, I would imagine that I did have a sister. I would tell her my problems and she would tell me hers. She was like me in so many ways, and she seemed so real."

Suddenly the color drained from Mike's face and his hands began to tremble.

"Daddy are you feeling ill?" said Frances, taking his hand.

"No, I'm fine. It's just an emotional day and I am missing my Minnie. Now, I'm going to leave you. I hear your girlfriends at the door. You need to get ready. I'll see you downstairs." He kissed her gently and said, "Frances, I am so proud of you."

The guests had gathered in the conservatory. Mixed in with the rather provincial group from Reading was a variety of chic women and dapper men from Connecticut and New York, dressed in the latest fashion. Skirt hems were shorter this year after descending below the knee during 1924 and 1925. Caroline and Mary wore elegant sleeveless shifts with asymmetric hems.

Each wore matching bandeaux with a discrete sprinkling of diamond-shaped crystal beads. Lois Long, ever the consummate flapper, wore a short sleeveless dress with the neckline cut too low and the hem too high.

There was an audible gasp and then a murmuring when Lois took her seat accompanied by a beautiful brunette. Tall, slim, and elegant, the woman swept the room with her large expressive eyes. The well-heeled crowd recognized Kay Francis from her performances on the Broadway stage. She was also notorious for two brief marriages before reaching the age of twenty-one.

The wedding march began, and Frances entered on her father's arm. Teddy's breath caught in his throat as he watched her walk down the aisle. She had never been more beautiful. Her long satin dress clung modestly to her slender frame. Her beautifully toned arms were bare, except for long white gloves. She advanced up the aisle with her eyes lowered, glancing up occasionally to meet Teddy's gaze. Before he took his seat, Mike lifted her veil.

The reception was held in the large living room and spilled out onto the expansive lawn. One of Teddy's business associates arranged with his bootlegger to bring in a supply of champagne, scotch, and wine. As the wedding party continued until the early hours of the morning, the fathers of the bride and groom retired to Theodore's study with two bottles of scotch.

Although they came from different worlds, the two men found that they had much in common. Their deepest connection lay in the heartache that each felt after the loss of their wives.

"You don't realize what you have until it's gone," said Theodore as he finished his third scotch. "I was busy working, sailing, and spending evenings at my club. I knew that she adored me and Teddy. She took care of both of us. And you can see what a fine boy she raised."

Mike was bleary-eyed. He spoke in a low wistful voice. "My Minnie was a beauty. Yes, she was. And I loved her. She's been gone over a year, and I expect to see her waiting for me every day when I come home from the hospital."

"I can imagine what a beauty she must have been when I look at Frances," said Theodore.

Mike looked puzzled. "They didn't tell you? Frances was adopted."

"No, they never mentioned it, not that it matters."

By that time, Mike was finishing his fourth glass of scotch and had let down his guard.

"Actually, that's not completely true."

"I don't follow," said Theodore.

"She's mine. I admit that I wasn't always the truest husband. I had my share of girls on the side. But there was one, well, let's just say things went too far. She got pregnant and I arranged to adopt the child. My wife never knew the truth."

Theodore sobered up enough to ask for details. "I assume that Frances knows nothing of this."

"No, I could never bring myself to tell her the truth, even after Minnie's death. How could I tell her? She adores me and I couldn't risk losing her respect."

Mike was about to pour another scotch, but Theodore had stopped drinking. "Listen Mike, I don't know if you should tell me anymore. You have had a lot to drink and perhaps you may regret telling me all your family secrets."

Mike sighed. "Yes, you're right. I will keep my secrets. And you must promise never to reveal to Frances and Teddy what I just told you.

"Of course not. I would never assume to interfere, and I certainly wouldn't do anything to hurt Frances. But if you will allow an observation, I think that your daughter is a kind and understanding woman. Don't you think that if you told her the truth, she might forgive you? It might even bring you closer together."

"No Theodore, it's too late. It's best to leave things as they are."

"Mike, I don't know what to say. That's perhaps the saddest story that I have ever heard. I understand why you don't want Frances to know. In this case, the truth would only bring pain and sadness. Of course, I will not tell a soul."

The two men grew quiet and emptied their glasses. They came from different worlds, but they shared the grief and regret of losing their wives. Mike had the added regret that he had not respected his marriage. But he certainly was paying for his sins now.

ADDIE AND THE RABBI

BROOKLYN, NEW YORK, AUGUST 1926

Walking slowly up the subway stairs, Addie looked around for the street signs. Evie had told her that the synagogue was two blocks down from the subway exit. She had also expressed her opinion that she was crazy for agreeing to convert to Judaism. Under the best circumstances it would be an onerous undertaking. But given that the new rabbi was such a curmudgeon, the experience would be even more unpleasant.

"He's relatively young," Evie had said. "But he comes across as an old man, so old school. I was not at all happy with how he officiated at my wedding." She shook her head and narrowed her eyes. "Addie, this is not going to be easy. You must really love my brother to go through with it."

"Well, what do you think? I've waited for him to propose for years. Of course, I love him! I'm doing this so that your mother will finally give us her approval. I don't expect her blessing."

"If I know Mama, she might never fully approve of you, even if you convert."

"I will just have to win her over with my brilliant personality. Maybe I can learn to speak Hebrew and dazzle her," said Addie with a smile.

She opened the large wooden door of the synagogue and

entered a stunning foyer with marble floors and gorgeous stained-glass windows. An officious elderly woman greeted her in a brusque manner.

"I suppose you are here to see Rabbi Levinson" she asked.

"Yes, I called last week for an appointment," said Addie. "Today is my first lesson, if that is the correct word."

"That'll do," said the secretary. "Please follow me. The rabbi is waiting in his study."

A thin, pale man with wiry hair and a patchy beard stood up behind his large desk to greet her. He bowed his head slightly, refusing to shake her outstretched hand.

"Please have a seat, Miss Stanford." She tried to make herself comfortable on a hard wooden chair. "Let me begin by asking you about your motivation for converting to our faith."

His question took her by surprise. If he was questioning her motivation, she worried that he might have already decided to put a spoke in her wheel. She had assumed that he would be supportive of her decision. She considered her answer cautiously. "I believe that you know the Segal family quite well."

"Of course," he answered proudly. "The Segal's are longstanding members of our shul. Mrs. Segal is extremely active in the sisterhood, and I performed Evie's wedding ceremony last year."

She tried not to smirk, recalling Evie's complaint. "Then you must realize that the family, especially Mrs. Segal, feels that Sam must marry within the religion. Since I have not been raised in any particular church, I have no strong objections to converting to Judaism."

"I see," he said, not trying in the least to hide his contempt. "You have no deep convictions. In that case, can you honestly say that you will form a deep attachment to our faith? Does it hold any appeal to you?"

"I can't honestly say. I know so little about it. I assumed that would be your role, to help me discover the beauty of the religion in our classes."

"I see," he said, visibly annoyed. "I can teach you the tenants of our religion, the Torah and possibly how to read and pray in Hebrew. I can't teach you to love the faith. Besides there is so much more to learn then what is done in shul."

"I realize that it will take time, perhaps months," she said before he interrupted her.

"Yes, at the very least. As I was saying, there are other things that you must learn.

As a Jewish wife and someday mother, you must learn to keep a kosher home. Mrs. Segal can help you with that. But you must also learn how to respect the traditions of the sabbath and the high holy days."

Addie looked at the young rabbi in astonishment. His tone was bordering on hostility. She had the impression that he was trying to discourage her from converting. She certainly couldn't imagine spending months under his tutelage. Besides, it all seemed an absurd waste of time. Kosher! How many times had she seen Sam eat a ham and cheese on rye? Suddenly, she felt the skin on her neck beginning to prickle, as she hid her clasped fist under the desk.

And still he continued. "And then there is the question of blood."

"Blood?" she asked.

He sighed. "Miss Stanford, although we do perform conversions, it is always preferable for a Jewish man to marry within the religion. It is not so crucial if it is a Jewish girl marrying a Gentile man."

"And why is that the case, Rabbi Levinson?" she asked, trying to control the anger in her voice.

"I guess I must spell it out for you," he said with disdain. "We take into consideration that if a Jewish woman marries a Gentile, any child that she bears will be Jewish. In Judaism religion is passed on through the maternal line."

Addie looked at him, waiting for further explanation.

"Come now. Do I have to be blunt? We simply believe

that you always know who the child's mother is, but the identity of the father is always open to question."

She had reached the end of her patience. "So, you're telling me that if I marry Sam and have a child, the Segal's will worry that he will be the result of an affair with an old Irish Catholic beau!"

Addie tried to stand up. She suddenly was experiencing painful cramping and felt that if she didn't leave at once that she might be sick. Her head was spinning, and she felt faint.

"You must excuse me Rabbi, I am not feeling well," she said finally managing to stand.

She looked down and noticed that there was a large blood stain on her skirt. 'Thank God!' she thought. 'It's not too late. What was I thinking?'

FRANCES AND TEDDY

MIXING BUSINESS WITH PLEASURE, CORAL GABLES, SEPTEMBER 1926

It had been easy to convince Teddy to take a week off from his work on Wall Street, even though it was a busy time for the traders and the financial advisors, coming off their August vacations. He had no desire to be parted from her. They had been inseparable during their two-week honeymoon on Cape Cod. The nights were spent exploring each other's bodies during lovemaking. The days, as they walked on the beach, they talked about their past and their dreams for the future. Frances talked about her childhood and shared her shame about trying to deny her Jewish heritage. She even told him about her attempted elopement with James Whitman when she was at Bryn Mawr, confessing that she had been asked to leave after her first year. She was surprised by his reaction.

"Baby, you were young, and you were trying to fit in. I would never judge you for anything you did in the past. But from now on, I want you to be proud of who you are and never deny your origins."

For his part, he told her about his escapades in college, the fast girls and booze. But none of this shocked her after living with Lois and Kay.

The first week in September, Dore Roberts summoned her into her office and informed her that her article on Florida real estate that had appeared in *The New Yorker* had made quite a splash in the advertising world. As a result, Albert Lasker had convoked a meeting in Florida made up of a panel of advertising executives, lawyers, and heads of various corporations. She had to admit that without Lasker's influence and offer to advertise heavily in the magazine, Ross might not have published it. In the end, he was impressed with her work and even offered to print any follow up articles that she might write after the Florida meeting.

Frances was thrilled that Mr. Lasker was heading up the panel himself. He was the most influential advertising man in the country and his interest in her article was a matter of great pride to her. She also felt reassured that Dore would be there. They had become close, both professionally and socially. Dore often invited her to dinner at her home in Brooklyn. She had gotten to know her husband Christiaan, who was a distinguished journalist. It was a pleasure to hear him speak on salient topics, especially with his charming South African accent.

Their two children were lovely, a boy and a girl, both with Christiaan's light blue eyes.

Teddy and Frances traveled by train and arrived in Miami on a Friday afternoon. The meeting was scheduled to begin on Saturday, September 18th. Since it was being held at the Biltmore Hotel in Coral Gables, they had reserved a suite and extended their stay for an additional four days. Frances rented a car and took her husband on a tour of Miami and the surrounding area so that he could have an idea of the problem over development. All the while, she could not help thinking about Marjory Stoneman Douglas and her campaign to preserve the balance of nature in Southern Florida.

Later they ate supper in the hotel and settled into their suite. For the first time since their wedding, Frances refused to make love to Teddy.

"Darling, I'm tempted, but I must go over my speech. Besides, I am a bundle of nerves tonight and I am afraid my mind and my body would be elsewhere.

ADDIE MAKES A DECISION

NEW YORK CITY, SEPTEMBER 1926

Addie met Sam at a coffee shop on the upper west side. If they were alone in his apartment, he might try to persuade her to change her mind about her decision. It would not take much for her to lose her resolve. A few minutes in his bed and she would change her mind.

Meeting in a public space avoided that temptation. Hopefully, he would understand why she changed her mind about converting. Her conversation with the rabbi had been so humiliating that it opened her eyes to what life would be like as the shiksa daughter-in-law that Mrs. Segal would never fully welcome into the fold. He would have to take her as she was, whether his mother approved or not.

It was a beautiful autumn day in New York. The air was crisp, and the sky was a brilliant blue despite the exhaust expelled by the passing cars. There were a few tables set up outside on the sidewalk. She quickly claimed a table away from the other customers so that they might have some privacy.

She had worked up the nerve to tell him about her decision and had just started speaking when he interrupted her.

"Addie darling, I have some news. I have known about it for a week, but I didn't want to tell you until I received certain confirmations."

"Sam, what are you going on about? I have something important to discuss with you. Can't it wait?"

"No," he said a little too curtly. "This is business. It's important to me and to you as well."

"Alright," said Addie, deciding to let him have his say. "What is so important that it can't wait?"

"This morning my superior told me that I am to head up an inquiry into the real estate debacle and related bank fraud in Southern Florida. He read all the reports that I compiled. I informed them that you and Donald contributed to the research by working undercover. He feels that having you present at the meeting would help fill in a lot of the blanks.

"Really," she said, surprised and suspicious at the same time. "You must have laid it on thick with your boss. I don't mind a free trip to Florida, but I don't think that Donald and I are indispensable to the inquiry."

"Don't underestimate yourself Addie," he said. "Your insight is important, as is Donald's. He has invaluable insight into how the binder system worked. The two of you worked directly with Fisher's lackeys and you know how they ran their scams."

"Well, I'm on board. But you will have to ask Donald. We're working hard to get the agency off the ground. I'm not so sure that he'll want to go out of town right now."

"The meeting will take place over the weekend of Friday, September 17. We will be meeting at the Biltmore, and I have reserved three rooms for us. Of course, you have to include travel time, about four days by train. So, all in all, the entire thing will take a little over a week."

"Fine," she said. "You can ask him. If he declines, then I must stay here and work."

"Okay," he said, sounding confident that Donald would accept. "By the way, what did you want to tell me that was so earthshattering?"

"It can wait," Addie said, deciding that she would tell him after the trip. It would make things awkward, especially with Donald being there. She would tell him on the train coming home."

A few days later, she entered the small office that she and Donald shared near Union Square. It was just a large room with two desks and extra chairs for potential clients. It was located in a rather shabby building, made up of similar offices that were occupied by other ambitious people trying to launch firms, insurance agencies, import-export companies, talent agencies and the like.

Donald smiled and shrugged his shoulders. "What do you think, old girl? Are you willing to go back to the scene of the crime?"

"So, he told you? I didn't want to be the one to ask," she said. "Do you think that it's alright to leave our clients hanging? I was sure that you would object."

"I don't know," he said. I was thinking that it might work out in our favor. The publicity could help attract clients. You know, good will and all that."

"Perhaps," she said with some skepticism.

"The timing isn't great for me on a personal level," he said. "I have been seeing a young lady recently and I think that she's just beginning to take me seriously."

"Why Donald!" said Addie. "You never mentioned her. Who is she?"

"She's a senior at Barnard with plans to go into law. A pretty girl, who is much too good for me."

Addie suddenly could feel a constriction in her chest. It struck her that she was feeling pangs of jealousy, which confused her. Donald had been her dearest friend and business partner for years. He was always there for her. It never occurred to her that he might fall in love. She had always taken it for granted that his heart belonged to her. She had no right to be jealous and she knew that she should be happy for him. But that didn't change what she was feeling at that moment.

"I would love to meet her," she said, trying to sound sincere.

"Maybe," he said cautiously. "Let's give it some time. It's a delicate dance with her and meeting you might scare her off."

"Oh Donald, sometimes you exaggerate. I won't press the issue. So, are we going to Florida or not?"

"Sure. I'll pack my white suit," he said with a broad smile.

THE SEABREEZE ROOM

THE BILTMORE HOTEL

It was a strange assembly of rogues, public officials and company executives seated at the long polished wooden table in the Seabreeze Room. The décor was classic South Florida, with hues of pastel greens and blues. There were large, arched windows with flowing white drapes.

Addie sat at the far-right end of the table between Horace Bronson and Donald. Across from her was Carl Fisher's lawyer, an unpleasant man who she had met on several occasions.

There were two men in dark suits, who she assumed must be federal employees like Sam.

She felt a little pretentious with her brass nameplate embossed with Miss Adelaide Stanford.

She did not regret changing her name from Lutz. After all her stepfather had abandoned her. She could not help wondering about her true name, her real father's name. She scolded herself silently for falling prey to her personal demons. Looking around the room, she wondered where Sam could be. It was unlike him to be late, especially for an important meeting.

A wry smile appeared on Donald's face, and his eyelids were half-closed as he concentrated on the report that was presented to each member of the panel. None of the information in the thick folder was news to him.

Horace, sitting erect and huffing with indignant frustration could no longer contain his anger. "This is pure hogwash, fiction! I swear that if you dare publish these claims, I and many of my colleagues will have grounds for libel suits." He then sat back in his chair, pounding his fist on the table for emphasis. His lawyer shifted nervously in his chair.

"Come now, Horace," said a middle-aged realtor with fleshy folds under his eyes.

"No need to fly off the handle and bring lawyers into the discussion. We are just trying to size up the situation and see how we can keep the market chugging along."

Addie found the statement ridiculous, given the recent precipitous decline in Florida's real estate market and the stunning failure of the latest projects. Glancing at Donald, she noticed his normally inscrutable demeanor was altered, the color rose to his hollow cheeks. She could almost feel the heat of his anger. Her attention was diverted when she looked out the window and noticed that a storm was brewing.

"My goodness, look at the wind! I have never seen palm trees bend like that." She stood up and approached the large window, noticing that the waves in the bay were rising. "What is going on?" she cried.

ADDIE

CORAL GABLES, SEPTEMBER 1926, THE PALM SALON

The meeting was about to begin as Albert Lasker took to the small podium in the Palm Salon. It was the larger and more luxurious of the two public rooms at the Biltmore, so it was generally used for weddings and parties, but the hotel management also rented it out for large conferences, which brought in a steady revenue.

Dore sat next to Frances and gave her hand an encouraging squeeze, as Mr. Lasker introduced her as the main speaker.

"I would like to introduce you all to a remarkable young woman," he said with pride. "She works for me in the New York office of Lord and Thomas, but it is for her independent work that we have chosen her as our featured speaker. Her article in *The New Yorker* magazine was the result of weeks of investigative work done here in South Florida. She was hired by George Merrick as an advertising executive."

Frances tried not to blush. She was not accustomed to public praise.

"I see that Mr. Merrick is not here today to defend himself," Lasker continued. "I do see his attorney, Mr. Clifton Benson, who I am certain will take copious notes for his client. But let me assure you that we are not here to place blame on any one man. We have a situation in Florida that was brought about by many actors in many fields. Of course, the bulk of responsibility lies with realtors and developers. We should place the blame with those at the top, those who devised the grand plan. But there are many others who took part and reaped profits at the expense of honest citizens, the banks, the city officials and even publishers of magazines.

We will be exposing the role of these publishers and the advertising that they employed to draw in the gullible public. If we look at the victims, we see not only the wealthy heiresses and the stockbrokers. Miss Austin wrote about the widows, the grocers and the farmers who made the trip to Florida in their Tin Lizzies. Many of these people lost their life's savings. She even mentioned her own father, a physician, who lost a large sum in a bogus investment scheme. But I will be quiet now and let her speak."

Frances stood and walked to the podium. She was about to begin her speech when the lights flickered and the doors to the Palm Salon flew open.

FRANCES

CORAL GABLES, SEPTEMBER 1926, THE HURRICANE

In the Seabreeze Room, a young journalist, who was there to cover the meeting for a local paper, stood up and joined Addie at the window. "I don't understand," he said with concern. "Our paper had a report from a most reliable weather service that the hurricane in the Caribbean was on course to hit the Bahamas and would then turn out to sea."

"Well, it looks like your source is not so reliable," Donald said with sharp sarcasm. "But why does that not surprise me? I mean if you're reporting on the real estate market is any indication of your accuracy."

The reporter turned and glared at him. He didn't like Jews as a rule, and this New Yorker only reinforced his prejudice. He was formulating a cutting response when his attention was diverted by a sudden gusting of wind.

One of the realtors went into the hallway to see what was going on. He returned with an assistant manager, who addressed them in a measured and sober manner.

"Ladies and gentlemen, I've been told that we are in the path of a strong hurricane. The management has decided that it would be prudent to gather our guests in interior rooms without windows. If you would please follow me, there is a large salon just down the hall. It will be crowded because it is occupied by another group. We believe that this is the safest course of action. We hope that what we are now experiencing will be the worst of the storm, but we have no such assurances."

Donald tried to grab Addie's hand to lead her down the hallway to the Palm Salon, but they were separated as the committee members pushed violently to exit the room, and then collided with terrified hotel guests who were searching for cover away from the hotel's windows and doors. Looking back, he could not find her, as he was carried into the large room by the panicked throng. The salon was twice the size of the Seabreeze room. Large mirrors lined the walls in place of windows. The large crystal chandeliers that normally would have illuminated the room were dimmed and flickering as the electricity began to fail.

He squeezed through the crowd trying to find some space along the wall of gilded mirrors. His eyes swept over the crush searching for Addie. Suddenly, he found himself pressed up against a mirror looking into her pale blue eyes. But there was no hint of recognition in them, they seemed to look right through him, as if he were a stranger. He sighed with relief and smiled, grabbing her hand. She drew back in confusion and fear.

"Excuse me, but do you mind!" she shouted warily.

Donald looked at her, realizing that this could not possibly be Addie. She was dressed differently than she had been a few minutes ago and her hair was bobbed. A look of confusion swept over his face. "Addie what is wrong? And yet as he said her name, he knew that she was not Addie.

She looked at him as if he were mad. "I don't mind pointing out that you are being extremely rude. Don't think for a minute that you can take advantage of these circumstances to try to pick me up."

He continued to stare at her, now realizing that her voice was identical to Addie's. He experienced a strange sensation of his body disassociating from his mind.

"Sir, will you stop gawking! You are really the limit!" she cried.

He felt his arms and the back of his neck beginning to tingle from shock. Finally, he held out his hand and introduced himself. "Please forgive me. I took you for someone else. I'm Donald Seligman. As he spoke the words to her, he felt that the situation was absurd and unreal. He tried his best to get a handle on his emotions, but his heart was racing and there was a buzzing in his head.

The girl looked at him and seemed to take pity. "Well, you are in a tizzy. Perhaps it has something to do with the sudden drop in the barometric pressure with the storm. My name is Frances Austin Pierson, not Addie. I'm on the Board of Advertisers that is investigating the real estate crisis in Florida. I'm down from New York with my husband for a few days."

Donald recovered as best he could. "That is a coincidence. I'm in a meeting next door. I am on a panel discussing realtors and bankers who are involved in fraud."

"I do hope that we are on the same side," she said.

"If you are investigating fraud in advertising, then we are. I worked undercover as a government spy looking into the realty scams."

"Then we definitely are fighting the same battle," she said, shaking visibly from the sound of the violent wind that was making the chandeliers sway and the mirrors shake. "Do you think that we are safe in here?"

"Yes, this hotel is well constructed. It's not made of wood like The Breakers that burned down a few years ago." Suddenly, his brow wrinkled as a shiver of fear ran through his body. He had to find Addie. He looked at Frances and said hurriedly, "Would you excuse me for a moment? I must find my friend. I really must see if she is safe. But would you mind staying right here?"

"I have no intention of moving, although I need to find my husband."

He had already walked away when she mentioned her

husband. He tried to wind his way through the swarm of people, all the while searching for Addie's light blonde hair. Why had he let go of her hand? He made his way to the center of the large room, when he caught sight of her standing next to the wall, directly opposite from the spot where he had left Frances.

She looked relieved to see him. "Addie, you must come with me immediately," he said in a tone a little too sharp. "Please, come with me."

"Donald, what is wrong with you? I was so worried."

"Please, come with me," he insisted.

"First you abandon me and now you're trying to corral me like a wild horse," she said with a tremor in her voice.

"Don't ask me because I can't explain. You must see her with your own eyes. You won't believe it. I can't believe it. Then he hesitated. "Wait. First tell me something. Let me ask you…I mean, do you have any relatives on your mother's side of the family, a cousin maybe?"

"What are you talking about? You know that I am an only child. My mother was an only child. I have no family now."

He grabbed her arm and began to lead her across the room. "I wouldn't be so sure of that," he said. The lights flickered as they approached the spot in front of the mirror where he had left Frances. The employees had brought in candles and the room resembled a nineteenth-century ballroom.

Again, he ran his hands through his hair, nervously. What should he say?

"Addie, I would like you to meet Frances Austin Pierson. Frances, this is Adelaide Stanford."

DR. MIKE AND ROSE

PHILADELPHIA 1904

Dr. Michael Austin and Rose Strauss met at Community General Hospital, where she had just started her job as executive secretary to the hospital's chief-of-staff. Mike felt like a teenager, falling in love for the first time. She was beautiful. But it wasn't just her looks that drew him to her. From the moment they spoke that day as he waited in Dr. Bauer's outer office, he admired the sweetness of her voice and her bubbly laugh. They chatted for a long time that day while he waited to be summoned by Bauer. Not long after, they began meeting for lunches at out of the way restaurants. After a few weeks, he began to visit her late at night at her apartment. He told his wife that he had emergency house calls. Minnie never objected. She encouraged him because it was important to be available to build up his practice.

Things became quite serious, at least as far as Rose was concerned. During and after their lovemaking, she would whisper that she loved him. He never responded. She would become distraught, often demanding that he leave Minnie. She had threatened to break off the affair several times. But each time he came to her door at midnight, she invited him in.

Rose was elated when Mike made arrangements to meet at a small restaurant out of town. They sat at a corner table hoping to blend in and pass for locals. After all, he was a local boy, born and raised in Philadelphia and graduated from the Pennsylvania College of Medicine, class of 1900. The restaurant was not in center city but was tucked away in a less tony area of the Main Line. There he could be somewhat confident that the cliental would not include his crowd, Jews and struggling medical school graduates. Still, he was cautious and asked for a corner table in a back room.

Mike squeezed Rose's hand and then gently stroked her wrist. She was absolutely glowing; the flush on her porcelain skin made her more enticing. In the six months that they had been meeting, he had never entertained the thought that he might be in love with her. Perhaps if there were any doubts about his devotion to his wife, for he loved Minnie without reservation. He had had several affairs before he met Rose, but they were casual and short-lived.

Rose had not made demands that he leave his wife in at least three weeks. Being a smart and somewhat experienced girl, he guessed that she finally realized the limits of their relationship. Even though their conversations were brief and superficial, he had intimated that his medical career could not survive the scandal of divorce. Reading was a small town, provincial and intolerant and the small Jewish community was insular. Infidelity was rare as secrets were hard to keep.

Mike wasn't particularly religious, he didn't even keep kosher when he dined in restaurants, but he was an immigrant and the son of observant Russian Jews. No, he thought, a little romance on the side was fine, but it could go no further.

"You know darling, I am so glad that you could get away tonight," she said, leaning close and enlacing her fingers with his. Arranging this dinner in Philly, well, it's marvelous. How did you manage?"

"Yes, it's one thing to steal way for an hour here and

there," he answered. "Minnie realizes that I have to make house calls. She encourages it. In her opinion, it's the only way to build up a busy practice." He sat back in his chair took out his immaculately pressed handkerchief and wiped his brow. "But tonight, wasn't so easy. I had to be creative. She thinks I am visiting a few of my classmates downtown. I told her that if things get a little too gay and the party went on too late that I would spend the night with one of the fellows."

"Does that mean we can spend the whole night together?" She asked breathlessly.

"Well, I kind of planned for it. There is a little inn down the street," he said with a mischievous smile. "I reserved a room, just in case."

Rose smiled and feigned a look of shock, which quickly transformed into an expression of delight. "Imagine, a whole night together and waking up in your arms. And Mike it couldn't come at a better time. I have to discuss something with you, a serious matter."

"I hope it's good news," he sighed. "I have had a rough week at the hospital."

"Let's wait until we are alone," said Rose with a nervous smile.

They sat on the bed in the small room with faded window blinds and a pretense of hominess provided by matching curtains and bedspread, both badly stained. Mike tried to hide his embarrassment for the shabbiness of the hotel, and for the fact that he had discreetly handed the clerk a five-dollar bill so he would ask no questions.

"Let's talk first," she said. "We rarely have the time to talk before we rush into it."

"Fine," said Mike. "As long as you're not going to bring up the song and dance about me leaving Minnie. We have hashed that out again and again. You know that I will never leave her."

Tears welled up in her eyes and began to fall from her long fair lashes. She threw herself into his arms and began to sob.

"Rose, please don't take it like that. You knew from the beginning how I felt. Besides…"

"No Mike, it's not that. You don't understand. I'm…I'm pregnant."

Suddenly, he felt light-headed, and his field of vision narrowed. As a physician he recognized that he was experiencing the symptoms of shock. Trying to calm his nerves, he took long deep breaths, as he often recommended to his patients. He stroked her cheek, comforting her while buying time to think of a response.

A few moments later he regained his equilibrium. "Are you sure, sweetheart?" he gently inquired. "You haven't seen a doctor in Reading?"

"Of course not!" she replied, annoyed that he would imagine that she could be so careless. "You don't seem to realize that I have no desire to hurt you or your precious wife. But as a physician, it must be obvious that missing two cycles leaves little doubt."

Running his hands through his hair and shaking his head, he didn't even try to hide his bewilderment. "I thought that we were being careful. I mean when we were together didn't you consider where you were in your cycle?"

Rose was petulant. "I tried Mike, but you would insist on stopping by when it was, well, inconvenient as far as taking precautions with the timing."

"It couldn't be helped. When I wanted to see you, to be with you, I didn't think of anything else. What do you think we should do?"

"Mike, what do you mean by that? I am having your baby. I should be asking you what you are going to do."

He hesitated, cupping her face in his hands. "I mean, if you want, I can arrange something. There are doctors that can solve this kind of problem. In my class many of the poorer students did that kind of operation."

She shot up from the bed. "Not on your life! I would never kill our child. How can you even suggest such a thing?"

He flushed with shame, and yet he felt oddly relieved. As a physician and as a man, he was opposed to abortion. Still, he worried that she somehow planned to entrap him. Did she think that he would feel guilty and leave Minnie? If that were the case, she was sorely mistaken.

Trying to relieve the tension, he kissed her gently. "Sweetheart, I am sorry. I never would have let you go through an abortion. We just have to figure out what you are going to do."

"You mean what we are going to do," she said as tears streamed down her face.

He held her and started to unbutton her lacy blouse. "Darling let's forget about it for tonight.

"Yes, Mike. We'll let it ride. I want to forget about everything and enjoy each other. We deserve it."

Dr. Michael Austin sat in his medical office, which was conveniently located one block west of Penn Street, the bustling main thoroughfare that bisected the growing city of Reading, Pennsylvania. His morning had been terribly busy, two minor surgeries in the office after he had performed an early morning delivery at Community General Hospital. He had just returned from a long lunch with Irving Bash, his accountant and good friend. Sitting behind a large oak desk that had belonged to Minnie's father, he shuffled mechanically through some medical charts. His mind wandered, his emotions vacillated between fear and confusion. He briefly entertained the idea that he might be in love with Rose after all. Then he quickly dismissed the thought. He loved Minnie, and he considered himself fortunate that she had married him. Who was he? Michael Austin, obviously a name changed by an official at Castle Garden when he arrived as a child in the 1870s. He, a son of a greenhorn from the Ukraine who had never learned to speak English properly, managed to wed the daughter of a German Jew. The Cohen family had been in the country for three generations and although they were not particularly wealthy, they were well respected by Philadelphia Jewish society.

Minnie proved to be a remarkable wife, especially for a doctor trying to make a name for himself in a new town. She was attractive, in the way many Jewish girls from her class were, long dark wavy hair, large brown eyes, and what was considered a fashionable curvy figure.

Moreover, she was tolerant of his long hours and frequent absences from their home. He mused that perhaps he could have done better, found a wealthier girl. God knows he needed the money in the beginning. After all he was a fine-looking man who always dressed impeccably. In his medical school Yearbook, his classmates described him as a social swell with a pair of glasses to go with every necktie. Yet when he really got down to it, he was a lucky man.

His mind returned to the situation at hand, and it dredged up an old concern. He had been married for five years, and Minnie did not become pregnant. He had always secretly worried that there might be a problem with his own fertility. But Rose was carrying his child, and after only six months. He decided that he had no choice but to take his wife to a specialist to see if there was something wrong with her. As he looked up the number of a colleague in Philadelphia, an idea threaded through his mind. At first it seemed absurd, but slowly the idea formed into a plan and became more and more feasible.

On the train on the way home from Philadelphia, Minnie cried silently. Mike glanced at her furtively but said nothing. Her pain and disappointment were palpable, and he thought it best to let her come to terms with the harsh reality before offering a solution.

Drying her tears with her handkerchief, she spoke softly. "Mike, I thought that there might be something wrong, but I always held out hope. Is there really nothing to be done?"

"I'm sorry, dear. Dr. Perry is the top man at Penn. And he said that your case does not call for further tests. It's the uterus, as he said. You cannot carry a pregnancy to term."

"But there must be a way," she said, almost in a whisper.

"Can't they perform surgery to rectify the problem?"

"No, Minnie. Let's not torture ourselves looking for solutions that don't exist. I don't mean to be cruel but it's futile. We were not meant to have children."

On hearing those words, Minnie burst into uncontrollable sobs. And this was the reaction that Mike expected and was counting on. He guided her to a quiet corner in the last car of the train. Encircling her with his arms, Mike gently kissed her forehead and waited until her crying subsided.

"It is alright, my darling. I love you, and that is enough."

"No, Mike. I want a child and I know you do too. You haven't spoken of it in the past few years, but perhaps you suspected there was a problem and you wanted to spare my feelings. But whatever the case, I cannot reconcile myself to a life without children, or at least one child."

For a few moments he held her in his arms, and they were silent. Then, he slowly lifted her chin and looked into her eyes. "Minnie if you are open-minded, I think I have an idea."

Her expression of grief transmuted into an air of confusion. "What do you mean? Open-minded? What are you trying to say?"

"I am saying that even though you can't carry a child, we can adopt. Would you consider raising a child that is not our own?"

She hesitated, and he thought that he saw a look of doubt cross her face. But then she nodded her head as if considering the possibility.

"You know that as a doctor I can avoid some of the usual legalities," he continued. "We wouldn't have to go through an orphanage or social welfare organization."

"You see, it's quite simple. I deliver babies, both in homes and in the hospital. Sometimes the mothers are single ladies. You know what I mean, girls who got themselves into a fix. In those cases, I call the county and they place the infant in an orphanage or home of some kind."

"I know," she said. "And it is such a shame. I feel for

these girls. But it's so unfair, Mike. They give their children away so casually. And I would give anything for a child."

"Would you," he asked. "Would you take another woman's child as your own? Would you raise it and love it? And would you do this without question as to who the mother is, or who the father is?"

"Oh yes! Yes, I would," she said, grabbing his hands. She was quiet for an instant, as if reconsidering. "But Mike, would we tell the child the truth?"

"I think it is always best to be honest. At the proper age, we could tell him, or her, that is if the situation allows it."

Minnie sighed with relief and a hint of sadness. "I would have wished to have your child, darling. That is my only regret."

Mike smiled and embraced his wife.

Mike found it almost impossible to find a pretext to leave the New Year's Eve party. The Bashes had rented out the party room at The Olympus Club, the only exclusively Jewish club in Reading. Located halfway up Mount Penn, it had been founded by a group of prominent professionals from Reading's Jewish community, including Mike and Minnie Austin. Esther Bash and Minnie had organized a themed costume party, "Inside a Harem." All the women were dressed in gauzy pants and sequined tops with elaborate feathered headdresses. Some of the men made half-hearted attempts to dress, donning turbans or mock caftans. Mike had refused to dress in costume on the pretext that he might be called out for an emergency. The truth was that he was expecting a call at any time from his friend Ralph Samuels, an obstetrician who had graduated a year before him. Ralph had a flourishing practice with a very tony clientele in center city. In addition, he had recently opened a small private maternity hospital on the outskirts of the city. When Mike had called him to ask a small favor, he enthusiastically agreed to help. After all, everyone liked Mike, such an amiable fellow. So, he arranged to have a bed available for a young woman who was expected to deliver sometime in late

December.

Mike had insisted that Rose take the precaution of going to Philly the third week in December. He put her up in a modest hotel and telephoned every day to see if there were any signs that her labor was imminent. Confounded bad luck! He received a call from Ralph just as they were leaving for the party that Rose had arrived at his hospital. Fortunately, he had decided to drive to the club, so he had a car and swift departure would be possible. He approached Irving and informed him that he had an emergency, a particularly complicated case, a nervous patient that would only let him treat her.

Esther sighed and rolled her eyes when she overheard the conversation. "Oh Mike, really, tonight of all nights?" She crossed the room to find Minnie, who was busy adjusting some balloons. "Oh, Minnie, what a bore! Go speak with your husband. He just can't leave. Sometimes I don't know how you put up with it."

Minnie moved slowly across the crowded room, her expression blank, but her heart was beating wildly. Reaching his side, she took hold of her husband's hand. "Mike," she said, trying to control the tremor in her voice. "What is this about an emergency? Really, I'm sure Kotzen can take care of it. He volunteered to take emergencies tonight. Madeline said he's staying at the Community General tonight."

"Darling," he said, drawing her away from the Bashes. "Listen, this is a delivery. A young single woman, who needs my help and my discretion. It is our chance. I haven't wanted to mention anything before because things were not certain. But I have to go myself and nobody must know."

Her face flushed and she bit her lip trying not to gasp. "Oh Mike! You mean now, tonight? Where are you going?"

His face tightened. "Do not ask questions. The less you know the better. That way you won't let anything slip. After all, you can't help yourself but to share everything with Esther.

I will take all the responsibility. Just play along and

confirm that I do have a difficult patient, an older woman who claims to have fainting spells and seizures."

"Yes, dear," she said, vacillating between elation and apprehension. "I'll get a ride home with Irving and Esther."

"Good. And try to act as natural and as gay as possible. Don't forget that it's New Year's Eve and it's your party."

Before heading for the door, he kissed her sweetly. "Happy New Year, Minnie."

Mike had taken an express train on the Reading Line and then caught a taxi. It was about a fifteen-minute ride to the maternity hospital. He rushed past the receptionist, but then turned back realizing he needed directions to the delivery room.

"Miss, I am Dr. Austin. Dr. Samuels is with one of my patients in delivery. Could you please direct…"

"Oh yes, Dr. Austin. We were expecting you hours ago. Dr. Samuels is with the patient and has told me to bring you up at once. Please follow me."

They ascended two floors in a large elevator and walked down a narrow hallway, where the receptionist pushed open a set of doors and announced Dr. Austin's arrival.

"Mike, finally!" said the exasperated doctor. "I thought that you were going to abandon me. I agreed to help keep things discreet and let you use the facility, but it was understood that you would be delivering the baby."

"I'm so sorry, Ralph," said Mike, out of breath. "I was at a party in Reading. I made my way here as fast as I could."

"Well, speaking of parties, I am expected at a formal affair at a friend's home in Rittenhouse Square. I'll leave you with Queenie here," he said indicating a slight woman who was putting on a pair of gloves. "She is a nurse midwife. She could probably deliver the child herself, but I would never presume to go against your instructions."

The young nurse nodded. Her face was small and a little pinched. She was not pleasant, but he had the impression that she was efficient and qualified.

"Good evening, Doctor. I guess it will just be the two of

us tonight," she said as they walked over to the bed where Rose lay sleeping. "We gave her something to calm her down. She was quite agitated. I'm about to give her an enema. It won't be long now."

A few minutes later Rose stirred and roused from her sleep. She began to writhe in pain from a strong contraction. "Mike, is that you? Where have you been, damn it?"

"Language, young lady," Queenie scolded. "I know you are in pain, but show a little respect for the doctor, and for me."

"It's alright, nurse," said Mike. "I can take it. We'll show her a little compassion."

He had put on a surgical gown and asked Queenie to help him with his gloves. Then he went over and waited for the contraction to pass. Then he examined her.

"Nurse, she is eight centimeters dilated. Membranes are intact."

Rose started to grit her teeth and cry, this time more softly. "Mike I am glad that you're here, I really am. Am I going to be alright? I never realized that there would be so much pain."

"That's nature's way. The only way to avoid it is to knock you out. I prefer not to do that if possible."

"I prefer not to suffer."

"Quiet please," he said, as he placed a small wooden stethoscope on her belly. "I think I can hear a heartbeat. Just try to bear it. It shouldn't be long. You are making good progress."

He took her hand, which she squeezed tightly.

"Doctor, her water just broke," said Queenie as she put her arm around Rose's back.

"Now it's time to push deary. Just listen to me and to the doctor and when we say push, you need to bear down and push with all your strength."

Twenty minutes later Rose let out one last guttural scream and a baby girl came into the world. The baby wailed loudly, and Mike cut and clamped the cord. Queenie took the child to clean her and was about to bring her back to her mother. But as Mike examined the placenta and then felt her abdomen, he realized that there was another baby.

"Nurse! You'll have to leave the child. Come here quickly. There is a second baby, and I am very worried about the position."

"I am coming doctor," said Queenie.

Rose began to flail in panic, as Mike examined her and felt two feet through the membrane. Should he turn the baby or deliver in bridge position?

"Nurse, bring some ether at once, hurry! I am going to do a bridge extraction."

Queenie quickly placed the cup with ether over Rose's nose and mouth. Meanwhile, Mike grabbed the feet with the intact membranes and gently pulled them until the membrane ruptured. The feet and abdomen followed.

"Listen, Nurse, we're going to have to move quickly. Is she out?"

"Yes, Doctor. She is under," Queenie said trying to avoid his gaze. She had never even seen a bridge extraction. She could see that things could go very wrong, and she didn't know this Dr. Austin from Reading from Adam. What could Dr. Samuels be thinking allowing him to deliver a baby in his clinic?

"I am afraid that if the uterus contracts, it could trap the head. We wouldn't want to lose the child. He skillfully delivered the shoulders, flipping the baby's back over her abdomen and the baby's head slid out. A second beautiful baby girl! After five minutes, the placenta was delivered. Adrenaline coursed through his body. It was not because of the staggering feat of the dangerous delivery, but rather the fact that there was only one placenta for the two babies. Two embryonic sacs and one placenta meant identical twins. Rose had given birth to two beautiful and identical girls. He cut the second baby's cord and looked at Rose who was sleeping, blissfully unaware of the reality that awaited her.

JANUARY 1, 1905

PHILADELPHIA

Rose awoke at dawn, confused and sore. The room was dark and hazy, but little by little objects became clearer, sharper. She felt constrained under the tight sheets of the hospital bed and wanted to call out, but she was afraid. She wasn't sure why she should be afraid. Then things began to come back to her, one after another the facts reentered her consciousness. She had delivered her child. Mike had been there. There had been pain, a cry and then darkness.

Now as it all came back to her, all she could feel was grief, a piercing pain in her soul. Her baby that she had carried for nine months would be taken away. No, she thought. She could change her mind. Maybe Mike would understand. No, she knew that she was being absurd. She had promised herself that she wouldn't cry, but she felt her face wet with tears. She never dreamed it would be so hard to give up her child. The haze returned and she fell asleep.

At seven o'clock the nurse from the night before, Queenie was her name she thought, came into the room, followed by another nurse. Each had a baby in her arms. One began to cry and the other chimed in. She thought there had been a mistake.

"Good morning, Mrs. Strauss." Said Queenie. "We have

quite a surprise for you. You were awake and alert for the birth of little girl number one, but while you were sleeping, we delivered her sister. Look, aren't they beautiful?"

"First of all, it's Miss Strauss. Let's not be hypocritical. Secondly, you must be mistaken." She couldn't absorb the facts that were being presented to her. She had two babies!

She had been unusually large towards the end of her pregnancy, but it never occurred to her that she was carrying twins.

"No, Miss Strauss," said the second nurse. You have two daughters, and I must say…"

"Daughters? Really, how are they? Is everything alright?"

"Yes indeed," said Queenie. "What's more. They are identical twins. So, we need to have names as soon as possible. You know, to avoid confusion. I imagine that you have at least one name for a little girl."

In fact, she had not considered names since she didn't plan to keep her child. She wrinkled her forehead and glared at the nurses. "I would like to see Dr. Austin as soon as possible, if you don't mind."

Queenie looked down the hall. He is just coming. We'll put one of the babies in the bassinette and you can hold the other.

Mike stood in the doorway, his eyes shifted from Rose, who held one of the infants in her arms, to the other baby lying in the bassinette. Then he scrutinized her face trying to determine her state of mind. But her expression was vacuous, her eyes glassy as she turned her head slowly away possibly trying to hide the tears that wet her face.

"Good morning, Rose. How are you feeling?"

"I imagine you must have some idea. I need something to alleviate the pain. You never told me how bad it would be."

"My dear, I had no idea what would happen during the delivery, no idea. I examined you every month and there was no sign that you were carrying twins. So, of course, the delivery was complicated and dangerous. I must be honest with you. We came awfully close to losing the second baby."

She tried to regain her composure, but her throat tightened, and her voice was raspy.

"Yes, how extraordinary! I have two daughters and I was told that they are identical. Two beautiful girls, now that sure does cast a new light on our arrangement. To be completely honest, I was having doubts about giving up my child. But now, I don't know what to do. Raising a child without a husband was a daunting proposition, but I was beginning to believe that I might be up to the task. I even thought about moving here to Philadelphia where nobody knows me, maybe passing myself off as a widow."

Mike stiffened and frowned. "Now Rose, we have an agreement. I have already paid you a great deal of money and I am willing to help you resettle in Philadelphia. When you get back on your feet, you can find work. I am not a rich man, but I will do what I can."

Rose noticed that Queenie was still in the room, hovering over the bassinette ostensibly swaddling the baby. "Mike," she said, making no effort to hide her anger, "could we have some privacy?"

Mike turned to Queenie. "Nurse, you can leave. Take the babies down to the pediatrician. He had just arrived when I came up."

Queenie huffed, "Of course, Dr. Austin. In my opinion the little ones should have been seen hours ago. Anyone can see they are underweight."

Once they were alone, Rose abandoned any effort to hide her emotions. Her mind was in turmoil, and she unconsciously gouged her hands with her nails. How could he just stand there, so silent, so calm? What did he expect?"

Finally, he spoke, softly and with compassion. "I know this is difficult, but really Rose, you cannot care for two children on your own. I will take them. We agreed that I adopt one, and it will be no hardship for me to raise the two girls."

"Hardship!" she spat. "You speak of hardship. Does it ever occur to you how I am suffering? My body is in agony, not just from the delivery. My breasts are hurting. What am I supposed to do about that?"

"The nurses will help you bind your breasts and there are homeopathic remedies to prevent the milk from coming."

"You seem to have an answer for everything, Mike. How about answering this? What would you do if I refused to let you have my babies?"

He stood mute; his heart was pounding. She was right. There was absolutely nothing he could do. They had made no written contract, and no one else knew about their understanding, for that was all it was, an understanding.

She sat up in the bed and held her head erect and gazed at him defiantly. A thought had been forming, and gradually things became clear. A solution emerged, brilliant and cruel, offering her both revenge and joy, having her cake and eating it too.

"Rose, I beg you to be kind. Remember that these are my children as well."

"Yes, I know," she said with a chill in her voice. "You will see how I can be kind. I will keep my promise…"

"Lord, thank you, Rose."

"But I promised you a baby. I never promised you two. And just think, we can both be parents. I will take one child and you may have the other. And isn't it, oh what's the word, "ironic" that they are identical. They are beautiful, aren't they? Two beautiful girls, one for you and one for me."

Mike's mind froze. The idea of twins had never entered his head, so he could find no argument for keeping them both. Yet, the idea of losing one of his children was as painful as if Rose had miscarried or delivered a stillborn. Still, she held all the cards, and he knew he would have to accept her decision.

"I guess there is nothing that I might say to change your mind."

"No, not a thing!" She said, straightening up and

squaring her shoulders. "I will take one of the girls and you the other. Now that I have delivered on our bargain, it's your turn. As I have promised I will leave Reading and settle here in Philly. But it will be more expensive. I want a house, oh nothing elaborate, just a small row home in a nice neighborhood. I will still need an allowance. I do not ask for much, just enough to pay a woman to take care of the child when I go back to work."

Mike lowered his eyes, trying to hide the fact that he was calculating how much her demands would cost him. "If the house isn't too expensive, I can just manage without Minnie noticing that our savings are shrinking. And she is only expecting one child. But what about me? When will I see my daughter?"

"You have a daughter," Rose snarled. "That's the agreement, so don't be greedy."

"It's not a matter of greed. I am her father, and I would like to see her occasionally, even if she doesn't know who I am. You could pass me off as an old friend or a distant relative."

"Absolutely not! I would recommend that you accept my conditions, for I can still change my mind and keep them both."

He gulped trying to control the tremor in his voice. "No, please, I accept."

"That's better. I will give you the name of a friend who will be an intermediary. You will give her the money every month."

"I understand. Perhaps she could let me know how the child is doing?"

"I don't think you quite understand, Mike. You will never know how she is doing or where she is. I won't even let you know her name. And if you start sending friends or detectives around, well just imagine the damage that I can do. I could tell Minnie everything. It's almost too perfect. I mean, there I would be at the door with my daughter. Imagine the shock and grief."

"Enough!" he hissed. He realized that he had to give in. "I agree to your terms. I always knew that you were a smart and beautiful girl. But cruel and devious, I never would have labeled you. I can only hope that our girls don't inherit those traits."

"They will be beautiful, that's for sure. You raise your girl and I'll raise mine. Time will tell."

THE PERFECT STORM

Donald turned his head, looking from Addie to Frances. It was hard to know where one stopped and the other began. Their reactions were as identical as their faces. Both girls appeared disoriented and confused. Each inhaled abruptly and wore the same expression of bewilderment. They approached each other in the faint candlelight, scrutinizing every feature.

Addie was the first to work up her courage as she touched Frances' hand. Their identical blue eyes flew open at exactly the same moment, as the touch seemed to complete a long-lost connection that had been severed by time and circumstances.

It was Frances who spoke first after almost a full minute of silence. "I don't understand," she said looking first at Donald and then at Addie. "Who are you? No, that's an absurd question. I know who you are. My whole life I have known that you were there. But I thought that I had conjured you up. I called you my secret friend. But you are real!"

Addie couldn't hold back another second. "You won't believe it, but I have seen you too, or dreamt about you since I was little. How is this possible?"

They stood side by side and looked into the large ornate mirror. Two identical faces staring at their reflection. Each girl had looked into many mirrors over the years, not realizing that the mirrors were empty, empty because one of the faces was missing.

Frances was ebullient. "We even have the same voice. It's so strange, like I'm talking to myself."

Donald interrupted. "Ladies, do you understand what is happening. You are identical twins. Identical! What are the odds of you finding each other?"

"I see. But I don't understand. How can I possibly have a sister? My mother never spoke of my father. When I would ask about him as a child, she would not answer. Her eyes would turn hard and cold. I asked many times, but she told me he didn't love us, so there was no need to speak of him. So, I stopped asking. She gave birth to us, then she separated us. How could she? It's too late to ask her now. She died last year."

"I'm afraid that I can't help," said Frances. I was adopted, and I know nothing of my birth parents. As a matter of fact, I always thought that my father had found me in an orphanage."

Addie started looking around the room. "Donald, have you seen Sam? I didn't see him in the Seabreeze Room."

Donald scanned the crowded room. "I don't see him, but it's hard with all these people. Come to think of it, you're right, he wasn't in the meeting."

"Where could he be?" She asked, starting to panic.

Meanwhile, Frances had a foreboding expression on her face. "Listen, do you think you could help me? I need to find my husband, Teddy. I left him in our suite upstairs."

Donald tried to ease her anxiety. "I am certain that they have taken the same precautions in other parts of the hotel. Perhaps the phones are still working, and you could call up to your room."

Frances began to shake uncontrollably. "No, look the electricity is out. I need to find Teddy!" she cried.

It struck Addie that she did not have the same concern for Sam that her sister had for her husband. It was at that instant that she realized that she was no longer in love with him.

"Donald let's see if we can help her," she said. She drew close to Frances and put her arm around her, trying to comfort her. "We will come with you, and we won't leave you until you have found him."

Suddenly, they heard smashing glass in the distance. One of the hotel employees came in and tried to quiet the crowd. "A strong gust has uprooted several trees and one of them crashed through a window in the Seabreeze Room," he said, trying to speak over the noise and commotion. "Remain where you are, please. This is the safest place in the hotel."

Many of the guests appeared unconvinced as they watched the swaying chandeliers. Frances blinked back tears, trying not to lose control. Addie could feel her sister's fear and put her arm around her, trying to console her.

Maybe you can ask where the other guests are taking shelter," she asked Donald.

"I'll try," he said. But at that moment a tall, blond man made his way through the mass of people and enfolded Frances into his arms.

"Teddy! Thank God!" she said, finally allowing herself to breakdown into uncontrollable sobbing.

It seemed almost impossible, but the fury of the storm increased briefly and suddenly the wind stopped. The crowd became eerily silent. Then abruptly, the chandeliers stopped swaying and the lights flickered momentarily.

Teddy looked into Frances' eyes and then kissed her. "Are you alright? I was mad with worry."

"I'm fine now that you're here. What is happening? Is the storm over?"

Teddy noticed that some people had begun to exit the room, most likely with the intention of leaving the hotel. "No, it's not over. Someone should tell those people to stay where they are."

Donald agreed. "Yes, they need to stop them! This is the eye. It's not over."

Teddy looked at him and was taken aback when he noticed the young woman standing next to him. His gaze bounced from her to Frances. For the first time in his life, he was utterly dumbfounded.

For a few seconds, nobody spoke. They understood that he needed a minute to process the situation. Finally, Donald tried to offer an explanation.

"Let me start by introducing myself," he said. "I'm Donald Seligman. This is my friend and business partner Addie Stanford. We don't have all the facts but be assured your eyes are not deceiving you. In the middle of this chaos, these two sisters have found each other."

Frances swallowed her tears and found her voice. "Darling, I have never seen you speechless before, and you should see your face." She turned him around so that he might see himself in the mirror. It only served to heighten the confusion and absurdity of the situation.

He looked into the mirror, paying no mind to his own reflection, and tried to understand what he saw. Frances was in his arms, and at her side was this girl. What was the word that he had heard to describe it? Doppelgänger?

Addie looked at him and tried to form a coherent explanation. "Teddy, if I may use your Christian name, we were trying to put it together. We are sure of one thing, we are sisters. Apart from that, we know nothing."

Frances took Addie's hand. "We will find out. I will speak to my father. Perhaps it may be a difficult conversation. But he is the only one left who may know the truth."

"In any case," said Teddy with a broad smile, "I am happy to meet you Addie Stanford, sister-in-law. How fast our family is growing."

AFTER THE STORM

CORAL GABLES, SEPTEMBER 1926

Donald and Teddy had been right. The calm that they had experienced in the Palm Ballroom was the eye of the hurricane. They later learned that winds of 132 miles per hour had been recorded. Freight trains had been flipped over; telephone lines were snapped in half. Waves reached across Miami Beach all the way to Collins Avenue. Yachts sank. Hundreds of people had ventured out into the streets as the eye passed over the city. Over 300 people had died with over 6,000 injured. Over 18,000 people remained homeless. Later it was revealed that it was the most expensive catastrophe in American history to date.

But despite the devastation, John Bowman, one of the investors in The Biltmore Hotel, declared that "Miami would rise out of the ruins." Carl Fisher almost immediately began replacing telephone poles and powerlines.

But Donald and Addie had had their fill of Florida and speculation. Their future was up north. Teddy and Frances were fortunate enough to find two seats on a small plane that Albert Lasker and Dore had rented and returned to New York within two days of the calamity. Of course, the two sisters exchanged telephone numbers and addresses. They would untangle the mystery as soon as possible.

Meanwhile, Sam searched for Addie everywhere in the hotel before finding her sitting in the lobby with Donald. Chairs and lamps had been strewn all over the large room and sand had poured in, ruining the expensive carpeting.

Sam approached Addie and took her into his arms. He noticed that she stiffened when he tried to kiss her. "Are you okay? I was late to the meeting because I got a call from Washington. And then when the wind started really blowing, they put a bunch of us in a utility closet. They told us to keep put. I was crazy with worry about you. But they wouldn't let us out."

Addie flashed a half-hearted smile. "We muddled through. A lot has happened, and I don't mean just the storm." She turned and looked at Donald. "Do you think that we could have a moment alone? I have a lot to say to Sam."

Donald smiled and gave a clipped nod. "Sure. I'm going to buy our train tickets."

"What's going on?" asked Sam. "I really am sorry. You surely can't blame me for not finding you sooner."

"No, Sam. I don't blame you for anything. I just think that we should not see each other, at least for a while. I had wanted to tell you before this trip about a decision I made. I will not be converting."

Sam looked disappointed and surprised. "Why? You met with the rabbi, didn't you?"

A frown transformed her face into a mask of contempt. "Yes, I did. He was most unpleasant to say the least. You should have warned me Sam. He's a horrible little man. How could you imagine that I would allow him to handle something so important and so personal?"

He shrugged his shoulders, not seeming to grasp the extent of her anger. "Yeah, I guess he is a wimpy little putz at that. But we can find another rabbi. I might be able to work something out with the reform temple."

Her patience grew short. "You're not listening to me. I will not convert. Apparently, Gentile women lack something called Jewish bloodlines. I was humiliated and I don't plan on subjecting myself to months of work and embarrassment to please your mother."

Trying to calm her down, Sam put his arm around her, but she pushed it aside. "Addie, I love you. We'll find a solution."

"I'm tired of looking for solutions and trying to please your family. Besides, something incredible has happened to me, and it has nothing to do with you. You see, I have discovered that I have a sister, an identical twin. She is my priority now. For once you will have to wait for me. I'm going back to New York with Donald tomorrow. I'll call you when I'm ready to talk."

Sam was stunned. "A twin sister? What are you talking about?"

Addie's face was flushed with anger. "If you had been with me, you would understand. But you weren't, Donald was."

"What does that mean?" he said, his eyes glaring. "Is there something going on between you and Donald? I'll kill him."

"Nothing is going on," she sighed, realizing that her feelings for Sam were falling away and that she might really care for Donald more than she thought.

"I'll be back in New York next week," he said. "We'll have dinner and talk this out."

"No," she said adamantly. I will call you when I'm ready to talk. I have a lot to think about.

Sam walked away looking dejected. For the first time, he was not in control, and he didn't like the feeling.

ADDIE AND DONALD

GOING HOME

After getting a ride up to Jacksonville, Addie and Donald boarded a train for New York. They only managed to find seats in the second-class day car, so the two-day trip would not be pleasant on top of the exhaustion and shock experienced during the hurricane. But they were grateful to be alive and unharmed. Since there was little privacy, she was hesitant to broach the subject of finding her sister. Besides, there were moments when she wasn't so sure that the whole thing hadn't been a dream.

"Do you want to talk about it? He asked, unsure of the wisdom of bringing up the subject. They had hardly spoken in the past several hours. Both stared out the windows at the passing fields and small town, which looked as if they had sustained serious damage during the storm.

"What is there to say?" She said with a sigh. "Frances and I are going to see each other next week. She wants to talk to her father to see if he knows anything about our birth and our real father."

"Do you think that he will be of any help? Sometimes these agencies and orphanages don't keep information about the mothers."

"We can try. We can go around to adoption agencies in

the Philadelphia area. Even if my mother used a different name, I could show them a photograph. Somebody might remember."

He didn't want to disillusion her, but he felt the chances were slim that anyone would remember after over twenty years. And if they did, it was doubtful that they would divulge such confidential information. "If I were you, I wouldn't waste my time with agencies and orphanages," he said. "I think that they are not legally permitted to give out information on the parents."

"I suppose that you are right," she said, looking defeated. "I just never understood my mother. She drove off anyone who ever loved her. My stepfather was a wonderful man. He would do anything for her, including adopting me. But she drove him away. Sometimes I think that she was incapable of loving a man."

"Well, there are many explanations for that, beginning with being abandoned by your father. Have you ever given that any thought?"

"Yes, of course. She made it clear that she hated my father. That was the only thing that she would tell me about him."

"That's what I mean. You can't know what happened to your mother. Perhaps she was attacked."

Addie's expression turned into one of shock. "She may have been raped! I never even considered that possibility. Or perhaps she was coerced by an unscrupulous employer."

"It's possible," said Donald. "But if that were the case, why would she have kept you and given up your sister? She would have wanted no reminder of such a horrible experience."

"I don't think that we will ever know the truth now that she is gone. Our only hope is Frances' father. Did you know that he is a doctor?"

Donald's expression became inscrutable, and slowly a light came into his eyes. "A doctor? Now that is interesting. A doctor might be in a position to adopt a child outside the usual legal channels."

Addie's eyes widened. "Yes, he must know something about my father. I'm sure of it."

The conductor came by and checked their tickets. Donald asked if she wanted something from the dining car. When he came back with two coffees, Addie's mood had lightened.

"Thanks," she said as she took the cup. "Listen, I know this is quite a sharp change in topics, but I was wondering if you were making any progress with your girlfriend? I'm sorry, what is her name?"

"Her name is Anita. It doesn't look good. I thought that she would be upset or angry with me for leaving her and going to Florida. But she took it a little too well."

She tried her best not to smile, feeling a sensation of relief wash over her.

"Donald, do you mind if I ask you something personal?"

"Since when do we have any secrets?" He laughed.

"Tell me. Are you in love with Anita?"

"That is personal!" he said. She had caught him off guard. "I haven't let myself fall into that trap. I don't mean to be blunt, but I made the mistake of falling too fast for you. Now, I am much more careful with my heart."

They said nothing for several minutes. Finally, Addie broke the silence. "Look, I need to tell you something. I have broken things off with Sam. I have been a fool as far as he is concerned. The last straw was the business of converting. The plain truth is that I am not Jewish, and that shouldn't matter, not if he really loves me."

Donald's face was flushed; perhaps it was relief or maybe joy. "I told him that he was a fool for making a federal case out of it if you'll excuse the expression. I told you that it never made any difference to me, and I have a Jewish mother too."

Addie laughed. "It's absurd. I wasn't raised in any religion, and I don't feel that I am a less moral person. Sam doesn't follow the traditions. He's not even kosher. He has this inexplicable fear of how his mother would react to a Gentile daughter-in-law. Evie thinks he's a fool."

Donald lowered his eyes. He appeared pensive and Addie could imagine what he was thinking. She was tempted to tell him that her feelings for him had changed, that he was much more than a friend to her now. But she decided to let things unfold slowly and naturally.

RETURN TO READING

The girls kept in touch after they returned to New York, phoning each other almost every day. Sometimes the calls were brief: "How are you? How's Teddy?"

Other days calls lasted for over an hour: "Have you given any thought to what you might say to your father?"

The following week, Frances called her father. "Daddy, I'm coming home to see you this weekend, if that's okay. Teddy will be coming too. There is something I need to discuss with you."

"I'm happy that you're coming. You don't need a reason, you know."

"Of course, I know that. It has been too long. There is something that I need to say to you, and I can't talk about it over the telephone."

Mike was silent for a moment. He didn't want to spoil her surprise, for he was certain that she was going to announce that she was expecting a child. "Alright darling. We'll talk when you get here. When do you expect to arrive? Shall I meet you at the train station?"

"No, we will be driving in. You can expect us sometime on Saturday afternoon."

"I can't wait. I've missed you," he said

"Me too, I love you, Daddy," she responded.

Frances had not told him that she and Teddy were not coming alone. She had asked Addie to come. But she hesitated. "I don't know, Frances. It might be a shock for him to see me, not to mention how awkward the situation will be. I think that you should speak to him alone."

"That is precisely what I plan to do. I will speak to him on my own. You will meet him later. I'll prepare him by explaining how we met. Oh, and I was wondering if you could give me a recent photograph. I mean, how does one tell her father that she has an identical twin that has shown up out of nowhere? I'm hoping in this case, a picture will be worth a thousand words."

"Sure, I'll find a suitable photo," said Addie. "I'm just incredibly nervous. So many questions about my mother have been running through my mind. I have to say that Donald has been incredible, like a rock for me. Would you mind if he came along?"

"I don't see why not," said Frances. "He's a wonderful young man. I can see that he really cares for you. I think that he will help you to steady your nerves."

"Thanks. He means a lot to me, more than I have ever realized."

It was an overcast, chilly fall afternoon when Teddy dropped Frances off two blocks from her father's house. She was glad that it was not raining because her plan was to have the others wait for her at Carsonia Park. She knew that Addie would be nervous and hoped she might be distracted by the beauty of the lake and the activity of the amusement park.

The door was unlocked as usual. She didn't see her father in the living room, so she went into the kitchen, where she found him pouring himself a beer.

"Hi Daddy," she said, embracing him a little tighter than usual. "Can I have one of those?"

"Are you sure?" he said looking at her with a strange expression.

"Why not? Are you suddenly respecting prohibition?" she said, laughing.

"No, I just thought, well I mean you said that you had

something to tell me. I naturally thought that you meant that you were expecting?"

"Expecting! No, it's nothing like that. I wish it were. But I must talk to you about something very delicate."

Mike sat down slowly. She noticed that her father was aging quickly. His gait was uneven, and his hands were shaking. She had never noticed that before.

"Where's Teddy?" he asked looking puzzled. "How did you get here?"

Mike began to worry. His mind suddenly shifted to a vague memory of a drunken conversation with Theodore Pierson. How could he have been so foolish? He trusted Teddy's father to keep his secret. But when his daughter started to speak, he realized that the old man had not revealed the truth about the fact that he was her real father.

"Daddy, I am going to tell you a story, an incredible story. I want you to listen until I have finished and then, I need you to answer some questions."

"Alright," he said, his voice trembling. "Tell me this story."

"When I was in Florida, in the midst of a hurricane, I literally ran into my sister, my identical twin sister." She handed him the photograph that Addie had provided. The face was identical. The only difference was that the girl in the picture did not have bobbed hair.

Mike looked at the picture and his hands began to shake even more uncontrollably. He dropped his glass on the floor and blurted out, "You found her?" He seemed to stop breathing for a few seconds and then exhaled loudly. "It's a miracle, plain and simple. I've been searching for her for years. I never imagined that the two of you would find each other."

"You knew about her?" asked Frances, her emotions somewhere between incredulity and anger. "Have you always known that I have a twin sister? Did they tell you at the adoption agency or did you find out later?"

Mike stared at the floor, hesitating, searching for the

right words. The time had come to tell the truth. There was no avoiding it. If his daughter ended up hating him, at least he would no longer have to live a lie. Besides, she deserved to know the truth.

"I knew about her. I delivered the two of you in a private clinic in Philadelphia."

"I don't understand," she said. "I thought I was adopted through an agency. Was my adoption even legal?"

"There was no adoption. I have your birth certificate listing your mother and I as your parents. Your real mother agreed to give you up."

"But that doesn't make any sense. Why would she give me away and keep my sister?"

It took several seconds before he could summon up the courage to respond.

"She did it for spite. To hurt me."

"To hurt you!" she cried, trying to fathom what he was saying.

"You see, she was your mother. I was your, I am your father."

"You're my real father? Then she was your mistress," she said, her chin began to tremble as she tried to control her emotions. "Did Mother know about her?"

"Your mother never knew about her. But she knew that I was unfaithful to her many times during our marriage. I am ashamed to admit it. Still, I loved Minnie so deeply. And she yearned for a child. Then chance played a role when the girl became pregnant. I did something unforgivable."

"Exactly what happened? Tell me the truth, Daddy!"

"I promised this woman, Rose, her name was Rose Strauss. I promised her that if she would let me adopt the child, then I would set her up in a house in Philadelphia and give her some money to get her life started."

"So, in essence, you bought me," she said, not believing her ears.

"I guess you could say that. But it was an arrangement that was meant to help out both of us. Your mother and I wanted a child. Rose did not want the stigma of being an unwed mother and she needed money to start over. But during the delivery, things went wrong. I had no indication that she was carrying twins. I didn't realize it until the first baby was delivered. I don't know if it was you or your sister who came first. But the second baby was breech. Do you know what that means?"

"Yes, Daddy. We studied biology at Bryn Mawr."

"Well, I almost lost her and Rose. But thank God and a great nurse, you both survived. Since she was under anesthesia, Rose didn't know about having twins until the next morning."

"I imagine that was a shock. Two identical girls and no husband," Frances said with a hint of sarcasm.

"Exactly. I naturally assumed that she would give me both babies. That would have been a wonderful surprise for Mother."

"So, Rose Strauss obviously did not agree. What did she say when she saw the two of us?"

"She told me that I could take you, but that she would be keeping the other child. At first, I thought that she was kidding. But she was dead serious. I thought that I knew her. She was not a bad person. After all, she was willing to give us her baby, even though she expected to be paid. I can't blame her for that. But something happened to her. Perhaps it was the trauma of the difficult birth. She was full of bitterness and looking for revenge. I begged her and then I threatened. I knew a lot of important people in Reading and Philly."

"You did fight for us, Daddy! You tried to keep us both."

"I did my best. But then she kept repeating that I could only keep one of you. If I insisted on her giving up the second baby, well then, the whole deal was off. I couldn't disappoint your mother. She wanted a child so badly, and I didn't know when I would have another chance of finding one. I had no choice but to accept. All the while, I secretly hoped that at least I could keep track of my other girl, maybe even visit her."

"But you didn't!"

"No, I didn't. It was as if Rose read my mind. She threatened that if I ever tried to see my daughter, she would bring her to our front door and show her to Minnie, then tell her about our affair. You can see why I couldn't let that happen. One look at the identical sister and she would know the truth."

"But didn't you ever try to find her?"

"I tried, but Rose left Philadelphia and I had no way of tracking her down. After your mother died, I started looking again. As long as she was alive, I didn't want the truth to come out. I couldn't bear the idea of hurting her."

"I know that you loved her. I don't understand how you could be so foolish. Did you love this other woman?" she asked incredulously.

"No, I didn't love her. She was beautiful and always so gay. I can't say that I regret what I did, because I have you and…" Mike stood up and took her hand.

"I have her. Frances, I have my girls. You are my child. I wish that you could have grown up knowing the truth. Now that you do, I hope that you will still love and respect me."

"Of course, I love you and I will always respect you. Do you really think that any of what you have told me could change that? Quite the contrary, knowing that you are my true father makes me love you even more."

He drew her close and stroked her cheek. "My darling girl. I am so proud of you." They sat silently for a few minutes, trying to compose themselves. "When can I meet my daughter," he finally said. "God, I don't even know her name. Frances, what is her name?"

"Her name is Adelaide Stanford. She goes by Addie. She changed her last name when she graduated from business college. She thought it sounded more professional. She is so bright and so sweet."

"I'll pack a suitcase and we can leave as soon as Teddy gets back. Where is Teddy anyway?"

"You don't have to pack. She is here in Reading. Teddy drove us. She is waiting down at Carsonia Park with him and a close friend of hers."

"She's here?" he blurted out. "I was going to think about what I was going to say on the trip to New York. What am I going to say to her?"

"Why don't you let me handle it," she said. "But I think it best that we don't tell her the exact truth about her mother. She died not long ago. She would never tell Addie anything about you. She only said that you didn't love either of them. So, you see, she already thinks of her mother as a bitter woman. I don't want to hurt her anymore by telling her she took her out of spite. That would be unbearable. Why don't we tell her that she couldn't give up both of her babies? We can say that she loved them and decided that she had to keep one. I don't think that it would be such a sin to alter the truth, not if it will spare Addie any more pain."

"You're right. I will let you explain the situation to her. I only hope that she will not resent me for not fighting harder to keep her."

"She won't. She has already found a sister. Imagine her joy when she finds her father."

CARSONIA PARK

READING, PENNSYLVANIA, OCTOBER 1926

Donald, Addie, and Teddy had spent several nerve-racking hours at the amusement park, watching the children on the rides and the youngsters roughhousing. On Saturdays the park was usually crowded, but this being the closing day of the season, it was packed. There was to be a dance at the Casino. The band had arrived, and the staff was setting up tables and chairs.

Donald spent some of the time trying to distract Addie by talking about business. He had plans for advertising for the agency and asked her if she had any ideas. But he realized that her mind was occupied with other thoughts.

"How about a walk around the lake. It looks like the sun is finally coming out."

Addie nodded. "Why not? It's beautiful here. Frances told me that she loved coming to this lake as a child."

The wind had scattered the heavy gray clouds and her spirits lifted when she saw the sky painted with pink, wispy clouds. The sun was beginning to set, but there was sufficient daylight to see the reflection of the sky and clouds on the placid lake. The reality and the reflection were separated by a row of tall trees on the opposite shoreline.

Donald turned to Teddy. "Do you want to come along?"

"No thanks," he said. He was restless thinking about what was happening with Frances and her father. "You two go ahead. I'm sure that they won't be long, so don't go too far."

Donald took her hand as they walked and was pleasantly surprised when she stopped and put her arms around him. "Donald, I'm wondering if you know how I feel about you." She drew closer and kissed him, first tentatively and then a second time with considerably more fervor.

"I think I'm beginning to understand," he murmured, incredulous at the turn of events. "But I am not sure that what you're feeling isn't more gratitude than love. Just tell me one thing. Have you really gotten Sam out of your system? I can't risk getting hurt again. Besides, we are not only friends. We are also business partners. I have made a big investment in you, young lady."

"Yes, I know," she said, nodding her head. "You took a huge risk. But I am telling you that it has paid off. Everything I am professionally; I owe to you. Of course, I am grateful. But that has nothing to do with what I feel for you. I think that if it weren't for Sam, I would have realized a long time ago that I was in love with you. What I felt for him was real, but it was based on physical attraction. I allowed him to play with me, mistreat me really. That was my mistake. All the while it blinded me to what I felt for you. If it hadn't been for Anita, I don't know when I would have acknowledged my real feelings."

"Anita?" He said, his brows shooting up. "What does she have to do with anything?"

"What do you think? Whenever you talked about your girl, I felt like I would explode with jealousy. I never realized how much I wanted you until I thought that I might lose you."

He hugged her tightly. "Thank God for Anita! Why didn't I tell you about the other girls I went with? We would be married by now."

"Yes, I'm sure we would be. By the way, may I consider

that a proposal?"

His face reddened. "What do you think?"

"I'm going to hold you to that," she said. The next second her eyes opened widely, and she squeezed Donald's hand. Frances was walking towards Teddy with an elderly gentleman.

"That must be Frances' father," she said. "Maybe he has told her something about your real father."

Donald and Teddy watched discretely from a distance as the two sisters spoke with Dr. Austin. They could not hear what was said but watched as Frances seemed to spend a long time talking to Addie, whose expression altered every few minutes; at first quizzical, it then took on an air of shock and then finally relaxed into a countenance of pure happiness.

Teddy did not know what was happening, but he had his suspicions. He had been worried about what Frances might learn about her father, but his concern vanished when he saw both girls embracing Mike. All three were in tears, but he could see that they were joyful tears.

Afterwards, Frances left Addie and her father alone. She took time to explain what she had learned to her husband and Donald. It was difficult for Addie to absorb the facts and then to accept them as true. Her emotions were muddled, first she was overcome by confusion, followed by disbelief. Finally, she was filled with joy.

When Frances left her alone with her father, she was suddenly shy. She searched for the right words. What could she say?

"Shall I call you Father?" She asked timidly.

"Frances calls me Daddy," he answered. "I hope you will do the same."

"Daddy, I've been struggling to find the words…Perhaps it would be best if I told you what my mother said before she died. She said, "He doesn't deserve to know you." And then her last words to me were, 'He got what he wanted; he got his child.' I didn't understand until today what she meant. She was so bitter, but now I can fathom the depths of her suffering. Perhaps no one is to blame. But it's alright now, Daddy."

"Yes, my girl," he whispered softly. "No one is to blame. It's alright now."

"It's unbelievable. Are you alright, darling?" Teddy said, putting his arm around Frances.

"I'm ecstatic! I was worried about how she would react, but she is marvelous. She said the exact words that I was thinking. It's as if she read my mind."

"What did she say?" asked Donald.

"She said, 'There has been enough bitterness and sadness. How can I be anything but overjoyed to have a family? I was alone, and now I have a sister and a father."

Donald smiled shyly. "This might not be the time to bring it up, but she will soon have a husband too."

Frances was stunned and almost jumped into his arms as she hugged him.

Teddy said, "This family keeps growing. It's astonishing!"

Later when they were back at Mike's house, Frances made some tea.

"Daddy, you don't have a thing in this house to eat. We need to think about dinner."

"How about we all go to Nick's?" He said with a sly smile directed at Frances. It was her favorite local restaurant and Nick was practically a member of the family, even though he was a Greek immigrant. She had called him Uncle Nick from the time she was a small child.

"Oh yes, let's do. I'm starving."

As they sat around the table, Donald and Addie spoke of how they met and later had gone into the real estate business together. Addie and Frances described their bizarre meeting during the hurricane. There was so much to say, so much that Mike had missed out on. But what was absent that night at the dinner table was regret. They all realized that there was no time for that.

In a rare moment of silence, Donald worked up the nerve to address Mike.

"Dr. Austin, it may seem like an odd time to bring this up, but I have a request to make of you."

"Well, tonight is the time to ask, young man. I don't think that I could refuse anything tonight."

"Well, Sir. I would like to ask for your daughter's hand in marriage."

Frances kissed her sister. "I'm so happy for you both. And you can be sure that I will take charge of planning the wedding."

Mike cast his eyes down, looking almost embarrassed. "If I have in any way earned the right to do so, I give you both my blessing. If only my Minnie could be here. By the way, what is your last name, young man?"

"Seligman, Donald Seligman, Sir. Obviously, I'm Jewish. I hope that you have no objections."

Mike looked confused. "What are you talking about? How could I object? You do realize that I am Jewish, as is Frances?"

Addie and Donald looked at each other in amazement and started to laugh uncontrollably. When she finally caught her breath, Addie said, "So that means I am Jewish."

"Yes," said Mike. "You are my daughter. I am a Jew; you are a Jew. Now, I don't know how you were raised, Lutheran or whatever. But that does not alter the reality of who you are."

"Oh, it's fantastic," she said. "It's just that I had no idea. Frances never mentioned it."

"Well, it never came up," said her sister, a little defensively. "Teddy and I have not discussed religion since before our marriage, however, now I'm thinking that it's important to revisit it. After all, someday we will have children. I think that children need a religious foundation and tradition."

Mike smiled. "I'll be happy to get in touch with the rabbi if you would consider being married in Reading."

Addie laughed and hugged her father. "Yes, Daddy, let's

have the wedding here, and soon. I don't need any conversion classes, do I?" She winked at Donald.

A BRIEF INTERLUDE WITH SAM

DECEMBER 1926

Evie saw Addie approaching the restaurant where they had arranged to meet. She wanted to warn her that Sam was inside.

"Addie, Sam is inside," she said, stopping her friend at the door. "I told him that you weren't ready to see him yet, but you know how he is. He must have overheard me talking to you on the phone and he just showed up. He has been desperate to see you."

"It's alright Evie. I had to face him sooner or later. He has sent me a few letters, but I haven't answered. Let me go in and get it over with. He deserves to know the truth."

"Truth? What truth?" She asked, her voice brimming with curiosity.

"I'll tell you. But first I want to speak to Sam alone, if you don't mind. I've been waiting a long time for this moment, and I want to hear what he has to say."

"Yes, I can only imagine. Let him dig his own grave," she said, her eyes twinkling. "You aren't thinking of taking him back, are you?"

"Not likely," said Addie.

Sam rose expectantly when she walked over to his table. She almost felt sorry for him.

He tried to kiss her, but she rebuffed him. "Look Sam,"

she said, "I'm here out of respect for the love that we once felt for each other. But…"

"Once felt," he said so loudly that a few customers turned their heads and started. "I still love you. Didn't you read my letters?"

"Yes, I read them. But there was nothing new in them. Yes, I believe that you love me, but not as much as you love yourself and your own peace of mind. If only you had stood up to your mother. If you had loved me enough to let me be true to myself."

"I always loved you for who you were," he insisted.

"No, you didn't. You couldn't have because I didn't even know who I really was."

"What do you mean? You're Addie Stanford, a beautiful, intelligent woman, who I adore."

"No Sam, I'm not. I'm Addie Austin, daughter of Dr. Michael Austin. And I have saved the best for last. The name Austin was assigned by an immigration officer when my father arrived at Castle Garden. He thinks it might have been Azimov, but he is not certain."

"What father? You always told me that you didn't know who your father was."

"Well, I do now. I told you in Florida that I have a sister. Through her I met my father in October. Sam, my father is Jewish and so am I. I always have been. Isn't it wonderful, and without having to subject myself to one lesson with Rabbi Levinson."

An ecstatic smile appeared on his face. "But that's wonderful, now we can…"

"Sam, stop. Now there is no more 'we.' Last week Donald and I were married in Reading, Pennsylvania by a rabbi, a lovely man. I am sorry that we didn't invite you, but it was just the immediate family, my father, my sister Frances, and her husband, and of course Donald's mother. I called Evie to meet me today so that I could fill her in and apologize for not inviting her. And now, she is waiting for me outside, if you will excuse me."

GREENWICH, CONNECTICUT

MAY 1928

"What are the odds, Dr. Mike?" Asked Donald. "Identical twins are rare and here we have two generations in a row."

"I couldn't say. I'm just an old-fashioned general practitioner. That's a question for medical researchers."

"Donald loves to ask questions, Daddy," said Addie. "He's fascinated by numbers and statistics. But I'm not complaining. It has been a great help in growing our business."

Addie was helping Frances with the last-minute preparations for the bris. It had been a difficult birth and eventually it had been necessary to perform a cesarean section. But mother and twin sons were doing well. Of course, the boys were identical.

Addie's little girl, Rose, was already crawling and had started grabbing onto furniture to try to pull herself up to a standing position. She chided her husband. "Donald, could you please keep an eye on your daughter before she pulls the tablecloth and the dishes come crashing onto her head?"

There had been a lot of discussion about what to call the boys. But in the end, one was named Edward a tribute to Teddy's father. Teddy had wanted to name his other son

Michael in honor of his father-in-law. But Frances gently explained that according to Jewish tradition, it was considered bad luck to name a child after a family member who was still living. However, it was acceptable to use the first letter of the name. So, in tribute to Michael Austin and in the memory of Minnie, Edward's twin brother was named Mathew.

Teddy shook his head and couldn't stop himself from saying. "It's really astonishing how this family is growing."

Frances kissed him and tried not to roll her eyes.

ACKNOWLEDGMENTS

I would like to thank my editors, Hadley Passela and Cory Hott, for your knowledge, skill, and patience. Your encouragement has helped me bring *The Empty Mirror* to life.

Thanks to my daughter Mia Valenstein and her husband, Adam. You two are always there to help polish and perfect my words.

ABOUT THE AUTHOR

Lisa El Hafi, born and raised in Reading, Pennsylvania, studied French language and literature in Paris. She pursued a career in teaching foreign languages while learning Spanish, Italian, and Arabic.

Because of her deep passion for history, especially the Progressive Era, she set *The New Woman* in New York during the first years of the twentieth century.

She lives in Houston, Texas, and Marrakech, Morocco. She is researching her next work, a historical novel that will follow the story of two families in nineteenth and twentieth-century Morocco.

ALSO BY LISA EL HAFI

THE NEW WOMAN

At the turn of the twentieth century, four women's lives intersect in a society that is transitioning from the predictable and rigid expectations of the Victorian age to the volatile and exciting world of the Progressive Era. Set in the mansions, brownstones, and tenements of New York City, with vistas to Alva Vanderbilt's home in Newport and an eventful trip to Paris, *The New Woman* captures a colorful array of notable people and places at this moment of historical inflection. Along the way we meet the women of the Colony Club and the young women of the Garment Union who are striking for better conditions in the factories. Bernadine, Flora, Dore, and Mae each represent their class, upbringing, and education. Through courage and independence, each manages to navigate the complexities of a turbulent time for women and society as a whole.

Made in the USA
Columbia, SC
20 December 2023